Dark Vengeance

EARTHLY WORLDS SERIES
BOOK TWO

BILLY WRIGHT

William Wright/Dark Vengeance
Printed in the United States of America

This is a work of fiction. Names, characters, places, and incidents are a product of the
author's imagination. Locales and public names are sometimes used for atmospheric purposes. Any resemblance to actual people, living or dead, or to businesses, companies,
events, institutions, or locales is completely coincidental.

Dark Vengeance/ William Wright. -- 1st ed.

ISBN 978-1-7347770-2-4 Print Edition

ISBN 978-1-7347770-3-1 Ebook Edition

ALSO BY BILLY WRIGHT

Earthly Worlds – Book One

I would like to dedicate this book to my kids big and small and in loving memory of my youngest son and their youngest brother Tatum.

My kids are my greatest success stories. I love them all so much.

ACKNOWLEDGMENTS

I would like to thank Mark, Travis, Christopher and Colin for the teamwork that has gone into making the Earthly Worlds journey come to life and grow into what it is becoming.

Part I

CHAPTER ONE

"Open it, Mommy!" Cassie said, hands clenched under her chin.

Liz Riley couldn't help but grin, in spite of how fast her heart was thumping. The kid was just so flarbing cute, even though she looked ready to explode with the conflict of expectation and fear. Liz had barely gotten in the front door of the trailer house before Cassie had pounced on her with pleas of "Did it come? Did it come?"

And now, standing in their modest living room, among newer furniture—secondhand now, rather than fourth-hand, thanks to Stewart's thriving cottage business—she held the official-looking letter in her hands, with a return address from America's New Star, Hollywood, California.

Her hands trembled.

"Mom," Hunter said, wearing his *gi* in preparation for martial arts practice. "You're *killing* us!"

Liz squeezed the letter to her chest. "Oh, I can't!"

Two weeks ago in Phoenix, Cassie had knocked her audition into the stratosphere, but Liz well knew that Mom-Vision was the most blinding kind of rose-colored glasses. What she really wanted to do right now was temper Cassie's blazing enthusiasm with gentle admonishments about how to handle disappointment, just in case she

1

didn't make it. It's what Liz's mother would have done, but without the gentle part. *Don't ever get your hopes up, little girl.*

The gentleness came from Stewart now. Her husband laid a warm, strong hand on her shoulder. "Come on, babe, before the poor kid explodes." He towered over her, and she leaned into him reflexively, habitually, her great rock of a man.

Dancing on her tiptoes, Cassie looked like the ten-year-old-human approximation of a skyrocket with its burning fuse disappearing inside, poised either to shoot into the sky—or fizzle and die.

Stewart handed her the letter opener he'd made from a dagger project gone awry. She was pretty sure no one else in the world had a letter opener made of Damascus steel. With it, she slit the envelope and pulled out the letter.

She unfolded it, and the first sentence nearly toppled her like a tree.

"Mommy!" Cassie said.

Liz took a deep breath, cleared her throat, and tried to keep her voice steady as she read, "Dear Miss Riley. The judges enjoyed your rendition of 'Let It Go' so thoroughly that we would like to invite you to appear as a first-round performer in the next season of *America's New Star*—"

Cassie's squeal not only cut Liz off; it went ultrasonic. Dogs in the next county would prick up their ears. Cassie's eyes filled with tears, bringing such a flood from Liz's, too, that she couldn't read the rest of the letter. Cassie clamped both hands over her mouth to stop from screaming.

Liz knelt and Cassie flung herself into her mother's embrace.

Hunter and Stewart high-fived each other. "I knew it!" Hunter said. "I had a feeling."

The hug became a swarm of arms around Liz and Cassie. When the exultation subsided, Cassie wiped her cheeks and hugged her father, too.

"I knew you had it in you, sweetheart," Stewart said. "Your voice could change the world."

"And stop giant chameleon grizzly bears dead in their tracks!" Hunter said with a sly grin.

Cassie slugged him on the shoulder, wiping her eyes again. "Shut up. That was scary."

"Scarier than getting up in front of the judges and all those people, I'm sure," Liz said.

Cassie said, "I don't think my stomach butterflies could tell the difference. And I miss Pooh. It was so long ago it feels like a dream now."

The dump-truck-sized grizzly bear with a coat that could change color and texture like an octopus, known as Pooh, was no doubt still safe and sound in the magical realm. There wasn't much that could actually hurt him, after all.

"Oh, Pooh is quite well!" said a tiny voice from atop the refrigerator.

Liz jumped and gasped, then chuckled. She would never get used to where the Little People might pop up.

The tiny voice went on, "Spotted the ol' thumper wandering the Borderlands a fortnight ago, I did."

"Peaseblossom!" Cassie yelped. "Did you hear the news?"

"Every word," Peaseblossom said with a pearlescent grin. About a foot high, she perched atop the refrigerator, legs crossed, wearing a dandelion-colored shift. Her eyes were big and brown, as were her pointed ears, as well as the froth of hair that added almost an inch to her height. "You'll do splendidly, child, of that I'm certain." Liz always had to remind herself that while the Little People were childlike in many ways, they were not miniature children. In human reckoning, Peaseblossom could well be a centuries-old woman.

The entrance to the Little People's burrow in the back yard still looked innocuous as a badger hole, but in the two years since Cassie had discovered it, and the family's subsequent harrowing adventures in the magical realms, its inhabitants had become like cherished next-door neighbors. After the Riley family's time in the Light Realm, Liz and Stewart could actually see the Little People now. Peaseblossom and the other Little People came and went as they pleased, and Liz was grateful for their presence and their friendship to her children.

It wasn't like any human neighbors ever came over to visit. Only Stewart's buddy and part-time employee Eddie and Liz's longtime friend Alice ever ventured this far out of Mesa Roja. Even Liz's parents never came to visit. Gatherings were always held at her parents' house or a suitably neutral location.

"Not to sound suspicious or anything," Liz said to Peaseblossom, "but what are you doing here? We just walked in."

"Like Hunter," the little woman said, giving the boy a nod, "I had a notion, I did, that something momentous was about to occur. Hated to miss it."

"Can she stay for dinner, Mommy?" Cassie said.

Liz raised an eyebrow toward the tiny, elfin creature. "You're always welcome. I think we're due for some serious celebrating."

Peaseblossom said with a bow, "I'll happily partake and thank you for the invitation."

"So how should we celebrate?" Stewart said. "Order pizza? Chinese?"

"Egg rolls!" Cassie declared. "And make sure we get vegetarian stuff for me and Peaseblossom."

"Absolutely," Liz said. All the sentient creatures of the Light Realm were vegetarian, some of them vegan, depending on whether they had a taste for dairy. The eating of another living creature was abhorrent to them.

"What else does the letter say?" Cassie asked.

Liz read more. "Filming starts in a month. Another package will be coming with a bunch more information."

Cassie sank to her knees, eyes wide, her voice going quiet. "Oh, my gosh. I'm gonna be on TV... I think I'm gonna die."

"Hello?" Hunter said. "We fought dark elves and demon badgers! *And* lived!"

Liz knelt and stroked Cassie's face. "Baby, you're going to be amazing."

Hunter said, "When I get back, we can work on some runes to fix your stage fright." He looked at Peaseblossom. "Want to help with that?"

"That would be lovely," Peaseblossom chirped, nimbly jumping down from the refrigerator.

Cassie nodded, still shell-shocked.

Stewart leaned over and kissed Cassie on the head. "I knew you could do it, punkin." Then he kissed Liz. "We'll pick up the Chinese on our way home."

She nodded and stood to hug him.

"Come on, Dad!" Hunter said. "We're gonna be late for class!" He hefted his duffel bag full of pads and weapons—a *nunchaku* (it was surreal to watch her twelve-year-old wielding it like Bruce Lee); a pair of *sai,* which were metal batons with two prongs that guarded the hands and trapped other weapons; and *bahng mahng ee,* otherwise known as eskrima sticks, a matched pair of long batons padded for practicing. Hunter had told her *all* about them, and so far she had kept her obligatory, motherly admonishments about weapons to a minimum. They would have felt hollow anyway, after what they'd all been through. Since their return from the magical realms and the harrowing battle at the mouth of the Cosmic Tortoise, Hunter had thrown himself into martial arts training with such focus and dedication that he'd gained four belts. He was a brown belt now. Just two weeks ago, he had won the Arizona state taekwondo competition in three categories in his age class: sparring, weapons, and forms.

Liz was so unbelievably proud of him, she teared up for a moment. Just looking at him brought a lump into her throat. Maybe his father's genes were catching up with him. He was the tallest boy in his seventh-grade class, the gangly awkwardness that was normal at that age tempered by the body control martial arts required.

Hunter and Stewart hustled out the front door.

"Hey, Peaseblossom!" Cassie said. "Want to go play?"

"Only if you let me try on your new doll clothes. I wear them better than Barbie," Peaseblossom said.

Cassie laughed, and the two of them scampered away to Cassie's room.

Leaving Liz alone to sink into a chair, eyes filled with tears of pride.

And other kinds.

Outside, she heard the minivan start up and back out of the gravel driveway. Stewart's reliable old truck had been destroyed by a well-aimed boulder during their journey into the magical realms. Upon their return and needing a new vehicle, she had convinced her parents to cosign a loan for them to buy one. He had rankled at the idea of buying something as staid and boring as a minivan, but Liz's mother had insisted as a condition of the loan, and Liz had gone along with it. A basic pickup truck wouldn't fit them all anymore, now that the kids were bigger, and the models that could were out of their price range. So, did owning a minivan make her a soccer mom now?

The kids were growing up so fast. How long before Cassie no longer wanted to play? Before she was a teenager, when boys, and probably some girls, too, would be showering her with crushes? And what on earth would happen if she did well on *America's New Star*?

"Holy cannoli," Liz said. "We're going to Hollywood."

And to San Antonio for Hunter's first National Taekwondo Championship.

Next week, Stewart was going to a trade show in Atlanta for knives and swords. So much traveling. She'd never been to any of those places, and in fact, any thought of doing so had been a pipe dream up until their trip to the magical realms, before which both she and Stewart had been trying to make ends meet with dead-end jobs. She still had her job at the day care—she loved kids too much to give it up easily—but Stewart's smithing business had taken off. He had since built himself a shop in the back yard that was almost as big as their drafty, old trailer house.

But here she sat, alone.

The wildly talented and successful members of her family were off doing their thing.

And she was exhausted from watching other people's kids for a sliver more than minimum wage.

How far the Homecoming Queen of fourteen years ago had come.

A couple of the men she'd dated in high school, including the captain of the football team, had successful businesses around Mesa Roja, with big houses and ex-wives. Everyone, especially her parents, had frowned upon her getting together with Stewart, with his checkered past and taciturn demeanor, but she'd never once regretted that decision. He loved her all the way down, she knew without question, and his soul was as deep as an ocean. She called him her personal Viking, a man born in the wrong century, but he was more than that. In the magical realms, he had become a powerful wizard. Here on Earth, the Penumbra, the bordering shadow forever caught between the Light and Dark magical realms, his power was much diminished, but he had learned to use runes to collect and focus magical Source into subtle but undeniable effects.

Magic had helped all of them. The kids were using it, too. It didn't give them outlandish abilities here, like it did in the magical realm, but it enhanced their existing gifts—Cassie's singing, Hunter's courage and martial arts skills. And they'd never used it to hurt anyone. They used it to help people. The family together had created runes of healing for Liz's father last year when he was diagnosed with Stage Three Non-Hodgkin's lymphoma. The runes had eased his suffering from chemo, and six months later, the cancer was in remission.

But what about her? What were her talents?

She'd never successfully used magic or created a rune.

Next to the greatness of her husband and her children, what was she? What had she become?

Mediocre. A cheerleader who had gone nowhere. A cliche.

She caught her fingers tracing the jagged eight-inch, pink scar along her belt line. She had come within a demon badgerine's claw of losing everyone, everything. She and Stewart could have orphaned their children. Or worse.

She still remembered how it felt, that monster's claws ripping into her, like a punch in the gut rather than a slice. The pain came later. The wisps of memory of Cassie singing over her, keeping her alive long enough for Claude and the bright elf Wyn Ar-Chaheris to work their healing magic. She still experienced dreams of being only half-conscious with a pitched battle swirling around her, unable to move, unable to see what was happening, and all she could do was cry out in despair over those dying on her behalf. Every time, it made her feel worthless, unworthy.

There was a weight on her chest now, like a big dog settling onto her ribcage and refusing to budge. She noticed it when she fell still for too long. It was easier to keep moving at life's frenetic pace—endless trips to martial arts practice, vocal lessons, work, groceries—than to pause and reflect about the whys.

That way lay despair.

An impulse drove her to the kitchen drawer where she pulled out a little notebook and a pen, then sat at their modest Formica table that was a couple of decades older than her.

She drew the rune for happiness and joy, which Cassie and Hunter had taught her. It was an easy one to remember, looking like an angular capital *P.* Then she took some deep breaths, attempted to still her inner turmoil, and focused her will on gathering motes of magical Source. Source existed everywhere, all around her. The kids had described the luminous specks to her over and over, what they felt like, what they "looked" like to the inner eye.

But Liz could never find them. It felt too much like she was just imagining them. They weren't real. They wouldn't come to her.

Just like all the other times she had secretly tried, nothing happened.

After five minutes of concentration, she gave up, tore off the page, crumpled it up and threw it in the garbage.

Then she grabbed the takeout menu for Golden Dragon from its refrigerator magnet and started writing down what to order for their celebratory dinner.

CHAPTER TWO

L ord Marvys Ar-Chaheris had a sickness he did not understand.
His stomach pained him. His chest felt cinched tight, his
throat thick. His favorite meals no longer gave him pleasure. He
passed through bright days in dark fog. He could walk through the
gardens of the Queen's mansion, bathed in sunshine, swimming in
the fragrance of flowers, herbs, and greenery, immersed in brilliant
colors—and drown in worry.

Perhaps right now, his worries were justified.

Because he now stood in the darkness of the earth where the only
light was the dim globe he'd apparently conjured himself, surrounded by the roots of the Great Tree which were as old as Time itself,
looking at a crystal urn that imprisoned something terrible.

And he had no idea how he got here.

Through the clear crystal, he could see the blackness swirling
within, a darkness deeper than the deepest subterranean depths,
blacker than the emptiness between the stars. Two scarlet pinpricks
peered out from the blackness, as if sensing his proximity. This mi-
asma of near-living Darkness churned and seethed. Did it have the
sentience to scheme? Lord Marvys didn't know.

For over fifty years, his sickness had gnawed at him. In a being as
long-lived as a bright elf, fifty years was but an eye blink, and Lord

Marvys's age could not easily be reckoned in the years of the human world. But this malady taxed him beyond the capacity for magic to heal. And he had tried. His elixirs and spells worked for shorter and shorter duration, until they no longer worked at all. The pain was there in his gut even now.

In the Light Realm above, whenever he passed through the cozy paths of the gardens, through little-traveled halls of the Queen's mansion, his subordinates in the Queen's Royal Guard gave him deference, bowing and offering greetings, but in recent days they had been giving him strange glances, thinking he would not catch them out of the corner of his eye.

Was it the inexplicable advancement of age, the new lines in the face of a being that did not age as humans did?

Had he forgotten to comb his hair again?

The constant physical discomforts distracted him from such basic tasks. He was spending too much time alone in his chambers, too much time in the embrace of dreamflower tea. It was not normal for one of the five Lords of the House of Ar-Chaheris to be so reclusive. He should be overseeing the Royal Guard, making certain everything was well with his fellow elves, especially now that the Princess had been rescued from the Dark Lord's imprisonment. The forces of Baron Tyrus were always scheming, always clawing at the gates of the Light Realm.

As Lord Marvys well knew.

He did not remember descending through the labyrinthine passages of the Queen's secret vaults to stand upon this spot, nor what spurred him to make this trek. The Queen's vaults went deep, deep through the ground into the fabric of the universe itself. He did not remember opening the massive door of this vault, which was fashioned from a diamond the height of a human. All but impenetrable on its own, the vault was keyed to open for the Queen and, it seemed, the Lords of House Ar-Chaheris.

But he felt like an impostor, coasting on his prestige. It would only be a matter of time before he was called before the Queen to face questions he dared not answer. How could he look her in the face, knowing what he had done? How could she know that every day since, he had been trying to make amends for it? But that would not matter.

If the truth got out, the House of Ar-Chaheris would be shamed. He could not bear the thought of bringing dishonor upon a lineage older than human civilization.

When nights fell and sleep would not come, he prowled the halls and rooms of the Queen's mansion. Deep within the roots of the mansion, sculpted of the living wood of the largest tree in all of existence, lay the chambers where secrets were kept, tomes of knowledge that were dangerous in the wrong hands and artifacts taken from Baron Tyrus's vile minions, sequestered in deep vaults where no hand could ever touch them. These days, it was in the shadows that Lord Marvys felt comfortable, as if the light of day might expose what he had done.

In the darkest of night, there was little chance he would encounter the Princess accidentally. Whenever he came upon her during the day, she would give him the most radiant smile and the warmest greeting. She was his friend after all, not just his sovereign. All the Royal Guard loved her, so sweet and innocent she was, even with all the wisdom of the universe residing nascent within her. He had loved watching her grow from an infant, watching her coming into her vast power, little by little. She was simply the purest, most beautiful being in the universe, the second-most powerful creature in the Light Realm. When she had disappeared, he wept inconsolably, and he had blubbered with joy when the human, Stewart Riley, had snatched her from the Dark Lord's clutches.

Stewart was the hero of heroes, and rightfully so. He had risked his very soul—and lost it—to return the Princess to the Light Realm.

Everyone believed Baron Tyrus, the Lord of the Dark Realm, had been the villain, but no.

Unknown to anyone, the true villain was Lord Marvys Ar-Chaheris.

Every day of the fifty years of the Princess's imprisonment in the Dark Realm, Lord Marvys's burden grew heavier and heavier. His nightmares got worse and worse, more frightening, more violent, more insidious. It seemed every time he tried to close his eyes and rest, he was plagued by images of Baron Tyrus and his awful minions.

For centuries he had suffered such dreams, and he faced them with nobility and compassion, recognizing that nothing in them could truly hurt him. But now, since the Princess's abduction, certainty of that had fled. Too often, he awoke terrified that the Dark Lord or one of his dark elf assassins was there with him in his bedchamber.

How could he have been so stupid?

It was just a jeweled locket, he thought, a beautiful bauble. He had discovered it on a patrol in the Borderlands. He and his troops had encountered a band of Baron Tyrus's dark elves lurking as close as they could to the Border of the Light Realm, clearly up to nefarious purposes. His larger force had defeated them easily and destroyed them to the last. He abhorred killing—except for dark elves,

14

those terrible cousins who, in ages past, embraced the Darkness and had been consumed by it. They were as vile as they were dangerous.

But as he and his troops were searching the bodies for clues about why the enemy was there, Lord Marvys's eye caught the glint of a lustrous, sky-blue gem, lying on the ground among the dead.

He picked it up and found it to be an aquamarine so deep and rich it matched the color of the Princess's eyes. The gem proved to be the front of a locket. Out of curiosity, he opened the locket and found it empty. But the moment he opened it he had the idea to present it as a gift to the Princess. He loved the way it sparkled, the way the light danced within it, and he had seen the Princess spend many hours staring into the facets of jewels she had just conjured from the earth, as if scrutinizing their crystal lattices with her naked eye.

How could he have been so stupid as to think to give the Princess spoils taken from a dark elf?

Nevertheless, he took it home to the City, and one day he spotted her playing alone amid the stones of Jewel Garden, spinning profusions of rubies, emeralds, sapphires, and diamonds in the air above her head. He approached and offered her the locket.

"Oh, what a beautiful color! It's like the sky!" she had said, accepting it.

And he showed her that it was a locket.

"I shall keep a dream inside!" she said.

And then she placed the loop of golden chain over her head.

The moment it settled into place around her neck, she disappeared from view.

The suspended jewels all fell to the ground.

At first, he thought she was playing with him. Who besides the Queen truly knew what powers the child possessed? She was not really a child at all, not in any known sense, but a newly born projection of the Source, just as the Queen embodied. He thought she may have been playing a trick on him, playful as she was, a game of hide-and-seek perhaps. He called her name and searched for her throughout the Jewel Garden, then the wider grounds of the Queen's mansion, then up and down the many floors of the mansion, joined by the Royal Guards in an ever more frantic search. Lord Marvys's panic doubled and redoubled.

Then the Queen appeared, shining like a galaxy of stars, her voice as thunderous as an earthquake. "Where is my daughter?"

Lord Marvys's voice trembled, tears streaming down his face. "She was in the Jewel Garden, my Queen. And then she was gone." The full extent of his courage and honor could not encompass the ability to speak of his innocent gift.

The search spiraled wider through the City.

But the Princess was gone, vanished. She no longer existed within the Light Realm.

For almost ten Penumbral years, the Queen used her vast powers of perception to search for the Princess in the Borderlands, then the Penumbra, but could not find her.

But the Princess was an immortal, nearly infinite being. It was impossible that she could simply cease to exist. It would break the very laws of the universe. So that left only one explanation. She had been taken to the Dark Realm. Because she was the Princess of the Light Realm, however, she should not have been able to exist in the Dark Realm at all. Light and Dark beings could not exist in the opposite realm. If they attempted it, they simply fell back into their own realm. The closest either could get was the Penumbra, the world of mortal humans, or with great effort, the Borderlands. The magic binding the Princess, however, must have been so strong, she could not simply fall back into her home realm. It could only have come from Baron Tyrus himself.

For years, decades, questions swirled around Lord Marvys's ears, each one as a dissonant screech across his soul. *How could this have happened?* He was the only person in the Light Realm who knew the answer, and he could not bring himself to speak it aloud.

It became a sickness that gnawed at him, inside and out.

And then, when Stewart Riley had appeared within the Great Hall, holding the beloved Princess in his arms, Lord Marvys had been overjoyed.

But the cost to Stewart had been high. His journey to the Dark Realm and the magic he had been forced to use to accomplish his mission had transformed him into something no longer human. Dark Source was painful, violent, difficult to bridle, but it was powerful. And if one used it, it would systematically corrupt all goodness, kindness, and compassion within that person, until there was soon nothing left but a bitter husk, ripe to become a minion of the Dark Lord.

Stewart's wife, Liz, the very heart of courage and devotion, had demanded the Queen try to save him. In gratitude, the Queen and the Princess agreed. The Source had grown so powerful that it was almost a sentient entity in its own right, as if the Darkness in Stewart's soul had bifurcated and made a new entity. But it was an entity of pure shadow and darkness, a conglomeration of his darkest memories and impulses, an *umbral.*

The Queen had ripped the umbral out of Stewart and imprisoned it in an urn of star-crystal, an incredibly dense substance fashioned from the matter of a collapsed star, far denser and more indestructible than even diamond. Even though it was only the size of a loaf of bread, the urn itself weighed more than Pooh, the giant grizzly bear, so heavy it took four ogres to carry it to its vault deep underneath the City.

Ever since the Princess had been returned, Lord Marvys expected her to declare how she had been captured, how she had received a locket from him and that locket had transported her to an awful iron cage. He had heard her account of her captivity, the way Baron Tyrus had siphoned power and blood from her to fuel his terrible machinations, but she claimed to not remember how she got there.

Lord Marvys had received this information with shameful relief.

By this time, he had determined how he could have been so foolish. The aquamarine locket had been imbued with *two* spells—one to ensnare a fool like him into giving it to the Princess, and another to spirit her away.

If he'd had any courage at all, he would have simply revealed his mistake and thrown himself on the Queen's mercy. And she *was* merciful. But should there be mercy for the elf who had put her daughter in the hands of the Dark Lord? No. Had he any honor, he would simply throw himself on his sword.

But perhaps he could wreak vengeance on the Dark Lord.

The thing imprisoned in the urn could not be called truly alive, nor was it truly not-alive. It was the part of Stewart Riley that had embraced the Darkness and used Dark Source to power its magic. Humans were never purely good or purely evil, but somewhere in between. Although Stewart was a normal man in the human world, his powerful imagination and force of will made him a powerful wizard in the magical realms. And as a human with nearly equal parts Dark and Light within him, the result of an awful childhood set against a kind heart and a powerful will, Stewart was rare among wizards in that he could channel both Light and Dark Source with equal potency.

This umbral represented Stewart's ability to channel Dark Source.

Lord Marvys could see in its simmering gaze that its only wish was to reunite with Stewart. In a sense, it *was* as much Stewart as the goodness within him. But Stewart had used so much Dark magic that it had all but consumed him.

Listening to Stewart tell his tale during his recovery, Lord Marvys realized that Stewart's Dark power surpassed all but the mightiest of Baron Tyrus's minions. Given time and practice, he might well have gained enough power to challenge Baron Tyrus for control of the Dark Realm. But such a struggle would throw the entire Dark Realm into chaos, igniting civil wars between dark elves and dwarves, destroying great swaths of the Dark Lord's resources, and expending vast quantities of Dark Source in the process.

In such a titanic struggle, with all the Dark Realm's foul denizens distracted by civil war, the Light Realm might find a respite, perhaps even find the space to bring more Light back to the universe. People in the Penumbra might become kinder again, more compassionate, less selfish, less greedy, less hateful. While the Princess was imprisoned, the mortal world had darkened considerably. Hatred, avarice, and corruption had become the norm.

With the Princess's return, the pendulum might begin to swing back.

But Lord Marvys could hasten the swing by releasing the only weapon in existence capable of destroying Baron Tyrus. Even now, he wondered at the wisdom of what he was about to do, but Baron Tyrus had to be destroyed, for the good of all the realms.

The urn sat upon a pedestal of black stone. It looked fragile, but something about it pulled at him like the force of gravity itself.

He drew his scimitar, this faithful blade that had served him all these centuries, summoned his will, and infused the metal with Source, making the steel temporarily indestructible, its edge finer and sharper than the bonds between atoms.

He raised the sword over his head, took the hilt in both hands, and slashed diagonally *through* the stone pedestal.

The cut was clean. The upper section of the pedestal slid to the stone floor and toppled over, dumping the urn onto its side with a sound like someone had just dropped a building from a great height. The ground—or was it the fabric of the universe—trembled under his feet.

The lid, about the size of a dinner plate, weighing several tons, spun loose and rotated ponderously, striking sparks as it ground into the floor.

The black substance within spilled out like tar, if tar could sniff about like a cautious animal. The substance spread, growing larger but less substantial as it did so. The more it seemed to sniff about, the bolder it grew, the angrier its movements.

Lord Marvys simply watched. It was not looking for him. It had only one purpose—to find and reunite with *itself.*

The entity, the umbral, expanded into a black specter, becoming less and less solid-looking, filling the chamber, as if trying to get a sense of its environs, a cat sniffing around an unfamiliar space.

And then it came to the open vault door and *whooshed* away like a foul breeze.

Lord Marvys stood alone in the empty vault.

His vengeance complete, he knelt on the floor, braced the pommel of his scimitar against the base of the pedestal, held the point to his heart, and took one last deep breath.

"Forgive me," he said.

Then he threw himself upon the sword.

CHAPTER THREE

It was a hot Saturday afternoon in the taekwondo training hall as Liz sat and absently surfed her phone while Hunter practiced. By this point, she'd seen all the moves so many times it bored her spitless. Watching her son compete was exciting. Watching him practice was most assuredly not. Sweat trickled down the side of her neck, moistening strands of hair. Catching some split ends out of the corner of her eye, she realized it was time for an afternoon at the hairdresser. Add that to a bazillion other errands, and she might be able to get to it by Christmas next year.

Being pretty took too much work.

Granted, she loved the way Stewart looked at her, like she was a goddess, the most beautiful woman in existence. And her looks had certainly opened doors for her, sparked random kindnesses, and made it easier to smooth over her failings. She knew this. But she often wished she could simply get up in the morning, spend five minutes in the bathroom, and be done, ready for anything, as Stewart could.

Sometimes, being pretty, being ladylike, being the perfect wife, the perfect mother, was too much pressure.

Checking the time, she saw that about half of the class time remained. So, she got up and excused herself to the parking lot, where the awning shaded her from the blistering sun. She thumbed in Alice's phone number.

Alice picked up immediately. "Girlfriend! I was just thinking about you."

"That's what you always say," Liz said.

"And it's always true. I pine shamelessly for children like yours who are old enough to go to the bathroom by them—Jamie! Get that out of your mouth! Right now!"

At Alice's sudden yell, Liz flinched away from the phone. Alice's two boys were three and five.

"Sorry," Alice said. "Kid was actually chewing on a lamp cord." In the background could be heard much wailing and blubbering. "Go play! Skedaddle!" She sighed again, and Liz could almost see her friend's exasperated fingers-through-the-hair technique. It hadn't changed since elementary school. "So, back to the purpose of my call."

"I called you," Liz said.

"Oh, well, I was *going* to call you, so now that you're here, this is most fortuitous." Her voice rose in arch exaggeration. "We need to go out. Specifically, *I* need out. With you. As soon as possible. I need a girl's date more desperately than any woman who ever lived."

"You need to feel like a person again," Liz said, well remembering those days. Several years of her own life had disappeared into a black hole. How many times in the lost days of Hunter and Cassie's preschool years had Alice—pre-marriage, pre-motherhood—reminded Liz that she was not just a wife and mother, that she had once been a pretty-darn-cool person?

"With thoughts!"

"And dreams!"

"And conversation that doesn't involve bodily functions!"

Liz chuckled. "Well, what are you doing in a couple of hours?"

"Trying not to kill myself or anyone I purportedly love." Liz could imagine Alice shooting one of her boys a severely raised eyebrow. "Just like every day. Whatcha got in mind?"

"Coffee shop?" Liz said.

"How about tomorrow?"

Tomorrow was Sunday. No extracurricular activities took place on Sunday. "Make it happen."

"Jake owes me a day of unobstructed 'father time' with the boys. Tomorrow I'm cashing a piece of it in. I'm hoarding it like a dragon. Are you bringing the tequila, or should I?"

"You don't drink."

"But I *want* to want to."

Liz laughed. "Whipped cream and chocolate sauce instead?"

"You drive a hard bargain. Sold to the lady with pre-diabetes!"

After they made arrangements and disconnected, Liz went back inside, feeling much better, as if she had just been hugged in a warm, gentle embrace, so much so that she had to wipe a tear from the corner of her eye.

Knees squeezed against her chest, Cassie sat on the rock in the back yard, in the shade of a palo verde tree near the Little People's hole, rocking to a silent internal beat.

Peaseblossom lounged on a nearby branch, sipping lemonade from a tiny wooden cup. "What is it, dearie? I thought you wanted to practice drawing runes."

Cassie sighed. "I did. I do."

She fell silent long enough for Peaseblossom to prompt her. "And...?"

"And every time I think about having to perform *on TV,* my mouth goes dry, my heart stops, and I feel all oogy. I can't concentrate." The runes for *courage* and *skill* were already drawn in the dust at her feet, but she couldn't summon any Source to give them power.

"Stage fright then," Peaseblossom said.

Cassie nodded and rested her nose between her kneecaps, sighing again. She hated admitting this kind of silliness to her friend. She wanted to do well on the show. It was all she thought about since getting the letter. She wanted to get up there and sing her heart out for the world. Until she started thinking about "the world," and how many people that really was. Millions of people she didn't know would *see* her, judge her, and maybe think she was lame. *What were those judges thinking, letting this kid get on stage?* People could be so mean.

From her father's workshop a few dozen yards away came the steady *bang bang bang* of a hammer against steel, the clang and rasp of steel against anvil, the deep-throated hiss of the forge. She found the sharp rhythm comforting, telling her that her daddy was nearby. She could always run to him, always trust him. He would never be scared by something as stupid as stage fright. When he was in the Dark Realm, he'd had to fight giant, half-machine dragons and even the Dark Lord himself. After surviving that, nothing scared him anymore. Even Cassie herself had had to face some terrifying creatures in the Battle of Tortoise Mountain, as she and Hunter had come to call it. So being terrified of getting up in front of people, no matter how many, to do something she loved sounded all the sillier.

Peaseblossom jumped down from her perch and walked over to the two runes. "Let us forget about the show for a moment." She erased them with her foot.

"How?"

"We shall do some runes for something else, *someone* else, that have nothing to do with singing or performing or what have you. Do you think you could do that?"

Cassie nodded, eager to try. "Could we do something for Mommy?"

"Certainly. How shall we help her?"

"She's so tired lately, always wants to go to bed early. And I think she's sad sometimes. I see her face when she thinks I'm not looking."

"What do you think saddens her?"

"I don't know. Maybe she wants to go back to the Light Realm."

Peaseblossom rubbed her chin. Then she brightened, knelt, and drew a rune in the dirt that looked like an angular, lower-case *n*, with a slope instead of a hump.

"Yup, that's the one," Cassie said. This rune represented endurance, survival, physical strength.

"And what do you reckon will happen if we draw it upside down?" Peaseblossom asked, like a tiny schoolteacher.

"We don't do that," Cassie said. "It would be like a curse to take all that away from somebody."

"And that requires...?"

27

"Dark magic."

Peaseblossom grinned. "Good girl."

As Earth, also called the Penumbra, was the mid-realm between Light and Dark, both Dark and Light magical Source, motes of magical power surrounding everything like air, floated around, waiting to be harnessed and channeled by someone's will. There was as much of one around as the other. The Penumbra was the only place that was true. The intentions of a spell naturally attracted the proper type of Source. Curses, hexes, anything that caused intentional harm used Dark Source. The more often someone used a particular kind of Source, the easier it got to attract that kind, the more it clung to one's spirit, like what happened to Daddy in the Dark Realm. They had been lucky the Queen could save him.

"Very well, then," Peaseblossom said. "So we use this one and...?"

Cassie knelt and used a stick to scratch out the rune for joy and light, which looked like an angular capital *P.* And then the one for *motherhood, fertility, womanhood,* which looked like a similar capital *B.*

"Shall I help you with the channeling?" Peaseblossom asked.

"I can do it," Cassie said, closing her eyes. She took a couple of deep breaths and relaxed herself.

From the darkness behind her eyelids, she began to look for floating droplets of Source, with the intention of channeling them into the three runes before her, which, if properly invoked, would make Mommy's day much happier. Soon, the Source appeared behind her eyelids like rainbow sparkles moving around her, through her. She seized them with her mind and channeled them into the shapes of the three runes. In her mind, the runes took shape and grew in brightness until it was like they focused the light of the sun, too bright to keep looking at. That's when she knew they were properly charged and she could send them out into the world.

She opened her eyes and released them.

Peaseblossom grinned at her. "And you said you couldn't do magic today. Nicely done that was."

Cassie flushed with pleasure at her success. "It's easier when it's for someone else."

The little woman nodded, "And that, dearie, is the difference between the Dark and the Light. Concern yourself less about yourself, and more about the All, about the connections between us all. Too much selfishness, you'll be playing with the Dark. Never forget that once you start using the Dark, it gets easier and easier, because the Dark is more eager, more willing. So you must always beware your intentions."

Cassie nodded soberly.

Stewart put the cooling billet back into the forge, stripped off his leather gloves, and wiped the sweat from his brow. If all went well, this billet would be a finished rapier in a couple of days. He closed the door on his homemade forge, blocking the bright, yellow heat. The temperature in his workshop probably topped 120 degrees. A series of large fans kept the air moving, made the heat tolerable. He was long since used to it, but staying hydrated was a constant concern, so he put down his tongs and took a long pull on his thermos of ice water.

Using the burgeoning profits of his smithing efforts, Stewart had built himself a new workshop of concrete, lumber, and aluminum, including a larger propane forge he had put together from firebrick and welded iron beams. It was triple the size and heating capacity of his old forge, large enough to handle bigger weapons and drastically speed up his process. Under the benches and pegboards were his supplies of several types of raw metal: iron, steel, copper, tin, bronze, brass, nickel, even a little silver. The new electromagnetic power hammer worked like a dream. With its endless capacity, he could work for hours with a reduced burden of physical fatigue, and he could work on larger pieces without an assistant. It didn't relieve all the work on his arms, but it could strike over two hundred blows a minute. Swords, axes, and spears hung decoratively on the walls, among the carefully arranged tools.

He remembered making each of those weapons with intimate clarity, as if each of them was one of his children. Like children, each came with a unique set of challenges, quirks, imperfections that had to be accepted and worked with.

Stewart loved the nature of metallurgy. He understood it in his bones, knew its temperament, recognized its mood by the color of its glow, even as he recognized its mysteries.

Wiping a cool dribble from his chin, he heard Eddie call him from the small, enclosed office in the corner.

Stewart opened the door and let the wall of cool air waft over him. The swamp cooler in the corner reduced the office's interior to somewhere in the comparatively frigid upper eighties.

Eddie exclaimed, "Gah! Door!"

Stewart stepped farther inside and pulled the door closed.

"Were you born in a barn?" Eddie said good-naturedly. Since Stewart's old boss, Mr. Richards, had inexplicably disappeared, the locksmith shop where Stewart and Eddie had worked soon went out of business, leaving Eddie unemployed. Eddie started taking classes at Mesa Roja Community College to learn bookkeeping, so Stewart hired him to do the books for Bright Blades, Limited. He had let the kids come up with the name.

The two of them sharing the small space made it feel like a closet. There was just enough room for Eddie to sit at the desk with the computer, file cabinet, and several shelves full of reference books on metallurgy and ancient and medieval weapons. This was all Stewart needed to make anything from a Roman *gladius* to a nineteenth-century cavalry saber or a samurai sword.

Eddie leaned back in the creaky chair so he could see Stewart's face more easily. "Okay, I've got everything caught up in the expenses and receivables through this month. Everything looks fine. Steel and Shield is still paying you on time, and the check just cleared for that German guy's *Zweihänder*. I called the steel supplier, and they said the next shipment should be showing up on Tuesday. Is there anything else you need?"

"What are the profits for this quarter so far?" Stewart asked.

Eddie made a couple of mouse clicks and pointed to the computer screen. Stewart didn't exactly hate computers; they felt more like alien, parasitic organisms that he would never comprehend beyond the on-off switch and how to answer an email.

Seeing the profit figures for his hard work, Stewart nodded appreciatively. They really were doing okay. Would he ever shed himself of the expectation that his business was going to come crashing down around his ears at any second? Today was not that day. Old habits die hard, so seeing that he was firmly in the black, with

31

enough left over to do some nice things for Liz and the kids, always surprised him. After that moment of surprise always came the worry that the Dark Lord was working some secret machination to destroy Stewart's life. No doubt Baron Tyrus was out for revenge after Stewart had saved the Princess, depriving the Dark Lord of his favorite toy.

"Look good, boss?" Eddie said.

"Looks real good, Eddie. Thank you."

"My pleasure. Now I've gotta get to class."

The two of them walked outside, where Eddie paused, noticing Cassie over there under the palo verde tree, scratching something in the dirt with a stick. Stewart could see Peaseblossom there as well, watching Cassie's scratchings with a teacherly eye.

Eddie waved. "Hey, Cassie!"

But she didn't respond. Stewart recognized a kid in magical concentration when he saw one. "I don't think she heard you. She can concentrate pretty hard."

"What's she doing?"

Stewart shrugged and moved toward the corner of the house, subtly urging Eddie along. Eddie couldn't see Peaseblossom, didn't have the right kind of spirit for it. So, Eddie shrugged along with Stewart, but for different reasons, and followed him toward the driveway, their feet crunching in the gravel.

"You know," Eddie said, "it's been two years, but I still wonder what happened to Richards. I keep waiting to hear a news story about somebody finding bones in the desert or something."

"If he died in the desert," Stewart said, "I doubt there are any bones left to find."

"But if there ever was a dude the world was better off without, it was that guy." Eddie shuddered. "I make more working for you and it's way less hours, so I have time to go to school. So, thanks for that, buddy. You're a good guy—a weird guy, but a good guy—and a way better boss."

"I couldn't do it without you," Stewart said. "I always figure Richards died on the toilet of bitterness and self-loathing, and no one ever came to check on him." Mr. Richards had made Stewart's life a hell for too many years. Stewart still chided himself for putting up with it for so long. Once a mind has been expanded, it can't be jammed back into the same box.

"Maybe the javelinas got him." Eddie opened the door and slid into the rickety Honda Civic that was older than he was.

Stewart chuckled. "See you next week."

For the first time in its existence, it was free.

It had no name.

It had no form.

It had no memories, not really.

It understood only that freedom was new.

Once, it had been a man. Or part of a man, the heart of a man.

And together, they had been *powerful*, able to move worlds and wreak destruction upon their enemies.

It had reveled in the destruction, in the rending of flesh and the shattering of things carefully made, in the annihilation of the unnaturalness of order and returning the multiverse to chaos, the natural state of all things. It served the man, and the man served it. It changed the man, and the man fed it. It had known joy for the briefest of instants.

And then it was ripped from its body and imprisoned in a tiny, tiny place. Throughout its time in the tiny prison, it yearned to return to its home, to its body, the body of the man. It still felt him, always felt him, in some distant place. He had forgotten his Dark heart. That made it angry, to be forgotten. So, in its prison, it seethed and boiled and churned, always seeking escape.

It must return to the man. The man was its home. Without him, it was nothing. It wanted to destroy enemies again, to feel joy again.

Every mote, every molecule of its prison it scrutinized, and when it was sure it had checked every molecular bond, it had forgotten.

But then suddenly, its prison vanished, and it existed for the briefest of moments in a realm that would not suffer its presence, and it was cast out, away, deep into a different cosmos, an infinite landscape of desert and desolation. Beings of immense power existed here, immense cruelty, awakening a sense of kinship.

But it did not belong here. Without the benefit of physical form, it could not feel, could not see, could not scent, could not hear, could not taste. It was a blind, dumb thing that was not a thing at all, not really, having no more substance than an ill thought.

Not until it could be reunited with the man, and the man would come here to join his Brethren of Shadow.

It could sense the notice, however, the attention of the Dark Lord, for such a nexus of power and spite it could only be.

It sensed the Dark Lord's curiosity, his approval, his wonder, like a parent watching an infant crawl for the first time.

So, the not-thing crawled more, farther.

It moved across a bleak, desiccated landscape of thorns and sand and malice. When it encountered any living beings, it made certain those beings were not the man. They never were. So it moved on.

It had no sense of time, only that the man still existed, and that it must find him.

It had no other purpose.

It *would* find him, no matter where he was, no matter how long it took.

And it moved with the speed of instinct.

CHAPTER FOUR

Sunday brunch was a thing Liz would never have thought to go to; it always sounded like something her mother or people with more money did, but Alice had talked her into it. Nowadays the family budget could in fact, afford her a syrupy latte and a pastry once in a while.

It was a lovely Sunday morning at Caffeine Dreams, a lace-and-local-art kind of establishment that was her favorite place in Mesa Roja's Crossroads Mall. She wasn't a shopper by nature or habit, aside from spending many teenage weekends at Crossroads with Alice and other friends. Caffeine Dreams had been a boutique clothing store then.

Liz was a little early for her brunch date. Her family were off doing their own thing, leaving her with nothing to do but housework, and she wasn't in the mood for that today.

Waiting for Alice, she sat at a wrought-iron table in the interior courtyard area outside Caffeine Dreams. Sunlight pouring through the skylights painted stark shapes on the mall's many shuttered storefronts and empty floors.

The state of the mall saddened her, infused as it was with so many youthful memories. Maybe the heyday of the shopping mall was over. About half the stores were vacant, making the place feel strangely haunted. The grand corridors used to be thronged with people, but now with only a scant few. The entire place felt a little desperate. In the parking lot, tough brown grass peeked between slabs of crumbling concrete. The building facade looked like a sun-bleached skull now, the windows overdue for cleaning, the compass-rose logo, once a brilliant scarlet, now faded to a lifeless salmon color. Inside, the floors were scuffed, faded by age, overdue for an update. The food court had been reduced to Chinese fast food and a burger place.

How much of this malaise was attributable to the ascendancy of the Dark magical realm?

An expostulation of exultant joy grabbed Liz's attention, Alice quick-shuffling to the table with arms outstretched, her face beaming.

Liz grinned and stood to hug her.

"Oh, my god, you're a sight for sore eyes!" Alice said. She was a little taller than Liz, willowy and dark-haired. Liz had always admired her friend's cheekbones and rich, brown eyes, products of her Chinese heritage. Her ancestors had helped build the Southern Pacific railroad line from Yuma to Tucson. Today, she looked like she had stepped out of a catalog, wearing a stylish linen pantsuit and gleaming yellow pumps.

"And *you* look *fabulous*," Liz said. All of sudden, she felt like Frumpy McFrumperson in her (slightly worn) jeans and (five-year-old) white lace blouse.

"You know how long it's been since I've been able to dress up like a normal person?" In spite of Alice's immaculate hair and makeup, a definite tiredness lurked in her eyes.

"I can imagine," Liz said.

"Shall we order? I'm starving," Alice said.

Liz hooked Alice's arm, and together they went into the coffee shop, where the grinder was grinding and the steamer was steaming, and the air smelled deliciously of coffee, chocolate, and fresh-baked scones. Southwestern and native art adorned the walls, paintings and sculptures and beadwork.

They approached the counter, and Alice said, "I wore a maternity blouse because I'm going to order one of everything."

They laughed along with the high-school-age barista who took their order.

Alice proved to be a little more sensible, ordering a still-warm blueberry scone and a coconut mocha with extra whipped cream and sprinkles. Liz ordered a cherry cream-cheese Danish and the same extravagant latte as Alice. When they returned to their table in the courtyard, they had to be very careful to balance the towers of whipped cream, sprinkles, and chocolate syrup atop their drinks.

Liz took the initiative. "How are things? Tell me everything."

"I could write the Encyclopedia Big-Yawnica. It would kill you from boredom." Alice ticked each thing down on her fingers. "Seriously, my life is: making food no one wants to eat, arguing about where pee is supposed to go, scrubbing marker from walls, slathering on sunscreen, and shepherding play dates. At least I get to sleep through the night now, mostly." She slurped some whipped cream with an expression of ecstasy. "If only Bobby didn't wake up at the crack of five thirty every single day."

"I feel your pain," Liz said, squeezing her hand. "It'll get better."

"I know," Alice sighed. "When you're going through hell, keep going, right?"

"How's Jake with the boys?" Liz asked.

39

"Oh, he's great," Alice said with another sigh. "He doesn't even give me anything to complain about like a proper wife. He even manages the toilet seat like a conscientious human. When I told him about how today was Mom-Gets-Out-of-Jail-Free Day, though, he got this thousand-yard stare..." Her eyes widened and went dead for a moment, then she chuckled devilishly.

"Photos, please!" Liz said. "I'm sure both of them have doubled in size since I saw them last."

Alice whipped out her smartphone and produced a series of photos of her boys playing or in various stages of misbehavior. They really were adorably cute.

"How are Jake and your mom getting along?" Liz asked. Long ago, Liz and Alice had bonded over their problematic mothers.

Alice had broken family tradition and married a white guy, much to her very traditional mother's disapproval. She said, "Jake is a loan officer now, so that has helped assuage Mrs. Wang's reservations. But she do love them grandbabies."

They talked for a while about little things, munched on their pastries, and sipped their coffees. But the longer they talked, the more Liz sensed something behind Alice's veneer of urbane charm and ordinary motherly woes.

At a pause in the conversation, Liz fixed her friend with steadfast scrutiny.

"What?" Alice said, eyes narrowed.

Liz raised an eyebrow.

"Okay, fine," Alice said, her mask of joviality fracturing, revealing something raw underneath. "Most days I feel like the worst mom on the planet. Some women are born to be moms. I am not one of them. I miss being wildly in love with my husband. I miss fun. I miss *sex*. Neither one of us seems to want to make time for that anymore. After all day runt-herding, I'm just dead and numb, reduced to the mentality of algae." She carefully dabbed a tear with her finger so as not to smear her makeup. Alice and Jake had lived together for years before getting married and having children. Liz and Stewart had taken that leap much sooner. "Don't get me wrong, I think the sun rises and sets over their dirty little faces, but I feel like my whole life is on hold, in limbo. I want to *live* again, dammit!"

Her words resonated like a tuning fork with what Liz was feeling lately. Alone, isolated from her own family, her entire life swept up in theirs. She squeezed Alice's hand and let her own tear slide down, nodding.

"I mean, we're too smart to be housewives!" Alice said.

"Hey, being a housewife and mom takes a whole pile of intelligence, efficiency, problem-solving."

"And patience!" Alice said.

"And patience. Besides, I have a job. I work."

"Yeah, but we could've made something of our lives."

Liz leaned back, bristling at the implication that she hadn't made anything of her life. Or maybe it rubbed her wrong because deep down she felt the same way.

Alice didn't seem to notice. "My whole life is spent appeasing *somebody*. Crying toddlers. A husband who likes his wife to be beautiful, be a doting mom, *and* have dinner on the table when he comes home. And a mother who never knows when to shut the hell up."

Liz crossed her arms. "Women are expected to do it all, be everything to everybody. Mom, servant, lover—"

"Goddess!"

"Goddess," Liz said with a sigh.

Silence hung between them as they simmered.

Alice said, "Tell me you feel the same way. Tell me I'm not wasting my life."

"When I was in the middle of what you're going through," Liz said, "there might have been flashes of it. On those sleep-deprived, baby-puke-on-the-bathroom-wall days. But I've never regretted marrying Stewart, not once. He is my rock."

"Yeah, he's always worshiped the ground you walk on," Alice said, her voice tinged with envy.

"And the kids, I can't imagine a life without them. They're my everything..." Liz trailed off, feeling like she was at the verge of some momentous epiphany. Even as she meant every word of what she'd said, the realization settled into place like a boulder. "And if I give my everything to everybody else..." Tears came. She wiped them. "...What *am* I? If Stewart and the kids disappeared from my life tomorrow, what would be left of me?"

It was Alice's turn to squeeze Liz's hand.

Liz said, "The world expects everything of us. Women who put aside family for careers are frowned upon. They shouldn't be so selfish. Women who throw themselves into motherhood, giving up careers, are just 'housewives' and isn't *that* a loaded term?"

"Preach it, sister," Alice said.

"And women who try to do both, especially single moms, run themselves into the ground and disappear. Working at a day care, I could fill an auditorium with women I know who are just like that. And they wake up at forty-something, when their kids are grown, or almost, and wonder how they got there. And then, if they're *my* mom, they spend the rest of their lives being bitter about that." She looked Alice in the eye and stopped herself from cracking wide open with what felt like emotional scotch tape. "I don't want to be my mom."

"Oh, honey," Alice said, and they hugged across the table.

When they sat back down, teary eyed but smiling, Alice sniffled and dabbed her eyes. "Makeup!"

"So, what do we do?" Liz said.

"First of all, we do this more often. Jake is going to give up a couple of golf afternoons now and then. And you?"

"I don't know yet."

"Hire a nanny?"

Liz laughed. "I work in a day care! *I'm* a nanny."

"Become Queen Nanny?" Alice said.

They laughed again, louder this time, perhaps trying to dispel the heaviness of moments ago.

"Hello, ladies," said a deep voice attached to a man's face so handsome he looked like he should be a movie star. The man approaching their table looked about 25, all chiseled jaw and immaculately sculpted stubble.

"Uh, *hi!*" Alice said, beaming a smile at him.

"Look, I'm new in town, and I never do this but..." He ran fingers through his wavy hair, and Liz took him in, top to bottom, a perfect tapering torso, thick shoulders, trim waist, shirt and trousers that were stylish, but not ostentatious. And he wore a nice pair of leather wingtips. "I couldn't help but notice how absolutely stunning you both are," he said, giving them a flawless grin, with just the right mix of shyness and confidence. "I just had to come over and say something."

His gaze fixed upon Liz in a way that no one but Stewart had done in a very long time, almost worshipful but confident enough not to ogle, interested but not lascivious. Her cheeks and ears flushed.

"Uh, thanks," Liz said, not sounding confident at all, like she'd just fallen under the gaze of a godlike movie star.

Alice tucked her left hand—with her big wedding diamond—into her lap. Liz laid hers—with its plain, gold band—on the table.

Liz mustered her faltering confidence and said, "You are fortunate enough to have just met the two most amazing, married women in Mesa Roja."

Alice glared playfully at her.

He smiled wider. "Of that I have no doubt. Lucky fellas, your husbands. I hope they know it. I just needed to say it. Have a lovely day." Then he sauntered off, and they both pointedly watched him go.

When he was out of earshot, Alice said, "What the hell just happened? And more importantly, why did you put the kibosh on the first flirting I've had the chance to do since the last presidential administration?" She feigned a pout.

Liz laughed and shrugged. Deflecting an excess of male attention had become a well-practiced skill for both of them way back in high school. "Just remember, you have been reminded that you've got it *all* going on."

"But it wasn't me that had his full attention." Alice waggled her eyebrows.

Liz shrugged, "A guy like that probably drives a car worth more than my house." And it would take five of him, maybe ten, to measure up to Stewart.

The umbral felt the Border of the Dark Realm as it crossed into the Borderlands, the place where the magical realm and the Penumbra touched, overlapped, where Dark magic still thrived before it dwindled away.

From the immense desolation of the Dark Realm, the umbral passed into craggy mountains, where ravenous creatures stalked and hunted, things that were neither of the Dark Realm nor the Penumbra. But a few creatures of the Penumbra sometimes found their way into the Borderlands. It encountered small, fluttering things, and small, skittering things. All of them blackened and died at the umbral's touch. These would not serve its purpose.

Traveling through the Borderlands was more difficult than traveling through the Dark Realm, like swimming through tar. Its progress was slower.

And its quarry lived in the Penumbra.

The closer it got to the Penumbra, the slower its progress.

It would never be able to reach its quarry on its own. It needed assistance. It needed conveyance.

But all this it knew with instinct that lay far below actual thought. It simply knew, just as a predator knows that it must hunt, and what it must eat.

Days and nights passed as it churned at the edge of the Borderlands, unable to go any farther. Rage burned in its eyes. All along the invisible barrier it seethed and searched.

And then it came upon a pack of four-legged things, strong things. Predators like itself.

It chose the largest, strongest one and entered its body.

The creature howled and jerked and shook itself in protest, but the umbral settled itself within the creature's flesh, carving out a home.

When the creature's fighting ceased, when it accepted this new presence within its mind, within its flesh, it was ravenous, as the umbral was ravenous, starving as if it had never eaten.

The umbral helped the creature kill one of its own young, a convenient meal, as it was so close. That was enough to fill its belly before it left its pack behind and set off across the Penumbra.

CHAPTER FIVE

"Mommy, I'm nervous," Cassie said, wringing her hands, standing at the corner of the kitchen counter.

Liz put the skillet from this morning's breakfast back into the dishwater to soak and faced her daughter. "About what, honey?"

"About martial arts," Cassie said.

Liz felt a moment of confusion. "What about martial arts? Hunter's—"

"I want to try it."

Confusion turned to surprise. This child had never before expressed any interest in it to Liz. "Really? Is someone bothering you at school again?"

"No, but—"

"How about we sit at the table, and you can tell me all about what's on your mind." Liz could tell by Cassie's expression that this was a Very Big Deal, something she'd been thinking about. It didn't take magic for Liz to tell that the kid's energy felt like an over-filled balloon, ready to be released.

Liz pulled out a chair for her, and Cassie scooted onto it.

From the cookie jar, Liz pulled two oatmeal-everything cookies, placed them on Moana plates, filled two plastic Merida cups with milk, and set them on the table. Cassie bit her lip at the sight of the cookie, but something else was way more important right now.

Liz sat down and squeezed Cassie's hand in empathy. "Okay. Let 'er rip."

"Hunter is brave. And I'm not," Cassie said.

Liz's first reaction was to protest, but she held back. Better to let Cassie speak her piece.

"Going on TV scares me really bad," she went on. "Like I freeze so bad I can't even talk whenever I think about it. Hunter says that doesn't make any sense at all. I mean, we fought evil goblins and bad-gerines and stuff. But...it's like if I mess it up it will kill me worse."

Liz stroked Cassie's hand. "Oh, baby."

"And I know it's doesn't make any sense. But Hunter is brave now. He used to be kind of a scaredy-cat. Back before. I want to be like that. Not a scaredy-cat. But maybe stage fright is like a monster inside me, and I have to fight it. Maybe I can learn how to be brave like Hunter, and this monster inside won't scare me anymore. And *don't* tell Hunter I said any of this!"

Liz suppressed a smile. As the words spilled out of Cassie, Liz sat in awe of this child that she had brought into the world. Then her eyes teared up, and she stroked Cassie's hand again.

Cassie went on, "And I've been having bad dreams. They start out good, but then they get scary. We're going back to the magical realms, and I get all excited about that, because we get to see every-body again. And we're in the Borderlands, but it's different, and in-stead of Pooh being there, it's another one of those giant badgerines, but even bigger this time, with tentacles or something. And instead of forest, we're in the desert, and we're in danger." She took a deep breath and released a quavering sigh, staring through her oatmeal-everything cookie. "I think we're going to go to the magical realm again, but it won't be any fun at all. I want to learn how to fight. Just in case." She picked up the cookie and took a bite. "So, can I go to martial arts class, too?"

A storm of thoughts swept through Liz's mind, but first and foremost, how her baby was growing up. "You've really thought about this, haven't you?"

Cassie nodded and took a bite, chewing, looking away.

"Do you want to go to tonight's class?" Liz said.

Cassie nodded again, her face flooding with a relieved smile.

"Then get some tights and a loose T-shirt on before it's time to leave. I'll call Sabom Jenny and let her know you're coming."

She expected Cassie to bounce out of her seat with a *Yay!* but instead, Cassie just sighed and said, "Did it hurt?"

"Did what hurt?"

Cassie's gaze flicked to Liz's waist, the scar.

"It did," Liz said, "but not as much as you might think. It hurt more when it was healing than when it happened. Probably because I had more time to think about it then."

Cassie nodded sagely and took another bite of cookie. "Maybe that's like stage fright."

Across the desert it had run for a long time, mostly at night because the sun hurt its eyes. There was more to eat at night, as well, when all the creatures that hid underground or in shaded crevices came out. It wanted to taste everything, small, scaly creatures, wriggling, serpentine creatures, stabbing, many-legged creatures. Some were sweet, some were bitter, some too hard, some too soft.

But it had a favorite prey now. The small, wild pigs were fast, but its spiny tentacles were faster, its venom nearly instantaneous. The javelinas stopped squirming quickly, and they were so *juicy*. The deliciousness of their flesh, their marrow, was like nothing the umbral had ever experienced before. Their blood lent it moisture against the desert heat.

It liked having a body to live in. Having flesh gave its existence dimension, sensation, exhilaration. It could *feel* things, *taste* things, and thanks to the incredible sensitivity of its host's nose, it could smell *everything*. It could feel the world under its feet, the air around its body.

To be sure, there were unpleasant sensations. Its footpads had been rubbed raw by relentless travel. Its muscles burned and weakened from constant running. Its body protested the changes the umbral had worked in its flesh to better suit its purposes, but sculpting, reshaping a physical form was a great delight. And it could sense its quarry growing nearer, night by night.

Then, as beauteous night was squelched by the heat of what felt like a hundred suns, it sensed the closeness of its quarry, and its excitement drove it to travel through the heat of the day, the last leg of its journey. This body would last that long.

The hot sand and rocks burnt its feet, but it did not care. Its strength flagged for lack of water, but it kept on.

And then, after nearly a full day's run, it arrived at the edge of a human settlement and saw its quarry for the first time.

A metal-skinned dwelling among a smattering of tenacious trees. A mechanical carriage. A workshop at the edge of the desert.

From the shade of a boulder, it watched as the human—*its* human—crossed from the house to the workshop, and it felt a shuddering thrill of anticipation. Pausing in the shade, tongue lolling, it retracted its spiny tentacles, and rearranged its aspect to resemble more closely its host's original form. It did not wish to frighten its human. It must appear to be a creature of the Penumbra. It wished for the exultant joy of long-sought reunion.

Then it leaped from the shade and charged.

It was a blistering afternoon, even for the desert. The sun was a hammer, the earth, an anvil, with Stewart caught between them.

The doors of his workshop hung open to allow airflow. Pausing from grinding an edge onto a Scottish claymore, a two-handed sword almost six feet long, he took such a long drink from his water bottle that he emptied it but still wanted more. The fans around his workshop cooled the sweat, but it was so easy to get dehydrated. He went to refill his water bottle from the back-yard hose.

Stepping out of the workshop, the corner of his eye caught swift movement in the adjoining desert. He focused on it just in time to see a large, canine form skid to a stop about thirty yards away, almost as if it had reached the end of a chain.

At first, he thought it was a coyote, which were common in these parts, but it was way too large.

Not canine, *lupine*. An honest-to-god wolf.

The wolf's yellow eyes regarded him with a strange want, not hunger, really, even though it looked half-starved. Its gray fur, so dark it was almost black, seemed to ripple with the lean muscles underneath. Its shoulders were hunched, trembling as if from exertion.

He locked eyes with it and opened up his intuition to assess his danger. Had the wolf been in the midst of attacking him when he spotted it?

He didn't think so.

It sat on its haunches, tongue lolling in the sun.

The wolf looked familiar somehow, and he sensed mutual recognition in the wolf's gaze. But when had he ever seen a live wolf, much less up close? Never once. He'd never been to a zoo, never traveled far from Mesa Roja, except for the journey into the magical realms. But the wonder of the moment held him fast.

Not wanting to raise his voice lest he scare it off, he went to the kitchen window and knocked on the glass.

Liz's voice came from inside, muffled. "What's up?"

"Come and look at this," he said quietly, keeping his eye on the wolf. He almost said *You're not gonna believe it,* but of course they'd both become accustomed to far more outlandish sights. If it attacked, he had a workshop full of weapons within easy reach.

Moments later, Liz came around the corner of the trailer, and her gaze followed Stewart's pointing finger.

Seeing the wolf, she froze, and her face brightened with wonder. "Wow!"

The sight of her seemed to make the wolf back up a few paces, then it sat down again.

"What's it doing?" she asked.

"Just that," Stewart said. "Watching."

"Is that strange?"

"I don't know."

"Where's its pack? Wolves aren't solitary. They hunt as a team. Maybe they're hunting us while this one distracts us."

That thought chilled him. He went into the workshop and grabbed a quite serviceable boar spear from a display rack, Liz hugging his shadow. When he came out again, the wolf had moved away a few more paces, but now lay panting in the shade of a six-foot-high boulder.

The relentless sun raised heat mirages in all directions.

"Hey, I got an idea," Stewart said. "Go and grab a mixing bowl."

"Should I get the kids? They would love to see this."

"Let's leave them in the house, just to be safe," he said.

"Okay," she said and went back inside.

While she was gone, Stewart turned on the spigot of the backyard hose, letting the water run through his fingers until, sunbaked and hot enough to brew tea, it began to cool. In the desert, this was the stuff of life itself, more precious than gold.

Half a minute later, she was back with a plastic mixing bowl, which he filled with water.

"Stewart, be careful, it's a wild animal, and it's acting strange. It might be rabid."

He raised the spear to quell her fears and carried the bowl of water out toward the wolf.

The wolf watched him with surprising calm, but also cunning. He would not want to get close to this thing without the spear.

Motionless, it watched him as he knelt about twenty feet away and set the bowl on the ground. It looked at the bowl, then at him, then at the bowl. With his fingers he splashed out a few drops of water.

The wolf rose to all fours, gaze fixed on the bowl.

Stewart backed away.

It moved toward the bowl, but stopped short about five feet away, a low whine emanating from its throat.

Back beside Liz, he said, "That's weird."

"Yeah, it really wants a drink."

"Maybe if we go hide behind the house," Stewart said.

They circled around the front and peeked past the corner.

The wolf padded toward the bowl and lowered its muzzle to the water, sniffing first, then started to drink.

Liz squeezed Stewart's arm. "So cool!"

They watched it drink until the bowl was empty. Then it returned to the shade of the boulder and lay down, still watching them.

"It's such a tough-looking thing," Liz said, "like it's been through heck."

She was right. This animal had been through a wringer.

"I'd love to stay and watch the wolf with you, but I've got to take the kids to taekwondo," Liz said.

"'Kids'?"

"Cassie wants to try it. We had a whole long talk about it earlier. I'll tell you about it tonight."

Stewart shrugged and nodded. "Can't hurt." They had enough extra money to afford Cassie's class, too.

She pulled him down to kiss her goodbye. "I'll see *you* later, big boy." With that, she went back into the house to marshal the children into movement.

Stewart went back to the workshop, the wolf's gaze locked upon him. He still had work to do today. Best get to it.

A couple of minutes later, he heard the minivan doors, then the engine. Liz tooted the horn in goodbye as tires crunched on the gravel driveway.

He switched on the grinding wheel and returned his attention to shaping the claymore's edge.

A minute later, movement in the open doors caught his eye, and there stood the wolf, watching him with excitement plain in its eyes.

Its unexpected appearance threw him back into alarm. He reached for the boar spear, which he had stood nearby, just in case.

That was the last thing he remembered.

CHAPTER SIX

S tewart stood in his living room.

The house was dark, silent.

Worms crawled under his skin, but no amount of rubbing would find them or halt the sensation.

He had been standing there for a while, in the center of the room, as the shadows gathered around him.

He blinked and sighed. Why was he standing here? How long had it been? Where was everybody? Where had the daylight gone?

His stomach felt like a merry-go-round. Was he hungry? Ill?

What was he doing here? He should be working on...something. He had a schedule...didn't he?

The silence seemed to roar in his ears.

Something had happened, but he couldn't remember what.

Had he just awakened from a dream? He hadn't been napping. He couldn't remember.

Was he dreaming now?

Had the living room always had this sharp, silvery cast late at night? How many sleepless nights had he spent prowling the house and never noticed how crystal clear the night became in his vision?

There was something in his hand, something round, like a hard apple.

It was a doll's head. Long, blonde hair. One blue eye half-closed, the other staring. Plump, pink lips of inanimate porcelain. A dark smear from his thumb across its forehead.

Why were his forearms wet?

In the strange starlight, blood flowed from several gashes and punctures, dripped from his fingers, from his elbow.

Why wasn't there any pain? His arms weren't numb. He could feel the cuts, but they didn't hurt. Had there been an accident in his workshop? There were so many dangerous things out there...

What had happened to the wolf? Had there been a wolf?

He remembered...something.

Where would he get a doll's head?

No.

Not that.

He ran back to the kids' bedroom.

He found nothing amiss.

Except Jaclyn and Jazlyn were not sitting in their customary place atop Cassie's dresser. They were Cassie's friends and protectors. He had seen them in the window of Claude's shop and thought them perfect for Cassie's birthday present two years ago. The family had soon discovered they were animate automatons, and deadly ones at that. The dolls had marched with the family across the Borderlands and across the Light Realm.

Which of their heads did he hold in his hand?

But the head was gone now. He hadn't put it down. It had been in his hand, and he'd walked directly from the living room to the bedroom.

Had he imagined it? Was he dreaming?

What had happened to them?

Overcome by confusion, he sank to his knees.

He called, "Jaclyn? Jazlyn? Are you here? Are you all right?"

His voice sounded strange to him, as if it were someone else's.

His hand had left a bloody handprint on the floor of the kids' bedroom. "Oh, we can't have that. That'll give the kids nightmares."

He went into the bathroom, flicked on the light. The harsh, fluorescent light made his arms look like he'd lost a fight with a barbed-wire fence. He took out the cotton balls, hydrogen peroxide, superglue, gauze, and medical tape that Liz insisted on keeping around. *You work with three-foot razors all day, buddy,* she had told him when he had smirked a protest.

He dabbed the cold, stinging liquid onto the wounds, watched it fizz.

But as he worked his way through the succession of cuts, he discovered some of them were already partly healed. They had scabbed over and were itching like crazy.

That was *really* weird.

At least that gave him more time to clean up all the blood he had dripped everywhere. He took a washcloth and started with the kids' room, then the mess he'd left in the bathroom. Liz shouldn't have to clean up after him.

All the abuse and deprivation he'd suffered as a boy had left him with a few useful skills—among them, he knew how to clean a house, especially bloodstains. One of his foster "fathers" had once bloodied his nose with a solid punch, then forced him to clean it up. How old had he been then? Eleven?

But where had these wounds come from? He couldn't get his head around that, couldn't remember.

59

The weight of piled-up questions prevented him from answering any of them.

Where the hell were Liz and the kids? He dropped his blood-stained cleaning rag and frowned. They should be home by now.

Something in his stomach slithered, along with the deepest growl ever.

He was getting hungry. What was he supposed to do for dinner, eat a peanut butter sandwich? Liz should have told him dinner would be late. He worked hard all day. It worked up an appetite.

"Jaclyn! Jazlyn! Where are you?"

He turned all the lights on—they seemed brighter than normal, hurt his eyes—and searched the house, finding no evidence of the dolls.

The moon peeked over the black silhouettes of the pine trees as he searched the back yard. Could they have gone into the Little People's burrow? No sign of Peaseblossom either. The burrow stood dark.

The interior of his workshop was dark and silent, but from outside he could see things scattered over the floor in a way they were not supposed to be. As a rule, he kept his shop tidy.

Then he flicked on the lights and saw tools and several finished and half-finished blades scattered over the floor.

The sense of the world being strange somehow, out of joint, wouldn't let him relax.

Cassie would be so upset if something had happened to those dolls. On the other hand, they could certainly take care of themselves, as they'd shown over and over.

So why had he seen a doll's head in his hand? Was he imagining it? But why would he imagine such a thing?

Then he heard the engine of the minivan coming up the road and felt a gush of hunger.

"It's about time," he grumbled as the tires crunched through the driveway gravel.

As he went to meet them at the front of the house, the headlights washed over him, hurting his eyes. As the minivan doors opened, he said, "What took so long?"

Liz hefted some plastic shopping bags from the side door. "I had to run a couple of errands. I left you like, three text messages." Seeing his face, she paused. "Are you mad?"

He bit back a sharp reply. "Just hungry."

She kept her scrutiny on him as she passed and went inside, but made her voice sound light, "Well, *that* I can fix. Right, kids?"

Hunter held up a paper bag. "Brought you a hoagie with double meat."

But why had there been a sneer in Hunter's voice? Had there? Hunter never spoke to his father like that. Was this an episode of early-onset teenager? Stewart would have to nip that crap in the bud immediately.

Cassie stood before him and looked up with a big grin. "I got punched in the eye!"

He frowned, and his voice turned sharp. "Who hit you?"

"Chrissy Jackson," Cassie said. "She didn't mean to. She's just clumsy. It didn't hurt as much as I thought it would."

Stewart didn't know Chrissy Jackson, but in that moment, he wanted to see her face full of terror.

"Mommy says I might get a shiner!" Cassie's grin widened.

"We had quite an adventure," Liz said.

"You should have told me you'd be late," Stewart grunted.

Liz wiggled her phone. "I did. Not my fault you didn't see it."

Stewart followed them into the house, looking around for evidence of the bloodstains he had cleaned up.

As Liz ping-ponged around the kitchen, putting away things from the shopping bags, she said, "Are you all right, babe?"

"Why wouldn't I be?" he said.

She shrugged. "You look nervous or something. Something happen in the shop?"

"No, why?"

"Your arms." She gestured to the gauze and tape.

"Oh, that, yeah," he said, trying to hide them. "Nothing serious, though."

She gave him a long, penetrating look, then shrugged. "Hunter brought you your favorite sandwich, so dig in." She thumbed over her shoulder to the paper bag on the kitchen table.

His stomach snarled and he went for the sandwich like a half-starved hyena.

Cassie called from the back room. "Jaclyn! Jazlyn! Where are you? Come and see my shiner!"

The memory of the doll's head in his hand chilled him for a moment, making him pause at wolfing down his sandwich. Where had that come from? Hallucination? Dream?

"Found 'em!" Cassie called.

Stewart deflated with relief at the lack of alarm or horror in Cassie's voice.

Then a sharp rap came at the front door.

"Who could that be?" Liz said as she went to the door.

She opened the door, and a familiar voice came from outside. "Good evening, dear lady. By me mother's graces, ye look lovelier every time ye grace me eyes."

"Bob!" Liz said, kneeling to shake the leprechaun's hand. She ushered him into the house. "Hey, everybody! Look who's here!"

Standing about knee high, Bob spotted Stewart and doffed his top hat in greeting. "Stewart, how nice to see you." He wore his customary waistcoat of emerald-green scales, starched white shirt, paisley trousers, and a pair of tiny, black shoes that gleamed with polish.

Normally Stewart would be happy to see the little man who'd led them on their journey across the Borderlands to the City, but right this minute he found himself sharply annoyed at the interruption of his sandwich.

Perhaps sensing Stewart's mood, Bob gave him a penetrating look, until the kids came bounding out of the back hallway to greet the magical visitor.

Bob took one look at the kids and whistled. "Why, me dearies, ye've doubled in size! Ah, human children grow up so quickly." He clucked his tongue.

"Would you like some tea, Bob?" Liz said.

"Alas, this is not a social call." Bob's face darkened. "I've come to deliver grave news."

Stewart spotted small, pale shapes in the back hallway, edging toward the living room, two little porcelain faces, azure eyes fixed upon *him*. Everything about the way they stood told him they were poised to spring into action that would be too fast for a human eye to follow.

He looked back at Bob and reluctantly put down his sandwich.

Something writhed inside his belly, and the sensations of worms crawling beneath his skin returned.

"Oh, no!" Liz said to Bob. "What news?"

Bob took a deep breath and let it out. "'Tis Stewart's dark half, the thing the Queen peeled away from his spirit when he returned from the Dark Realm. It is free."

Liz leaned against the counter, looking back and forth with a stricken expression at Bob and Stewart. "How did it happen?"

"We cannot reckon exactly, but we think agents of the Dark Lord infiltrated the City somehow. Again, we cannot fathom how. One of our most honorable elven lords was found dead in the vault where the beastie was imprisoned. Its urn was open, empty."

"Someone let it loose. Why?" Liz said.

"Someone up to no good," Bob said.

"Can't the Queen capture it again?" Hunter asked.

"Alas, no," Bob said. "Its Dark nature would have sent it straight to the Dark Realm, once it were freed. Perhaps it was captured or summoned by the Dark Lord, but that is not what the Queen thinks." Then he looked Stewart squarely in the eye, a gaze Stewart could not meet. "She thinks it's comin' for *you*, me boy."

Stewart's mouth was dry, his voice a rasp. "To do what?"

"To rejoin with you. It *is* you, after all."

"That *thing* is made of Dark magic," Liz said.

"Aye, but it's also made of Stewart's darkest impulses, the worst part of him. It remembers all the terrible things ye done in the Dark Realm. It knows ye, Stewart, perhaps better than ye know yerself."

Liz looked at Stewart, and he couldn't meet her gaze either. "He's never really talked about what happened in the Dark Realm."

"I daresay not," Bob said. "Stewart, I can only imagine what ye had to go through to find the Princess and set her free."

Like setting loose a beast from within him, a beast he never wanted to see again. Like slaughtering a roomful of dwarven smiths in cold blood and reveling in their deaths. But Stewart couldn't say that, couldn't admit that. The shame of it was too powerful. Liz and the kids had no idea how close he had come to embracing the Darkness forever, not because he had to, but because he wanted to. The Dark side of him wanted it more than anything. "You're right. I don't want to talk about it." His voice was little more than a whisper.

The silence hung like a funeral veil for several ticks of the kitchen clock.

Stewart said, "So, what, you're saying my Dark half is coming for me?"

"That would be the most likely event," Bob said. "I am sorry."

"But what can we do?" Liz said. "We can't just let it show up and take him over."

"It can't have my daddy," Cassie said. She stood beside Stewart and crossed her arms.

"The good news is this," Bob said. From his waistcoat pocket he withdrew a crystal disk about the size of a silver dollar, ensconced in a silver frame that hung from a silver chain.

The way the crystal glittered and caught the light hurt Stewart's eyes and made him angry. Suddenly his uneasy stomach felt like it had an angry rattler in it.

"Is that a diamond?" Liz said.

"Indeed," Bob said. "And it has been imbued with a warding spell that will keep the beastie away from you." He offered it to Stewart.

Stewart took it, but the snake in his belly and the worms under his skin started doing an insane rumba.

Get rid of it! The thought came so strong and so hard he almost ran outside to fling the amulet out into the desert. Almost.

Instead, he said, "So how long do I have to wear this thing?"

"Well, until the beastie is found and put back in its bottle," Bob said. "But the magical worlds are vast and complex. Even the Queen with all her power cannot see everything at once."

"What happens if it shows up and we see it?" Liz asked. "Can it hurt us?"

"It cannot hurt anyone unless it joins with a body. It has no substance of its own, only a sad half-existence."

"So it can possess people? Animals?"

Bob nodded.

Liz fixed her gaze on Stewart again. "The wolf?"

Stewart said, "I haven't seen it since you left."

Liz turned to Bob. "Today there was a wolf outside, acting very strange. Like it wanted to be friends or something. We gave it some water. It was weird because it was all alone, and there are no wolves this far south. We're over seven hundred miles from Yellowstone."

Bob scratched his chin. "That is peculiar."

Cassie said, "Can you stay with us, Bob? Watch for it? You can sleep in me and Hunter's room."

"I believe I will stay. 'Tis a long walk to get here. We don't know when the beastie might show up, but I daresay it shan't be long. Ye've a quite comfortable-looking tree out back I might have a kip in. If the beastie appears, I shall call the Queen, and she assures me she will come quicker than a pixie can change her mind."

Liz released a sigh of relief. "Thank you, Bob."

"Mommy, I'm scared," Cassie said. "I remember what Daddy looked like when that thing had him."

"Now, don't ye worry, lassie," Bob said. "Yer daddy puts on that amulet, and the beastie can't touch him. Then it's just for me to call the Queen, and the Queen puts it back into its prison."

Stewart's insides seethed with anger, but he kept his expression neutral.

Because they obviously expected him to, he slipped the silver chain over his head. But the thing inside him *roared* with fury, like a bull-ape gone berserk. With an immense effort of will, he held his body motionless, his face neutral.

Liz stroked Cassie's hair. "Everything is going to be okay, honey."

In the back hallway, the two dolls watched Stewart with cold, crystal wariness.

CHAPTER SEVEN

Hunter and Cassie sat cross-legged on the floor in their bedroom, facing each other, with Jaclyn and Jazlyn sitting cross-legged beside them.

"I got a really bad feeling," Cassie said. Her tummy hurt. The inside of the house felt like a monsoon storm that hadn't yet cut loose, like there was distant thunder everywhere, but no clouds in the sky.

"Me, too," Hunter said.

"I've been having bad dreams—"

"Like being on stage with no pants on again?"

"No, not that one!" Her cheeks flushed. That particular dream had been on heavy rotation ever since she'd gotten the letter. "Dreams where monsters are coming out of the floor, and sometimes they look like Daddy. What if that thing is already here somewhere? Jackie and Jazzie think so."

The dolls nodded vigorously.

Cassie remembered what Daddy had looked like when he came back from the Dark Realm, all hideous and mean-looking, with great raven wings, like a monster made from the man who'd been her father. The thought of him turning into that again made her eyes tear up and a sob come right into her throat. Her hands were shaking as over and over again her finger absently traced the rune for courage, which looked like two angular capital *R*s back-to-back, on the stubbly, green carpet.

Hunter's face looked like he wanted to say something, but he couldn't muster the words. Thoughts flitted behind his eyes. Finally, he said, "We should tell Mom."

Cassie listened for a moment and caught the sound of the grinding wheel in Daddy's workshop. "Let's go," she whispered.

They found their mother in the kitchen putting away the dishes. Bob had gone off into the night to prepare whatever magical defenses and alarms he could.

"Mom," Hunter said, "we have to talk to you."

Their mom turned and tried to hide her worried expression. "Sure, what's up?" Her voice was too perky.

Cassie said, "We think the bad thing is already here. Jackie and Jazzie do, too."

On either side of her, the dolls nodded again.

Mommy said, "But Dad's safe. He's got the amulet on. It will keep that thing from getting close."

Jackie and Jazzie glanced at each other in worry.

Mommy went on, "It's the Queen's magic, right? She bound that thing and put it in an urn. She made an amulet that will keep it away."

"Maybe so," Hunter said, "but don't you think Dad was acting weird when we got home?"

"Well, yeah," Mommy said, "but he gets a little moody sometimes since he came back from the Dark Side. It haunts him."

"But what if he's like, *really* haunted now?" Hunter asked.

Mommy looked away. "Well, we just have to hope that doesn't happen. Remember what Bob said? If that thing shows up, the Queen will come running. It can't get past the amulet, right?"

Cassie said, "The Queen can't know everything. She doesn't know everything. The bad guys were able to kidnap the Princess right out of the City, and nobody knew how."

Mommy's brow furrowed at that, then she threw her arms around them both and hugged them. "All we can do is keep our eyes open and hope that doesn't happen. And we're gonna stick together, no matter what happens. Right?"

"Right," Cassie and Hunter said.

But nobody sounded very sure.

Liz lay in bed, wide awake. Rolling, flopping, wrapping herself in covers, unwrapping herself, trying to find a configuration that would let her relax.

Bob had retired outside somewhere, telling Liz he had set up a magical perimeter that would raise an alarm if the umbral crossed it.

The kids were asleep.

The alarm clock beside the bed said 12:43.

Bob's sudden appearance with such dire news, stacked on top of everything with Cassie, Hunter, their worried little faces, and that strange wolf, was an endless churn in her mind. From where she was, she could see the precipice of being overwhelmed and useless.

She could tell that beside her, Stewart was awake as well, even though he remained utterly still and silent, as if meditating. She checked again to make sure he still had the amulet around his neck—he did. What she couldn't fathom was why he seemed to have such an aversion to it. He hadn't said anything to that effect, but she knew him better than anybody. He wore it, but grudgingly. And now he lay in bed, immobile as a stone, but there was an unquietness about him, as if he were waiting for something.

What could that mean?

He'd been acting strange, short-tempered, tense, since she and the kids got home.

She rolled over and threw her arm across his chest.

He did not move. Usually he responded in some way, with a nudge or a wiggle or a gentle touch, even asleep. But now it was like trying to cuddle a stone, and she really could use a little comfort right now.

His eyes snapped open.

"You okay, babe?" she asked.

"Can't sleep," he said. "I'm going to go work for a while, clear my head."

"Okay," she said, as he climbed out of bed and got dressed. "Want to talk about it?"

"No."

Out in his workshop, Stewart flicked on the lights and fired up the forge. The rumbling hiss of the propane heater filled the space, drowning out the sounds of the night creatures outside.

The moon seemed especially bright tonight. He could see everything as if it were high noon, hear the skitterings and slitherings of the creatures around him. The darkness comforted his crawling skin and unquiet soul, a feeling he remembered from his life as a young man filled with rage.

There was no denying it, especially to himself.

His Dark side had found him.

He could feel it writhing inside his body, twisting his heart and soul with urges and desires he couldn't allow.

He had to run fast and run far, somehow without causing a panic in Liz and the kids. He feared what he would become as the umbral seized greater and greater control. He controlled it now by sheer force of will, but he had to sleep sometime, and what awful things might it do while his conscious mind was asleep?

The way Liz had looked at him, spoken to him, told him she suspected. That she hadn't mentioned it told him she didn't want to frighten the kids, or maybe she wanted to be absolutely sure.

His brain felt ready to explode with unwelcome thoughts. His chest was on fire with panic. His stomach ached with hunger, but for what, he did not know.

Should he allow those urges free rein? *No!*

He couldn't bear the thought of his family's faces if he did.

Should he just destroy himself and the umbral with him?

How long had he lived a lie, living as if he were Liz's equal, but knowing he was not?

Love was a cage, a prison he had willingly entered.

Maybe he should destroy those who held him in that cage?

No!

But he caught himself laughing, a sinister, hateful sound. The nastiness of it snapped him back to the moment.

He loved his family more than his own life. He would die for them. He would destroy himself rather than cause them harm, of any kind. It was this love that gave him the strength to have lasted even these few hours since the umbral's arrival. The umbral wanted to *breathe*, to *live*.

He had to get away. Right now. He wouldn't last much longer. He wanted to grab the amulet—vile, hateful thing that felt like a coil of barbed-wire cinched around his chest—snap the chain, and fling it into the darkness, but it might be dampening the umbral's influence just enough for him to do one last thing.

It would be so much easier simply to succumb, to let Darkness complete his transformation, fulfill his potential. He would become the greatest Dark wizard in all the magical worlds, and he would wreak terrible vengeance on Baron Tyrus for endangering his family, for all the evil he had done over the millennia. The only way he could destroy Baron Tyrus was to embrace the Dark.

Stewart was not afraid to fight, especially for what he loved.

Just as he had allowed himself to slip to the Dark side to save the Princess, he would do it again to save his family. He would become the supreme ruler of all and—

Wait, no.

His hands were shaking at the effort of restraining such thoughts.

Destroying the Dark Lord required a powerful weapon that would allow Stewart to focus his power.

He had nearly finished a Scottish claymore for a commission, a two-handed, six-foot-long, double-edged blade. It lay on the bench, awaiting grinding and polishing.

If only he didn't have to worry about Liz and the kids.

They were holding him back.

He'd be better off without them.

He'd rather be alone.

He'd given them too much of his life already.

Besides, he might well be the most powerful human wizard in existence, even though here in the Penumbra his potency was greatly diminished, so what did he need them for? He knew how to gather and harness Source, both Light and Dark, and he knew the runes necessary to bind it to his will here in the Penumbra.

He was more powerful without them.

No!

The umbral's grip was tightening around his mind, his spirit. He had to hurry.

He took up the claymore, but his magical instincts told him it required modifications for his purpose. He put the blade through more heating and hammering cycles as he reshaped it from straight to wavy.

When that process was complete, it looked more like a flamberge, a "flame-bladed" sword.

As he ground out the edge, he wondered where Bob was. Skulking around in the darkness? Had he already sensed what happened to Stewart and summoned the Queen? No, if that were true, she would be here. Perhaps he was just observing. Creatures of the Light Realm were not allowed to interfere in the lives of mortals, despite the fact that the Dark side did it all the time. Stewart would no longer hobble himself with such trivial concerns as "rules."

But he had to protect his family, and to do that, Baron Tyrus must be destroyed.

He picked up the steel and returned to his task, heating and shaping and grinding as the sparks flew and the flames roiled and the quenching water hissed. For hours he worked. The muscles of his shoulders, neck, and arms alternately sagged and tightened with fatigue, his eyes gathering what felt like sand in them, but he worked with steadfast purpose, and his callused hands ignored the heat of the metal.

With the grinding complete, he inscribed a series of runes on either side of the blade, Light on one side, Dark on the other. As soon as he did so, the magic began to take hold, giving the Light side of the blade a bright, shimmering iridescence, and the Dark side a sullen, dangerous sheen. These runes would attract and store both Light and Dark Source, enhancing the combat abilities of the blade and the power of any spells he cast.

The more he polished, the more pronounced the color shifts became.

This sword would be his greatest creation, a kingly weapon, an Excalibur of Dark and Light. With it, he might be able to face Baron Tyrus and any other magical creatures that got in his way.

As dawn broke, he hefted the finished weapon. How he had managed to complete it in only one night, he didn't know, but there it was in his hand. Now he had to get out of here before—

And there stood Liz in the doorway, hands on hips, with a look of determination Stewart knew all too well.

"What is *that?*" she asked, her voice curious, with a touch of concealed accusation.

"Uh, a special commission," Stewart said, trying to keep his voice light. "Want to see it?" He offered her the hilt.

She took it in both hands and examined it. "Wow, this is beautiful, babe! Great work."

"Thanks."

"Why does it have runes on it? This isn't a Viking kind of sword."

He took it back in case she looked too closely at the difference in aspect each side of the blade presented. "You've been studying."

"Can't help it," she said with a smile. "Medieval weapons are just in the air around here. Just, hopefully, not flying through the air. What's that kind of blade called, a flamberge?"

He nodded.

She said, "And isn't the flamberge a Renaissance-era weapon? Centuries later than the Vikings?

"You're right, there."

"But the customer wants Viking runes on it?"

Stewart shrugged. "Special request from the customer. He likes runes, I guess." She was getting too close to the truth. "Say, are you hungry? I've been working all night, so I'm starving."

"I could be persuaded," she said.

"Then how about I run into town and bring home some takeout from Pancake Palace? I'll bring you that French toast you love so much."

"Mmm, crème brûlée French toast." Her eyes brightened, but there was something in her stance that said she wasn't buying it.

"I'll run into town and bring some back. Sound good?" he said.

Something glimmered in her eyes that wasn't hunger, though. Fear? Regret? She was going to stop him. He could feel it. Or she would try to. What would he do then? Now that his concentration on a task at hand had diminished, the umbral's tentacles of spite and greed were worming deeper into his mind. But instead, she said, "That sounds great." But her voice sounded close to tears.

She came forward to hug him, and he embraced her, feeling her warmth and softness around a core of strength like he'd encountered in no one else. This would be the last time. He lifted her chin, cupped her cheek, and kissed her goodbye.

"I love you," he said.

Her eyes sparkled and her cheeks flushed. "I love you, too." Then she said, "Hey, how about I come with you? When was the last time we had a little grown-up date at six in the morning?"

He smiled at her, a brittle mask. "Great idea. But can you please go get my wallet?"

She gave him a long look with sadness hiding behind a wistful smile. She sniffled a little. "Sure. Be right back." She spoke the last part pointedly, earnestly.

He nodded and waited for her to disappear into the house.

The moment she did, he snatched up the sword and ran for the minivan. The keys were in a dashboard cup holder.

It was now or never.

As he started the car and spewed gravel, peeling out of the driveway, the umbral's blackness roiled within him. He recognized this black fog around his thoughts. It had served him well when he was in peril in the bowels of the Dark Lord's fortress.

But *he* was in control, and there was no way he would give the umbral free rein anywhere near Liz and the kids. *He* was in control.
Him.

The umbral served *him,* not the other way around.

Stewart still had a score to settle, and this Dark creature thudding against the inside of his ribs like a caged beast would help him do it.

Behind him in the rearview mirror, Liz stood in the road, in the dust, agape, watching him go.

As Liz stood in the middle of the road, watching the minivan's taillights disappear in a cloud of dust, a glob of cold lead settled into her stomach. He wasn't coming back.

Could she have stopped him?

The blackness swirling behind his eyes had told her no, she couldn't have. She could never believe that her husband would hurt her, but she had no such certainty about the umbral. Who knew what kind of evil had attached itself to Stewart in the Dark Realm? And now, it was in her world.

A flicker of movement caught her eye, and she jumped at Bob's sudden appearance. "Yah!"

Bob said, "I was too late."

"Oh, thank heavens you're here!" she said, her heart pounding. "Why didn't your warning system work?"

"Regretfully, I suspect because the beastie was already inside the ring. Alas, the awful thing was speedier than we thought." He dangled the protective amulet from one hand.

"Why would he take the amulet off?" she asked, tears starting to run. She paced back and forth, clenching her fists, feeling helpless, hopeless.

"I suspect because the umbral already had him. The amulet might have done a bit to cramp the beastie's style, one might say. He chucked it in the bushes as he got into your contraption." Bob moaned. "I should've known! So sorry I am!"

"I *did* know," Liz said. "At least at some level. I just couldn't bring myself to believe it. It's not your fault."

"But it is. I watched him all night. That's the best I could do. Me magic isn't strong enough here to do much more than hide meself. He's so powerful there's nothing I could do against him."

"Should we call the police?"

"That would be mighty dangerous for the police. Them that cross his path would best keep a wide berth. That beastie wouldn't hesitate to snuff me. As soon as you went into the house, I saw something come over him, or rather, him throwing something off, like a costume. As sure as a snake shedding his skin. It chilled me spine from crown to cr—"

"Mommy?" came a small, tired voice. Cassie stood in the front door, the two dolls in combat stances on either side of her. "Where did Daddy go in such a hurry?"

"Oh, baby," Liz said. The girl idolized her father. How much had Cassie heard? What else had she seen? What could Liz tell her? She gestured Cassie to come in for a hug.

As Liz embraced her, Cassie spoke against Liz's chest, "Are you all right?"

Liz just squeezed her tighter.

"Bob was right, wasn't he," Cassie said. "Daddy's Dark side got him."

Beside them stood Bob, hat in his hand, his normally rosy cheeks an ashen gray. He lowered his eyes and pursed his lips.

"I don't know, honey," Liz said, unable to speak the words even though she knew the truth. Speaking it would be admitting it, and that meant she might never again see the man she loved. "We're going to try to find him and get him back. He's going to be okay."

Cassie shook her head with a sharp look, and her voice was angry. "No, he's not. And you know it."

CHAPTER EIGHT

The questions concerning "Is Dad coming back?" could not be answered when Liz had no idea herself.

Bob had offered to return to the Light Realm and inform the Queen and ask for advice, but Liz told him she needed time to think about this. Maybe Stewart could control the umbral enough to come back.

Bob looked doubtful.

Out of pure routine, she made the kids breakfast, even though they were too upset to eat it. She was numb, her brain fogged by worries and what-ifs.

In the midst of that, her phone rang. It was Alice. Liz shouldn't have been surprised, because the two of them had been psychically in tune with each other since high school. If one of them was experiencing an extreme moment, the other somehow knew to call.

"What's up?" Alice said.

Liz restrained more tears. "I don't even know where to start."

"No doubt. Your psychic whammy hit me like a logging truck. Want me to come over?"

Liz sniffled. "Yes."

"If your kids can watch my kids, I'll be there in fifteen."

Liz turned to Cassie and Hunter. "Hey, how would you guys like your first babysitting job?"

Hunter grimaced. Cassie managed a smile and a nod.

"You just have to play with Alice's boys for a while and keep them out of Dad's shop, so they don't hurt themselves. Can you do that for a little while? Hunter, you can bust out your action figures you don't play with anymore."

Hunter's shoulders slumped, but he said, "Okay."

She embraced him with one arm and a kiss.

"Mom, stop with the hugs!" Hunter said, shrugging off her embrace sullenly.

"Oh, you're too big now for a mom hug?" she said.

"No, but it's too much today," he said.

She clamped down on the lump in her throat. He was right. Since Stewart had left, she couldn't stop hugging her children as if they were the only things she had left in the world.

Cassie looked up from her untouched egg and peanut butter toast. "It's okay, Mommy. I'll take Hunter's extra hugs."

Liz chuckled in spite of herself and gave Cassie the twenty-seventh hug of the morning.

Then she got back to her phone. "We're go for babysitters."

Alice said, "Hang in there. The cavalry is coming."

After she disconnected, Liz gripped the kitchen counter with both hands, keeping her back to her children so they couldn't see the tears. Was she strong enough for this? Could she do this, whatever *this* was, without Stewart? Her personal Viking had just gone rogue. Could he possibly have become the *enemy?* She had faced this possibility when they were in the Light Realm, but after a couple of years of new normalcy, she had let such thoughts submerge into the past. But now...

She needed Alice's comfort and advice, but what could she tell her? How could she possibly explain that Stewart had been possessed by...himself? Even if it was a dark, magical version of himself created in another world? The police would come and take *her* away and give her a nice, white coat with really long sleeves. But no, Alice would never do such a thing. She'd take Liz's secrets to the grave.

Aside from the questions of what would happen to Stewart now that the umbral had him, there were larger questions Liz could not discount. Her husband had left, and she had no idea if he was coming back. Her intuition told her, screamed at her, he was not coming back. Her *husband* had *left*. Their marriage was strong, but how strong? She couldn't stand the thought of a life without Stewart.

If he had just disappeared from her life for good, what was she?

But those were all mundane concerns, shallow trifles, considering what had just happened to Stewart. She would never forget the sight of the Queen ripping the shadowy phantom from Stewart's body and soul, its hateful eyes like glowing coals, capable of unfathomable violence and cruelty. With that thing attached to his soul, he was capable of anything.

But where would he go? Was he even now headed straight for the Dark Realm?

Fifteen minutes passed in an eyeblink and a swirl of reverberating worries as Alice's big, silver SUV pulled up outside.

Liz went out to meet them.

Alice gave her a big, warm hug. "Whatever it is, we'll kick its tushie."

"Thanks," Liz said, and then helped Alice get the boys out of their car seats.

"Say hi to Auntie Liz," Alice said as she hefted the three-year-old out of his car seat.

"Hi, Auntie Liz!" Jackson said, with a wave of his pudgy hand, and a grin full of rosy cheeks and tiny chips of perfect porcelain teeth.

"Hey, Auntie Liz," five-year-old Philip said; he unbuckled his car seat like a big boy and jumped out.

In the house, Hunter and Cassie met them.

"Hey, you guys," Hunter said, "want to come and play with us?"

Philip's eyes gleamed with joy, and he led his brother, following behind like a duckling, off into the back of the trailer.

Liz sat Alice down at the kitchen table and poured two cups of coffee.

"Black, right?" Liz said.

"As my soul!" Alice said brightly.

Liz fumbled her spoon. It hit the floor and bounced under the table. "Ohhh...*flarb!*" She knew what a completely black soul looked like, in a way few other people did.

"Whoa, there, Miss Potty Mouth, that was almost profanity," Alice said. Her jovial tone turned serious. "It's bad, right? Something happen between you and Stewart?"

"Sort of." Liz sat down across from Alice, cradling her cup to warm her unnaturally cold hands.

"The car's gone, I see. It's too early for most stores in town to be open..."

Liz nodded.

"I thought you and Stewart were solid, the ultimate couple, impervious to temptation and strife."

"Me, too! We are! But..."

Alice squeezed her hand. "My cousin Mei Ling thought everything was hunky-dory, too. Next thing she knew, her husband was moving in with his personal trainer—"

"It's not like that." Liz's voice trembled. "I don't even know where to start."

"Is he hitting you? I'll personally make sure he—"

"No!" But could he have? Was he capable of hurting her now?

"You got any bruises I can't see?" Alice reached for Liz's shirt sleeve, but Liz pulled away.

"*No!* How do I even tell you?"

A new voice said, "Perhaps I should begin." Bob was standing at the corner of the kitchen counter, his emerald waistcoat gleaming, his expression grim.

The two of them jumped at the voice. Alice let out a garbled yelp and jumped to stand on her chair as if Bob was a mouse, not a leprechaun. "What the hell is that?"

"I beg yer pardon!" Bob said with a sniff, tiny fingers drumming on the head of his cane.

"That's Bob," Liz said.

Alice's eyes bulged, flicking back and forth between Liz and the leprechaun.

Bob whisked himself quicker than sight to stand on the table between them.

Liz said, "Bob, meet Alice, my best friend. Alice, this is Bob. He's, uh, one of the Little People."

Bob tipped his hat and bowed. "At yer service, charming lady."

"Uh, hi?" Alice said, apparently still struggling with the idea of settling back into her chair, crouching with both feet on the seat. "Can I...touch you?"

Bob offered his hand, small and hairy knuckled. Alice reached out and touched it with her finger. The moment contact was made, she almost collapsed from her chair in relief. "Oh, thank god!"

Liz took a deep breath. "You remember a couple years ago, when we went on a camping trip, and Stewart's truck got wrecked?"

"Yeah, and you were all acting really weird for a while afterward, cagey," Alice said.

So Liz launched into the story. For almost an hour, she and Bob told the story of the journey across the Borderlands and into the Light Realm, what they had seen, the Dark forces they'd encountered, and what they had done to rescue the Princess. Liz gave the events, and Bob offered the background.

Sitting in the dawn light slanting through the kitchen window, Liz showed Alice her scar.

Alice said, "Oh, my god! You almost *died*?"

Liz nodded.

Alice's brow furrowed with anger, and she leaned back, crossing her arms. "How could you not tell me that?"

Liz glanced at Bob. "If he weren't here, standing right in front of you, would you have believed it? Really believed it?"

Alice chewed on this for several moments, then finally said, "I'd have wanted to." Then she sighed. "But yeah, I probably would have laughed it off. Like you were writing your own *Alice in Wonderland* or something. I wouldn't love you any less."

"I couldn't stand the idea you might think I'm crazy," Liz said. "Who could?"

Bob said, "These 'modern' attitudes are precisely why magic is fading from yer world. No one believes in real magic anymore. Except Stewart, and that's why he's so powerful."

"Well, we don't all have leprechauns to convince us magic is real," Alice said, still frowning.

"Maybe in this case, you don't want to know how real it is," Liz said. "Last night, Stewart's Dark side found him and rejoined with him or something."

"The thing the Faerie Queen pulled out of him?" Alice said.

Liz nodded. "He took off, I think to protect us from himself. So, he still has some control, but we don't know how long that will last, and we don't know what will happen to him when it's gone, and we don't know where he's going. He took a huge sword with him, and he'd engraved magical runes all over the blade. He has a plan."

Alice said, "But what if Dark-Side Stewart comes back? You just said he's armed."

Liz didn't have an answer.

Alice asked, "So do you and the kids have magical powers like him? You could do some mojo on him."

"The kids do," Liz said. "Not me."

She caught Bob giving her a long and penetrating look.

Then Alice said, "I think you and the kids should come and stay with me for a few days, while you figure out what to do."

"I can't just sit in one place," Liz said. "We have to help him."

Bob's face turned skeptical again. "Dear lady, not so certain am I that we might help him at all."

"That is *not* an option!" Liz shouted. She stood and began to pace. "What are we waiting for?" Each passing moment felt to Liz like Stewart was getting farther and farther away, and the farther he went, the less likely she would ever have him back.

Her vehemence put the little man back on his heels. "That dark elf we faced last time, he used to be one of the good folk, a bright elf. But the Dark Lord got his hooks in, and Dark magic was just too seductive. He's hardly the only creature of the Light who's succumbed in such a way. It saddens me to say, they never come back."

"We have to find him," Liz said, quieter, her voice cracking. "I have to get to him somehow. Everything in my heart tells me I still can. I still believe in him. I still believe he loves me. I believe in his love for our family." She glanced at Alice. "Corny, I know, but it's true."

Alice raised her hands. "Hey, I'm the cynical one."

Bob gave Liz such a long, searching look that she started to squirm, as if he sought something she herself couldn't see. A glimmer in his eye suggested he'd found it. "Perhaps 'corny,' as ye say, is precisely what's needed. I shall send word to the Queen to see if Stewart can be found. It will take magic stronger than mine to find him in the darkest places in all the worlds."

Then the approach of little footsteps caught everyone's attention, and Jackson came around the counter from the living room. "Mommy, look!" His face was all grin and wonder. On either side of him were Jaclyn and Jazlyn. The dolls each danced a perfect pirouette.

Alice screamed and jumped back onto her chair, clamping off a stream of expletives.

Liz laughed in spite of herself.

It was noon when word came in the form of Peaseblossom's "*Pssst*" on the counter from behind the blender.

"Gah! Another one?" Alice said. "A girl this time!"

Bob said, "Ye don't think we spring from beneath cabbage leaves do ye, dear lady?"

Peaseblossom darted to where Bob was sitting on the table. She gave Alice a glare, but said, "The Queen sends word. She found evidence of Stewart's passage. He's on his way to the Borderlands."

"The campground!" Liz said, jumping to her feet. "We can catch him!" The Bent Knife Campground had been their gateway to the Borderlands on their earlier journey.

Peaseblossom shook her head direly. "Wrong Borderlands. Headed the...*other* way, he is."

Liz sank back down. "Oh, no! What do we do?"

"The Queen says to come to the City right away. She's a plan to track him," Peaseblossom said.

Hunter jumped up from the floor, where he'd been doing push-ups and generally impressing Philip and Jackson with his physical prowess, and came into the kitchen, having overheard Peaseblossom. He said, "So when do we leave?"

Liz looked him squarely in the eye. "I don't think I can take you guys this time. You need to stay with Alice."

"What?" Hunter said with a frown. "No way!"

Cassie came over, too.

Liz said, "Last time, your dad was there to protect us. I can't fight off a tribe of coyote-riding goblins."

"But I can," Hunter said, assuming a ready martial arts stance.

"*We* can," Cassie said, elbowing him.

"Look, last time was a different situation. We didn't know what we were getting into. I can't *knowingly* take you into that kind of danger again."

Cassie asked, "But what if you need magic help? You're not good at it yet, but we are."

"Not like that dark elf," Liz said.

Hunter said, "Well, no, but we could face those goblins again. And Bob will be with us. Right, Bob?"

Bob nodded.

Liz wiped at fresh tears and shook her head vehemently. "No. The answer is no. You're staying here this time."

Alice said, "Your mom and I have had all morning to talk about this. Jake and I will make it as fun for you as we can."

"We'll have Jackie and Jazzie with us again, too," Cassie said.

Hunter stepped closer to her, and his voice softened. "Mom. We did this together last time. All of us. We couldn't have done it any other way. Dad needs us. *You* need us."

Liz looked hard at her little man and soon-to-be young lady. Her voice cracked. "I can't."

"We'll just stowaway anyway," Hunter said. "No way you're going to just ditch us."

"We don't have anything for you to stowaway *in!*" Liz said.

Alice squeezed Liz's knee. "I'll drive you wherever you need to go."

"Even knowing what happened to Stewart's truck last time?" Liz said.

"That's what insurance is for. I'll take you as far as, what do you call it, that campground. I'm not much good for off-roading."

Liz looked at all their expectant faces.

Hunter said, "I'll bet the Queen will have it all figured out by the time we get there. She got it out of him once. She can do it again."

Liz took his hand, squeezed it, and solidified her resolve. She had to try.

Part II

CHAPTER NINE

After hearing Liz's account of everything they'd encountered on their last journey to the Bent Knife Campground, Alice decided to leave her boys at home with their father.

"I don't even know how to explain," Alice told him. "I have to give Liz and the kids a ride somewhere. Stewart ran off with their car this morning. Things are a little rough right now."

"Do what you gotta do, sweetheart," Jake told Alice. "Me and the boys will be fine." The concern on his face for Liz and the kids was plain.

"I'll be home tonight, but probably late," Alice said.

Liz could hardly look Jake in the eye, but she gave him a hug of gratitude.

While the explanations and preparations went on, Hunter and Cassie, Bob, and the dolls waited quietly, pensively, in Alice's SUV. Jackson and Philip were one hundred percent on board with the "Let's Not Tell Daddy About Bob and the Dolls" Game. Liz doubted either of them could restrain themselves for long, but even if they couldn't, Jake would be unlikely to take them seriously. A tall, trim man with wavy blond hair and a chiseled jaw, Jake was a golf course kind of guy, not a library one.

With goodbye kisses in place for her husband and the boys, Alice declared, "Road trip time." She clamped a desert camouflage safari hat onto her head and headed for the car.

Minutes later, they were on the highway headed north out of Mesa Roja.

Liz felt so hollow she didn't notice the passing of miles. The weight of worry on her chest got heavier and heavier as she thought about Stewart getting farther away from her—in ways that were not just about miles—with each passing minute.

The air-conditioning hummed. The desert slid past the windows. The dolls lay dormant somewhere in the back. She caught the whiffling whistle of Bob snoring somewhere out of sight. Hunter and Cassie stared out their respective windows at the passing desert, saying nothing, lost in their own magical worlds.

At one point, as the sun was still rising to pour its scorching heat on the desolate landscape, Liz said to Alice, "Thank you." Her voice cracked as she said it, and suddenly she felt more unmoored than she ever had in her entire life.

Alice gave her a solemn nod. "You'd do it for me."

It was true.

"Besides, this thing," Alice said, patting the steering wheel, "has never even left pavement. It needs a little breaking in."

Had Liz mentioned the thorny vines that had shredded all four of the tires on their old truck? "Once we get off the highway, we need to be careful."

Something else that was true was how profoundly Stewart's departure had rocked her world. Just a couple of days ago, everything had been normal—at least, normal for her family, what with Little

People scampering about and magic in the air. But it had been good magic. Now, a black cloud had rolled over her entire life, crackling with lightning and threat, and she didn't know what to do about it. Stewart, her rock, her personal Viking, was gone. It was just her and the kids now, and they had to find a way to get him back.

Just then, she realized she was grieving. It was as if he were already dead or lost to her forever.

No!

Maybe he wasn't lost to her.

He had faced impossible odds in the Dark Realm and had come back from it.

But this time, he wouldn't be able to do it without her help, of that she was certain. Deep down in her bones, she knew she would have to go after him. So maybe she was grieving for herself, too. What if she wasn't the one who made it back? She caught her finger tracing her abdominal scar. How much of her Stewart would remain, even *if* she were able to find him?

Alice reached across and squeezed her hand. "It's going to be okay."

Liz gave her a wan smile, then wiped away tears she hadn't realized were there.

Then Liz recognized the stretch of highway they were on. Up ahead was a decrepit gas station.

Hunter said, "Hey, Mom, is that—?"

"It sure is," Liz said, then turned to Alice. "That's the gas station where the old service attendant fixed our fuel line and put a magic rune on it."

As they neared, it became clear that the station was no longer in operation. In fact, it was so decrepit and weather-beaten it looked like it had been closed longer than Liz had been alive, ready to be swallowed by desert. The windows were broken out, the front door hanging ajar. It couldn't have looked any more deserted if there had been a vulture sitting atop the ancient light pole.

"One of the Queen's agents, I'll wager," Bob said, standing on the console between Liz and Alice.

Alice and Liz jumped with a yelp, and the SUV swerved just a little. Cassie and Hunter giggled.

Alice said, "So this Faerie Queen has agents all over Earth?"

"Calling the Queen a 'faerie,'" Bob said, "is like calling the Taj Mahal or the Vatican 'someone's house.' But yes, she does. And so does the Dark Lord, Baron Tyrus. His agents are everywhere, and they are much less prone to playing by the rules."

"There are rules?" Alice asked.

"Magical beings are not allowed to act directly in the lives of mortals. We can guide, help, but we cannot interfere with humans. But as I said, Dark things don't like playing by the rules. In any war, whichever side is willing to go the furthest usually wins. 'Tis another reason why Stewart is so dangerous. He has become a Dark magical being, but as a mortal human, he isn't bound by the strictures of the Light or the Dark. That makes him even more dangerous in this world, and to all the worlds."

"What happens if he breaks the rules?" Liz asked.

"It would weaken the barriers between the magical worlds. If the barriers are ever broken, breached, it will be the end of everything. Unfathomable destruction as the Light and Dark worlds bleed together here, in the Penumbra. First, your world will perish, after that...'tis beyond my ken to say."

Alice laughed manically. "So, no pressure then!"

"We got this," Hunter said.

Alice laughed again, more jovially this time. "I admire your confidence, kiddo."

"We can save Daddy," Cassie said.

"So, what happens when we get to the campground?" Alice said. "You all just walk off into the forest and boom, you're in Faerie Land?"

Bob rolled his eyes at her continued use of the word "faerie."

Liz said, "That's mostly what happened last time. But it's not just walking, it's...journeying. I mean, walking is what we did, but there's more to it. I can't put my finger on it."

"Journey is perhaps the best word that English has," Bob said.

Liz went on, "It took us a while—I don't remember how long—before we got there. We crossed through the Borderlands—"

"And saw the giant moose," Alice said.

"Right, and then the giant grizzly bear—"

"With chameleon fur," Alice said.

Cassie piped up, "That's Pooh!"

Liz said, "It all happened little by little. Sometimes it felt like days or weeks had passed before we reached the City." She glanced at Bob. "Stewart could be gone before we even reach the City. We've already lost so much time. Do we have to take the same long path we took last time? Isn't there a faster way?"

"As ye said, 'tis a journey that cannot be measured in leagues or hours," Bob said. "I daresay it will feel quicker this time, as ye're more aligned with the Light Realm now, more attuned to it, than ye were before."

As the highway snaked around a mesa, the old gas station disappeared behind the landscape as if it had never been.

Alice's GPS led them straight to the turnoff for Bent Knife Campground, but from there, the digital map was blank. The dirt road was roughened by monsoon runoff and undulated across the desert floor just as Liz remembered. The kids' faces were glued to their windows, lost in the same memories as Liz.

"This is rough country," Alice said. "I'm surprised the Park Service goes to so much effort to keep this road open."

Liz leaned forward in her seat, scanning the road ahead for traps and threats. She gripped the dashboard, her shoulders tight as leaf springs.

As the road wound up through piñon pines into mountain slopes toward ponderosa forest, it skirted a slope that Liz thought she recognized as the place where the truck had been disabled. There was no sign of any unnatural rose bushes or thorny vines, just pine trees mixed with mesquite and dusty shrubs. She spotted a place in the embankment above the road that looked like it had been collapsed from above. That could be the spot where a boulder had rolled down the slope and totaled the truck.

And she had knowingly brought her friend into this kind of danger. And her kids, *again*.

She shook those thoughts off. Everyone was here willingly, enthusiastically.

But if anything happened to any of them, how could she live with that?

It was midafternoon when they reached the Bent Knife Campground, the meager patch of tent locations and fire pits, and the lone, cinder-block toilet, all nestled among pine trees.

"Looks pretty normal to me," Alice said. "Remote, but normal."

It did, indeed. Except that Liz's skin was crawling with memories of hiding, locked inside that smelly outhouse with Hunter and Cassie while Stewart held off a pack of snarling coyotes and their goblin riders. Her heart picked up speed. Those eyes in the dark. The menace in them.

There was no Stewart to hold off the goblins this time.

Fortunately, they had packed their coats of diamond mail armor and a selection of bladed weapons from Stewart's shop. Hunter had brought along real versions of his martial arts weapons.

As they unloaded their gear, Alice noticed some of these for the first time. Her eyes widened. "You look like you're going into battle."

"I hope not," Liz said, "but last time the only weapon we had was a hatchet. This time, we know what we're getting into."

"I thought you said the Dark magical creatures couldn't operate in our world," Alice said.

Bob said, "The Dark Lord views his minions as more...expendable. And he's willing to make them break the rules. This close to the Borderlands, the rules become a mite sketchy. Remember, magical creatures, Dark or Light, can come to your world. You could be standing in a field full of goblins, but not see them. Oh, and there's an ogre standing behind you, by the by, all eight feet of him."

Alice cringed and spun.

Bob slapped his knee and laughed.

Liz suppressed a smile as she shrugged on her diamond mail shirt over her T-shirt.

"Not funny," Alice said, fists on hips, glaring. Then she looked at Liz and the kids. "Geez, you guys look like you're about to walk onto the set of a fantasy movie. Except it's real, and now I feel terrible. I can't let you go. I can't leave you to do whatever you're going to do."

Liz hugged her. "You've done enough. We have to take it from here." As she squeezed, she felt Alice suppress a sob. Then they released each other, both wiping their eyes. She turned to Bob. "Can you put some sort of protection on Alice and her car so that she gets home okay?"

"Certainly," Bob said. "Perhaps the children would care to help me with that."

"Sure!" Cassie said. She pulled a small block of modeling clay out of her backpack. "We'll put a spell on this, and you can stick it to your dashboard or something."

She squeezed and patted the clay into a thick, oblong pancake. While the three of them worked on this, Alice took Liz aside. "Do you really think something will come after me for helping you?"

"I don't think so, but better safe than sorry, right?" Liz said.

Bob, Hunter, and Cassie all stood in a circle, all holding the lump of clay, eyes closed, concentrating, gathering Source with their collective will.

"Look," Liz said, "I know how weird this is, how crazy it all sounds. If we hadn't lived it, I would probably think so, too. But we'll be fine. We have Bob and the dolls to protect us. We have magic of our own. We're far from helpless."

"Those dolls are *super* creepy," Alice said, glancing around to see if they were near enough to hear, but they were standing near the spell-casting circle, holding hands.

"They're really very sweet. Like ninja toddlers, though. And they're sworn to protect Cassie." Then Liz sighed. "We need to get moving. You need to go. We'll be home soon. I'll call you as soon as we get back."

Alice sniffed a little. "You can't send selfies from the other side, I suppose."

Liz laughed, and they hugged again.

Cassie called, "It's ready!" She held aloft a palm-sized lump of clay with several runes carved into it. The glow of the runes was fading, but Liz could sense the magic in it.

Bob said, "This will shield you from the notice of Dark creatures and bring you good fortune."

Cassie climbed into the SUV and stuck the clay to a flat spot on the console. "That will work as long as you leave it there."

"Thanks, you all," Alice said.

"Let's be off, then," Bob said. "We must be well into the Borderlands by nightfall."

CHAPTER TEN

As Stewart drove west, his mind was a storm fueled by dark lightning and vengeance, churning with his intention to crush Baron Tyrus and cast him into oblivion. The Darkness coursing through his veins muted the tiny whispers of concern that this might not be the wisest course. His heart thudded against his breastbone.

Endless, sun-scorched miles of empty desert passed behind him, a vastness of low-lying sagebrush, dry lake beds, rattlesnakes, gila monsters, scorpions, and vultures.

He could sense his destination by the Darkness drawing him to his throne. How would he look sitting on the throne in the Metropolis? It would be his will that controlled the Dark magical kingdom, and thereby he would arrange his minions to restore balance between the Dark and Light Realms. He would cast away the greed and ambition of Baron Tyrus's reign.

You're fooling yourself, said a tiny voice in his head. *The Darkness will consume you, like it does everything.*

"Shut up," he mumbled. He had power now, and he would use it in the *right* way.

He knew that the closest entrance into the Dark Realm's Borderlands grew closer. He had to keep moving. He had to consider with certainty that Liz and Bob were marshaling the forces of the

Light Realm to stop him. He couldn't let that happen. His thoughts ran away from him with all the different possibilities, all coming back to one thing. This was the only way that his family could ever be safe, be free. Even free from him.

He must complete his mission. Or nothing would matter. Either way, they would be better off without him.

Where he was going, they couldn't follow. And he was going to the end of the line. This journey was one-way.

In the opposite front seat, his newly forged weapon gleamed dully, throbbing with power and purpose. It was the finest thing he had ever created, and he hoped it would serve him well in what was to come.

At about midmorning, he paused at a truck stop for a refuel, paid for his gasoline with cash, and parked among the resting semi-trucks.

Atop a light pole at the edge of the sprawling pavement sat the hunched shape of a vulture looking out across the desert. Its bald, black, wrinkled head hung low between dark, dusty wings.

Soon after returning from the magical realms, Stewart had engraved a palm-sized stone with the rune for *secrets* and placed it in his dresser drawer. With time and concentration, he could reach out with his awareness from anywhere and channel it into the stone. The stone would become an anchor for his awareness. He could, in effect, see his bedroom as if he were standing in the room, and from there, move around the house like a floating eye. He had conceived this idea in the worry that the Dark Lord's minions would attempt to hurt Liz and the kids while Stewart was away, and that he needed a way to check in on them, a magical surveillance system.

His own voice yelled in his head: *And now that Dark minion is you!*

No. He was doing all of this for *them,* however little they might understand that. He felt a pang of sadness that he would never see them again, but that was how it had to be. He wiped a trickle from his nose, then took a deep breath.

The density of free-floating Source in this area seemed higher than normal, with a more abundant accumulation of Dark Source than Light. He guessed this was because he was nearing the Borderlands to the Dark Realm. Both worked equally well in this case. He settled into a relaxed state of concentration, feeling the magic he had gathered resonating with the stone back home.

From his seat behind the minivan's steering wheel, he began to smell his bedroom, Liz's cooking, but in the house there was only silence. Then he could see the dark enclosure of his dresser drawer, a thin line of light coming in over the top of the drawer. He ghosted through the wood into the bedroom, seeing 360 degrees all at once. No sign or sound of Liz or the kids. Roving down the hallway, he checked the kids' room and found it empty, then propelled his awareness toward the living room and found it empty, too, as well as the kitchen. There was no sign of Bob or the dolls. Given what Stewart had done, Liz would have called Alice. He had always liked Alice, but now she was meddling in things in which she had no business. She had always been a bit of a busybody. What kinds of nonsense had Liz and Alice cooked up between them?

Bob would no doubt have informed the Queen immediately. That little rascal could go pound sand. Stewart would allow no obstacles. He would destroy any that appeared. His quest was too important. To make an omelet, you had to break a few eggs, just as he'd done to those dwarven smiths.

He moved through the house again, looking for clues he might have missed. This time, he entered the kids' bedroom and scrutinized the space. Everything in slight disarray, as if they'd just gone outside to play. A couple of drawers hanging open, like usual.

Hunter's gym bag was missing, the one where he kept his martial arts weapons. There was no practice today. The boy would not have taken the bag except to practice...unless he had protection in mind. Protection during a trip through the Borderlands.

Of course, Bob would try to take them to see the Queen. The Queen could fix anything, or so they foolishly thought. But she couldn't. There was no fixing Stewart this time. He didn't want to be "fixed." He was now his truest, most powerful self, giving free rein to the Darkness within.

But Bob couldn't just open a magical bridge to the City for them. They had to make the journey again, back to the Bent Knife Campground, then into the Borderlands and onward into the Light Realm. They might already be on the way. Could Liz have convinced Alice to drive them there? Maybe. Liz might even convince her parents to loan her a car. Her mother might even say yes if Stewart were not present.

He couldn't allow them to reach the Light Realm and cook up some sort of interference. They might be on their way right now.

He opened his eyes, returning his awareness to the quiet driver's seat of the minivan. The desert sun had already turned the interior into an oven.

The heat felt good on his flesh, warming his breath like a sauna, raising a sheen of sweat across his arms, soaking through his T-shirt. It reminded him of the furnaces under the Metropolis where he had forged the magical key that opened the Princess's prison. That was the moment he became truly alive for the first time, a moment that he reveled in. Looking back, he felt like he could have taken on the Dark Lord himself with just a little more knowledge and practice with magic.

And the Dark Lord was going to answer for what he had done. His family would never have to fear Baron Tyrus or his minions ever again.

Stewart's gaze fixed upon the quiescent vulture atop the light pole.

Then he gathered another draught of Dark Source into him. In his mind, the glimmering motes of magic essence congealed into a molten ball of crimson sparks that curled and arced like fishhooks. He savored the pain as the sparks ripped through him, a thousand pinpricks attracted by the presence of so much other Dark Source. He gathered them, focused them, squeezed them through his fingers until his hands dripped with Dark magic that only he could see. It would be invisible to any adult passersby. A child who had not yet abandoned their imagination might see the magic in his grasp, but they would not understand what they were seeing.

He stepped out of the minivan and reached out toward the vulture with his fistfuls of Darkness.

The bird flinched as if struck. But then it twisted on its perch and faced him, its beady eyes glinting red.

With his fingers he gestured for it to come to him, and it did. It lit upon his outstretched forearm like a falling brick, its talons squeezing with shocking strength, like steel hooks driven into his flesh by a vise. He hissed at the pain, swallowing it, and the creature hissed back at him, a low, guttural sound from a throat with no vocal cords.

Its five-foot wingspan stretched around him, encircling him for a moment, until it folded its wings.

He'd had such wings himself once. Perhaps someday he would have need of them again. The sensation of flying was a fond memory.

Collecting the bundle of Dark Source in his other hand, forming a coruscating ball of crimson that caught in the vulture's unflinching gaze, he infused the ball with his will, his intentions, and mental images of his targets. Then he thrust the ball into the vulture's breast.

The vulture leaped into the air with another dry hiss, unfurling its great wings into the desert's hot updrafts. Higher and higher it spiraled, until it banked toward the east. Stewart was pleased to see that its shape was already shifting and growing before it became a speck against the endless blue.

His eye caught movement through the windshield of a nearby semi. A pudgy, gray-haired trucker, mouth agape, eyes wide, stared at Stewart. Stewart met the old truck-driver's gaze and held it.

The trucker blanched, then ducked and scrambled into the sleeper out of sight.

Stewart got back into the minivan, started the engine, and continued toward his destination.

The farther he traveled, the more excitement rose in him. The tiny shred of guilt was replaced with a sense of calmness, knowing his family free and safe.

How far would the minivan take him across open desert if it came to that? It was hardly an off-road vehicle. But over miles and miles of highway, there were no exits, no turn-offs, nowhere to go except forward. Occasionally he passed a branching of a dusty track that looked more suitable for a jeep or a horse, leading off across desert flats.

But he trusted his instincts. He would find a way. He would walk if he needed to.

He passed an innocuous sign that read *Creech AFB* with an airfield and huge hangars in the far distance, then through a tiny town hardly lasting more than a couple of eyeblinks. There was no sign of human habitation as far as he could see. He kept driving, occasionally reaching out to touch the sword and run his fingers over the engravings on the blade. Their edges were still a little rough and unpolished, but the cutting edge was flawless.

As he drove, the desolation comforted him. He was alone, and he liked it that way. His sense of drawing nearer to his destination strengthened, driving him onward.

An arrow pointed toward a pull-off heading north, and his instincts tingled with the rightness of it. The tug at the horizon felt stronger.

A while back, he'd passed a large sign that read *Death Valley National Park.* Other signs said, *Caution: Extreme Heat Danger* and *Elevation Sea Level.* The surrounding hills resembled enormous sand dunes.

The paved road leading toward his destination was empty of cars, but somehow, he had the sensation of being watched. There were eyes upon him.

He turned off the highway onto a sandy track leading into nowhere. But it would take him places most humans never dreamed existed.

CHAPTER ELEVEN

"Mommy, I'm tired," Cassie said, with the kind of whine only a ten-year-old can produce, her upper body going so limp and boneless her backpack almost slid to the ground.

"I know, baby," Liz said, pausing in her tramp long enough to look back at the kids and the dolls. "Me, too. It's been a really long day." And the physical rigors of the hike bore no comparison to the emotional wringer she'd been putting herself through since the moment Stewart had driven off.

Bob had disappeared a few hours earlier without a word. The abrupt abandonment annoyed her, but he was a leprechaun after all.

The mountainside's pine forest was too thick to the see the sunset, which left Liz with some surprise at how quickly the light was dimming. From their previous journey two years before, Liz had somehow forgotten how rugged this area was, as if the Borderlands were an intentionally difficult obstacle. And they didn't have Stewart's bottomless well of strength to lead and inspire them this time. How many ways did her life depend on him? His absence highlighted new ones every minute.

Liz said, "We need to keep our strength up, don't we?"

Cassie said, "My strength is lower than a snake's belly in a wagon rut."

Liz chuckled at the analogy. "Where did you hear that?"

"A movie." Cassie shifted the weight of her backpack. "Did somebody put rocks in this thing when I wasn't looking?"

Hunter surveyed the area, a shaded forest glade with a stream trickling through. "I think this would make a good campsite. Nice and flat. Water over there."

Liz also took a look around. He was right. There was a minimum of rocks, a flat spot wide enough to set up the tent, and a stream of cool, clear water running across the mountainside. It would be best to have the camp set up before dark. She shrugged off her pack. "All right. Hunter, you start gathering wood and setting up the fire pit. It looks like there are enough rocks around here to make one."

He set down his own pack and got to work.

"Mommy, I have to...you know..."

Liz gestured to the forest around them and gave Cassie an apologetic smile. "The world is your bathroom. Toilet paper is in your backpack, right?"

Cassie frowned skeptically and looked around.

Liz said, "There are some bushes over there."

Cassie frowned deeper. "Tell Hunter to stay over there."

"Don't worry, I will make sure he does."

Cassie unzipped her backpack, grabbed a roll of toilet paper, and hurried off out of sight.

"Don't go too far!" Liz called after her. "It's already getting dark."

The dolls marched after Cassie, their expressions unchangeable as ever, but they moved with sharp alertness.

"Don't look!" Cassie told them.

Liz got to work unpacking the tent. Her stomach growled at the sight of the bags of jerky and trail mix, as she realized she hadn't eaten anything since yesterday.

How different the trip was this time. They knew what was ahead of them now. They knew not to be afraid of Pooh. In fact, she was wishing for Pooh's presence as some protection. The giant, magical grizzly bear would give any Dark creature pause.

Hunter returned with an armful of sticks and branches and went back to look for more.

She took a deep breath and tried to marshal her own strength. Her shoulders and back felt like a mass of knots, sweat soaking through the T-shirt she wore beneath her mail, plastering strands of hair to her face. With her ever-watchful Mom-Eyes, she spotted Hunter about forty yards away picking up sticks. But Cassie still wasn't back.

Amid a sudden burst of worry, Liz called out, "Cassie!"

No answer.

The burst became a spike. She called again, louder.

In response, Cassie came tromping out of the bushes about fifty yards away, looking sour.

Liz released her breath, hands on her knees. It was too soon on this journey to worry about battling Dark magical creatures. "Are you okay, honey?"

"Yeah, but..." Cassie's voice trailed off, and her eyes went wide, staring at something above Liz's head.

A winged creature the size of a cow hit the earth with a thump, right on top of Liz's backpack. Great, dark wings stretched twenty feet.

Hunter yelped a warning.

Reflexively Liz scrambled back. All her weapons were *in* the backpack.

The bird—not a bird, a creature—turned its malevolent gaze upon her. Its face was something between vulture and human, dark gray and scaly, with tufts of ragged hair or feathers sticking up from its wrinkled scalp. Its hooked beak was sickly yellow, sticking out from a human-shaped face. Its breast was also mostly devoid of feathers, as if they'd all fallen out in clumps from a bird-monster version of mange. It stood almost as tall as Liz, its gaze like crimson embers burning into her with malice so pure it turned her blood to cold soup. Its talons seized her backpack. The stench of death and putrefaction filled her nose, making her want to gag.

"No!" Liz yelled.

The thing *laughed* at her—a dry, hissing sound—and vaulted into the air with a great beat of its wings, blowing dust and grit into her eyes, her backpack clutched in its talons. And with it, nearly all their food, Liz's weapons, the first-aid kit, her sleeping bag, her change of clothes, her canteen...

It disappeared into the high shadows of the forest canopy.

Cassie came running, clutching her roll of toilet paper, the dolls flanking her. Hunter threw down his armload of wood and seized his gym bag full of weapons. He yanked out a pair of nunchucks and ran to protect her, scanning above for signs of the creature's return.

Cassie was crying as she threw herself against Liz's waist.

Liz's heart was pounding so hard she could barely speak. "We've all got our armor on, right?"

The kids nodded.

"Bob!" Liz called into the deepening night. "Where are you?"

The dolls' faces were turned skyward, their unblinking azure eyes intense and alert. In each hand they held what resembled dagger-like shards of obsidian.

The shadows of the forest canopy seemed to darken as the seconds ticked by. The memory of the creature's laughter was not something she would ever forget. Somewhere nearby, pine needles pattered over the ground, falling from on high.

Liz knew how strong the talons of vultures and raptors were. Attending a raptor show in middle school, she had gotten to hold a red-tailed hawk on her arm. She'd never forget the strength of its talons, painfully squeezing her arm even through the thick, leather glove. And this creature was giant-sized, with the talons to match. She hadn't gotten a clear look, but the claws must have been ten-inch daggers.

Wingbeats rustled through the branches, as if jumping from tree to tree. The great trunks trembled. More needles showered around them.

"You two stick close to me," Liz said. "Cassie, do you have any of Daddy's weapons in your backpack?"

Cassie nodded. "A really sharp dagger. He told me to be careful with it."

The backpack lay about ten feet away.

"Mom!" Hunter cried, pointing. "It's coming!"

Liz didn't look. She just dove for the backpack. Hunter and Cassie stuck close beside her.

Cassie yelped a terrified noise and grabbed onto Hunter.

"Leggo!" he yelled, shrugging her off, his nunchucks poised to strike.

The dolls turned into whirling dervishes, becoming little lacy blurs, flinging shards of obsidian skyward. The creature hissed and veered away, giving Liz the chance to grab Cassie's backpack. She fumbled the zipper open as if her fingers belonged to someone else. With enough room to stick her hand inside, she felt the wooden scabbard and the cold, metal hilt. She whipped it out and drew it. It was a brightly polished blade about a foot long, straight and double-edged. In Cassie's hands, it would be practically a short sword. Liz tested the edge with her thumb, and Cassie hadn't been kidding. It was as sharp as a fillet knife.

Watching for the creature's approach, she lamented the loss of her backpack. Strapped to the side of it had been a camping hatchet and a short sword of Damascus steel that Stewart had made just for her. It had been a beautiful weapon, now lost. At least she'd had the sense to put on her armor right away, even though it wasn't exactly comfortable wearing it all day.

The three of them stood back to back, watching the shadows above.

Cassie pulled a notebook and marker out of her backpack and started drawing. Liz knew they were runes, but she didn't focus on which ones. Cassie took a deep breath, closed her eyes, and fell into concentration, hand upon the paper.

The beat of great wings echoed among the trees like a slow, dusty heartbeat. *Thop. Thop. Thop.* Impossible to tell which direction it came from.

Cassie opened her eyes.

Liz felt something tug at her, as if a zephyr had just passed *through* her. It was the magic Cassie had just enacted. "What did you do, honey?"

"Protection spell," Cassie said, tearing off the sheet of paper and holding it out like a weapon.

Then, like a bomb, the thing plummeted out of the dark, straight toward them, talons outstretched. Both Liz and Hunter swung their weapons at it, but it turned sharply away before coming in range, as if it had bounced off an invisible wall. It hissed with frustration.

Cassie's sheet of paper burst into crimson embers. With a yelp, she flinched, shaking her hand and rubbing it against her shirt.

"Looks like it worked," Hunter said with a grin.

Cassie frowned. "Yeah, but only once!"

"Can you make us another one, honey?" Liz asked.

But Cassie was already drawing again.

Liz called again. "Bob! Where are you?"

"Right here, dear lady!" Bob's voice drew her gaze to the base of a tree about forty yards away. "Come! Let us away!"

Liz turned to run toward him. "Come on, you two!"

The three of them pelted toward Bob's voice.

Hunter snatched up his backpack and gym bag as he passed, but then tripped and splatted face-first on the ground, sending his nunchucks flying.

Liz came back, yanked him to his feet again by his collar.

"This way!" Bob called.

She could just see his diminutive shape at the base of the thick tree. Where was he suggesting they go?

With a heavy *whump!* the creature landed on Hunter's backpack, ripping it out of his grip. Then it launched airborne again.

"No!" he cried.

Liz swiped at the monster with her dagger but came nowhere close before it was gone again.

Bob stood at the mouth of a burrow leading down into the roots of the pine tree, gesturing. "This way, everyone!"

"Bob!" Liz said, skidding to a stop before trampling him. "We're not Little People!"

"But you can be!" Bob said. "Quickly! Hold hands and get in a circle." As Bob chanted and spoke in a language Liz didn't recognize, the air around them seemed to burst with tiny, winged creatures that came out of nowhere, thousands swirling around them as if they had sprung from the air itself.

Liz's skin tickled with tiny sensations. The touch was like the dew of a summer morning on the skin of a fresh apple, or like a dream of childhood, or like a smile from a beautiful stranger.

Even as this was happening, the urge to run, not stand stationary in a circle, a target, made her heart pound faster. Her eyes scanned the forest above, and a sudden wave of vertigo washed over her, like trick camera shots in a horror movie where reality itself is warped. The trees didn't grow, they *swelled* and *stretched* and...

She looked at Bob again, and they stood eye to eye.

The forest now towered above them like gigantic sequoias.

And the black-winged harpy rocketing toward them was the size of a T-rex.

"Go!" she yelled.

The four of them jumped into the burrow, followed by the dolls, tumbling over each other into the scent of verdant earth. The creature hit the ground outside the burrow. Dirt clods showered them as they scrambled to their feet and scurried away from the burrow's entrance. The creature's beak tore into the earth and roots but could not reach them. Its bloodcurdling hiss of rage and frustration turned Liz's muscles into noodles. Its breath was the most horrid stench she'd ever experienced, washing over her like fetid vomit that might cling to her hair forever. Its yellow beak was so enormous it could have bitten her in half.

Bob seized her by the shoulder of her shirt and dragged her deeper, down into the earth. Ahead lay a flickering light.

Not far below, a familiar figure held a matchstick-sized torch.

"Peaseblossom!" Cassie yelled in recognition.

Peaseblossom smiled and opened her arms. Cassie ran toward her, arms outstretched. They hugged each other with great relief.

"Weird," Cassie said. "You're the same size as Mommy now."

Peaseblossom smiled and kissed Cassie's forehead.

"You smell nice," Cassie said with a grin.

Now that they were all of a size, Liz could better see how beautiful Peaseblossom was, with great almond-shaped eyes and flawless, glistening skin. The usual size difference made seeing such details difficult. Peaseblossom was a stunner.

Hunter stared at the little woman, slack-jawed, his cheeks reddening.

Peaseblossom said, "I'm so pleased to see all of you. Now I get to show you *my* home."

CHAPTER TWELVE

The distant hills surrounding Death Valley kept their distance from what walked among them.

The feeling of rightness in Stewart's bones increased the deeper he went into the wilderness, like a musical instrument coming slowly into tune, into harmony. He had left the main road over an hour ago, taking ever more rough tracks into scorching nothingness. The minivan bounced and lurched over ruts and mostly buried rocks in what looked like a wagon track, which was now obscured at times by drifting dust. The engine temperature edged up toward the red line.

The sun seemed to grow larger in the sky, acquiring a lurid, reddish cast, but maybe that was just the approach of sunset.

A tiny voice in the back of his head admonished him for taking the family's only vehicle where he would likely have to leave it to die. He had deprived his children of their father, his wife of her husband, the family of their breadwinner. What would happen to them now?

But his mission was more important. The fate of all the magical worlds, the Penumbra, Earth, was more important than one family's hardship.

His way was the only way to save all of existence. If he failed, there would be no free worlds for his family to live in. All would be Darkness and chaos.

Baron Tyrus had to be destroyed. That certainty drowned out every whisper of doubt.

The engine coughed.

His gaze fell to the temperature gauge, now well into the red zone.

As he eased to a stop, engine chugging, he could hear the hissing radiator. He threw it into park and shut off the engine. Steam billowed from around the hood, with the strong scent of antifreeze.

He would be on foot from here.

He wrote a note on a scrap of paper with Liz's cell phone number. *Please contact...*

This he laid in the driver's seat. As an afterthought, he added, *I'm sorry.*

Then he gathered his gear and supplies. For this journey into the Dark Realm, he'd brought as much water as he could carry, about five gallons of it, along with beef jerky, granola bars, and trail mix he'd bought at a truck stop along the way. He hefted his backpack onto his shoulders; it had to weigh at least seventy pounds. Alongside, slung through a nylon loop, was his two-handed flamberge.

A truck-stop cowboy hat would keep some of the sun off. He clamped it onto his head and took one last look at the minivan. It might be the last time he saw something that tied him to his family.

Then he turned toward the scorching nothingness and started walking.

By the time the sun touched the distant hills, it took up too much sky.

He was in the Borderlands now.

His steel-toed work boots kicked up puffs of dust as he walked. Sweat soaked his shirt and dripped endlessly down his face. The only things he could see were the hills on the horizon, salt pan, scrub, and cacti. In the distance, two vultures circled something.

His only warning was a step into a patch of dirt that felt strangely soft, loose, pliable.

Then it exploded underneath him, flinging him into the air. He tumbled and spun, heels in the air, hat flying off, then crashed onto the hardpan, driving his breath out of him. The ungainly weight of the backpack pulled him onto his back.

Amid a burst of dust and grit, something big heaved out of its hiding place, bigger than a bull, bigger than *three* bulls.

Frantically Stewart unbuckled the waistband and shrugged out of the backpack.

A reptilian head the size of a Volkswagen Beetle swung toward him. A great, frog-like mouth opened with a deep-throated hiss.

He rolled out of the backpack and seized the hilt of his sword just as something shot from the creature's mouth—a huge tongue. The tongue's tip slammed into the backpack, and he glimpsed dozens of vicious hooks emerging from it, latching onto the backpack before the tongue yanked it away from him and into the cavernous maw. The creature swallowed the backpack in a single gulp. Left in the tongue's wake was a stench that punched Stewart in the nose. Not just bad breath, but a poisonous, chemical acridity.

Stewart was left with only his sword.

The runes on the Dark side of the blade were already glowing crimson with collected Source, gathered from the air itself, this close to the Dark Realm.

As the dust cloud dissipated, Stewart got a better view of the creature. Its shape and coloring resembled a gila monster, but its body was the length of a motor home. The spiny ridge along its back stood as high as Stewart's head. And a gila monster didn't have a tongue like a frog, much less spiky hooks on it. Its head was thrown up, still swallowing his backpack.

He needed that backpack.

His back near his shoulder blades had been itching all day, the skin crawling. He'd almost scratched holes in his shirt trying to relieve the discomfort. Gathering his will and all the Dark Source he could muster, he channeled the magical essence there.

Great black wings tore through his skin and sprang from his back. The feathers ruffled. The glossy, six-inch talons at the wings' knuckles gleamed wetly.

He stretched his wings and sprang into the air. Powerful beats bore him aloft.

The giant gila monster seemed unfazed by his transformation. Its terrible tongue flashed skyward. Stewart flipped sideways. The tongue grazed his leg, and its hooks tore gashes through his jeans, into the flesh of his calf and shin. The tongue disappeared again, quick as lightning, but the monster's beady eyes followed Stewart's flight with ravenous focus.

Gripping his sword hilt in both hands, Stewart summoned another swarm of Dark Source, sent it coursing through the blade—and set it alight.

The flamberge became a true flaming sword.

Stewart circled the creature. Its speed was greater than its bulk suggested, and its scuttling quickness threw up plumes of dust as it spun to keep him in view.

He dipped lower just once, and the awful tongue darted out again. But his dip had just been a feint.

Stewart jinked, spun, and slashed.

The tongue's hooks almost jerked the sword from Stewart's grip, but the flaming steel seared the member with a sizzling hiss. The beast loosed a breathy rumble of outrage as the tongue retracted, its eyes squeezed shut in pain.

Stewart dove, sword point foremost. Flames licked at his knuckles. Down, down...

The point plunged into the beast's neck, just ahead of one shoulder.

The titanic spasm wrenched the hilt from Stewart's grip, yanking him out of control. He bounced and rolled across the earth, losing feathers, his eyes, mouth, and nose filling with dust and grit. Still blinded by dust, Stewart launched himself into the safety of the sky until he could clear his vision. He spat and rubbed his eyes, hoping he was flying out of reach. The infra-bass rumble of the creature's pain vibrated through Stewart's bones like an earthquake.

When he could finally see again, he saw the flaming sword was embedded almost to the hilt in the creature's neck and shoulder. The stench of searing flesh reached Stewart almost a hundred feet above. The monster spun and thrashed, trying to seize the sword in its great jaws.

Now, it was time to finish this fight.

Gliding, spiraling downward, he gathered Source in a gleaming ball between his hands. Here in the Borderlands, he no longer needed runes as foci.

When he was only a few feet above the creature, he released the magic straight down into its head.

It spasmed once, then its legs collapsed under it. Its massive, crocodilian body *whumped* against the earth, heaving a tremendous sigh.

Stewart landed on its back, tugged his sword free, and extinguished the flames. Under his feet, the beast's great ribcage still rose and fell. It was only knocked unconscious, as he had intended.

He still had time to work before his stunning-spell wore off. Time to retrieve his backpack.

Going down the beast's gullet had left the backpack only a little worse for wear, having been swallowed whole. The only real damage appeared to be what the tongue's hooks had done upon seizing it. The stench of the gastric juices was hardly pleasant, however. He doubted the smell would ever come out.

Before the creature could die, Stewart gathered great draughts of Dark Source and used it to knit the beast's organs and wounds. This proved his theory that Dark Source did not always have to be destructive. It could be used to heal, to create. How else had the Dark Lord been able to build his incredible Metropolis? How much of what the Light Realm's inhabitants—the Queen, Bob, Claude, all of them—had told him was a lie?

When the healing was complete, there were livid scars across the creature's scales, but it wasn't about to win any beauty contests in any case.

As it stirred, Stewart fashioned one more spell, held it in his palm like a scarlet softball, and then pressed it into the beast's great scaly head. The spell found the strands of the beast's tiny brain and infused itself into neurons and synapses. It jerked once, as if dreaming, then its eyes blinked open. Slitted pupils focused on him. It heaved up its bulk and gathered its tree-trunk legs. Its stubby tail thumped the earth like a huge club.

Stewart stood before the immense mouth, furled his dusky wings, and began to reabsorb them into his flesh. He said, "Kneel." Where he was going, he would need all the allies he could muster.

The beast lowered its head back to the ground.

He laid his hand upon its snout. The scales were smooth and dry, perfectly interlocked. Acrid breath snorted from its nostrils.

"Up," Stewart said.

The beast stood again.

"Leg."

It raised a front leg for Stewart to use as a step, climbing onto the beast's back, dragging backpack and sword up behind him. The creature flinched as the sword caught the light of the deepening sunset.

Standing atop the giant gila monster's shoulders, he pointed toward the sunset and its lurid crimson sun. "That way."

CHAPTER THIRTEEN

Liz wouldn't have thought a burrow could be so homey. Lanterns kept it well lit. It was earthy and dry and comfortable.

As she and the kids followed Bob and Peaseblossom, she couldn't help looking over her shoulder for signs of pursuit. Where had that horrid creature come from? Could it shrink like they had and follow them down the Little People's burrow? Would some other creature more suited to burrows chase them?

Cassie peppered Peaseblossom with questions about what life was like in the burrows, but Liz was too worried about pursuit to pay much attention. It was weird being the same size as Bob and Peaseblossom. Their bodily proportions weren't quite human, with heads and eyes just a little too large. It gave Peaseblossom an ethereal beauty but somehow made Bob look a little misshapen in a comical way, like a cartoon character.

"What's the matter, my dear?" Bob asked. "Ye're safe now."

She kept her voice low so the kids wouldn't hear. "I still feel like we're being stalked."

"I'll not sprinkle yer bum with sunshine and tell ye we be out of the woods. The Dark Lord's shadow is spreading over everything." He frowned and rubbed his chin. "But ye're among friends. We'll not let aught harm ye if we can help it." He offered his elbow. She hooked her arm around it, and he patted her hand.

She said, "That's another thing that scares me. That the Little People might get hurt helping us. You might not be able to protect us. What was that thing back there?"

"I've never seen the like. Some sort of Dark magic abomination, I'll wager. Sent to slow us down. Dark magic can twist the flesh of Penumbral creatures in frightful ways."

"But who sent it?"

"Speculation wouldn't be helpful," he said with a deepening frown.

Her words caught in her throat. "I felt so helpless. Stewart is the fighter, not me."

"Ye are a powerful force, my dear, a fighter in yer own way."

"All this time and I've never even learned to use magic."

"Reckoning on that question meself, I've been. I did me some reconnoitering before we left yer home. I found a wolf carcass; in terrible shape it was. Didn't ye say ye saw a wolf, acting strangely?"

Liz nodded.

"A lone wolf in yer neck of the Penumbra is nary a thing, unless it were ill. But what I saw, 'tweren't any Earthly malady. I reckon that wolf had been claimed by the umbral, used to carry the Dark creature across mortal lands. And when it abandoned its host..." He shuddered.

"So if that wolf was...the *thing*—the umbral," Liz said, "why didn't it take Stewart when we saw it?"

"That is the trick, innit? I think it was because of you, my dear."

"Me? How?"

"I don't ken that yet, but I think it had to wait for you to leave before it could act."

"I took the kids to practice..." But how could she have possibly kept the thing away? She didn't know any spells. Nothing she had ever tried had worked. "Bob, I don't think that could be. I don't have any magic."

Suddenly Cassie stood looking up at her, forcing her to stop. "Sure you do, Mommy. You're just as strong as Daddy, but in a different way."

"That's nice of you to say, baby—"

"No, for real," Cassie said earnestly.

"How do you know?" Liz asked.

"I just know." Cassie hugged her waist. "Don't worry. When we get to the Light Realm, you'll see. There's plenty of magic to play with there."

Liz had been tired before the monster-vulture thing showed up, but now felt a whole new world of exhaustion. Cassie's questions for Peaseblossom had finally petered out, and she hung in Liz's clasped arms, a sleeping noodle, cheek resting on Liz's shoulder. The moistness of drool soaked through to her skin. Cassie was ten, but Liz could still carry her baby if she needed to, even if she felt like an anvil.

Their little band reached a stone gate blocking the passageway. As Bob and Peaseblossom approached the stone, it rolled into the passage wall as if it had seen them coming.

Beyond the gate lay a wide-open natural cavern, expanded with stonework, filled with dozens of stone buildings. At first, the sky seemed to be open and glimmering with stars, until Liz realized it was the cavern roof, and the twinkling lights above were not stars but clumps of light that looked...bioluminescent. Their colors shifted among blue, green, and amber. Lanterns glowed here and there, but most of the cavern's light came from the walls and ceiling. The air smelled earthy and alive, with hints of baking bread and spices.

On the distant walls, numerous other passages branched away in all directions.

Peaseblossom grinned and spread her arms wide. "Welcome to Serenity Glen."

Hunter's eyes widened, even as he rubbed them with exhaustion, and his mouth dropped open.

Liz shook Cassie. "Wake up, baby. We're here."

Cassie let out a groan and rubbed her eyes.

Peaseblossom said, "This is home for me, where I was born a wee sprout."

"Cool," Cassie mumbled, then went back to sleep on Liz's shoulder.

"Let's get you all some rest," Peaseblossom said. "Tomorrow we'll set out for the City."

Hunter asked her, "Are we in the Light Realm yet?"

"Not quite," Peaseblossom said. "But Serenity Glen is the closest settlement in the Borderlands. All those other passages lead to more settlements like this one. 'Tis how we get around."

"Yeah, but doesn't it take forever?" Hunter said. "I mean, we're so small."

Peaseblossom winked. "You'll see. But for now, we'll put you in an inn where the beds are soft and the breakfast is hot."

The stone gate closed behind them, and Peaseblossom led them down a broad street of natural stone worn smooth by the passage of untold feet. On the far side of the cavern, a waterfall cascaded down the rock face into a glimmering pool that caught the clusters of bioluminescence.

Hunter couldn't help staring, even though he looked dead on his feet.

Peaseblossom brought them through the cavern to a building made of perfectly fitted stone blocks. On a slate shingle above the door was painted a friendly looking chipmunk holding a tankard of frothy something.

Bob's eyes brightened, "Ah, the Thirsty Chipmunk, the best inn in Serenity Glen!" He rapped sharply on the closed door with the end of his cane. With no immediate response, he rapped again.

"Fear not," Bob assured them. "Arbornelle is a gracious innkeeper, but it is the wee-est of hours. She'll fix us right up soon enough."

The door opened to a green-skinned woman, almost as beautiful as Peaseblossom in a leafy emerald sort of way. With pleased recognition at Bob and Peaseblossom, her face went from annoyed to curious. Her hair was golden curls, and her eyes were amber, filled with kind maturity. She was dressed in a fluffy saffron robe and big, fuzzy slippers. "Burning the early candle, are we?" she said with a smile. "Come in, come in. You all look like you've been dragged across a washboard a time or two. A soft bed is just what you need."

That sounded like heaven to Liz.

Arbornelle said, "Why, you're *humans,* if I'm not mistaken!"

"Guilty," Liz said.

The interior of the inn was an inviting mix of polished stone tables and wall hangings that looked like impressionistic art, as if Monet had created tapestries depicting Little People frolicking in forest glens with their animal friends.

"Aye, we don't see many humans nowadays," Arbornelle said as she picked up a lamp of some sort, then blew on the crystal within. Warm light rose from the crystal. "Haven't seen any of you around these parts in many a decade."

"You used to?" Hunter asked. "See more humans?"

"I haven't visited the Penumbra in some time," Arbornelle said, "but Bob and Peaseblossom tell me that magic has all but disappeared there. No one believes anymore."

"But this family is different," Peaseblossom said. "That's why they're here. They're going to the City to see the Queen."

Arbornelle's eyebrows rose in surprise and realization. "Oh! It was you all that visited the Great Tortoise and saved the Princess!"

"The very same," Bob said.

Hunter said, "You heard of us?"

"Oh, my, but you're heroes!" Arbornelle's cheeks turned a deeper green. "The bards have been singing songs about you ever since. My favorite is 'The Battle of Tortoise Mountain,' quite a stirring ditty. But I do blather on!" She waved her hands as if fanning herself. "Oh, I'm so honored to have heroes crossing my threshold I've forgotten my manners!" She yelled through a doorway, "Milkweed! Rouse yourself! We've guests! Famous guests!"

A groan of protest sounded from the doorway.

Arbornelle's voice grew shrill. "Milkweed!"

A small voice came closer. "'Famous' my rusty..."

But the voice trailed off as an amber-skinned, emerald-eyed child in homespun pajamas emerged from the shadows and saw Liz, the kids, and the dolls. The child's jaw hung agape.

Arbornelle said, "After you pick up your chin, hop to it."

"Are they—?" Milkweed asked.

"They are indeed. Prepare the Crystal Suite."

Milkweed jumped and ran for the stairs in the back of the room. "Yippee! Wait till I tell the gang!" He disappeared in a flurry of skinny limbs and pointed ears.

"While we wait, shall I prepare you some Sleepy Night Tea? It will take out some of the weariness and let you sleep better," Arbornelle said.

"That sounds lovely," Liz said.

"Sit yourselves down then. I'll be back in a splash with a dash." Arbornelle winked, gestured to one of the polished granite tables, and hustled away.

With a groan of relief, Liz sank onto a stool. Still in Liz's lap, Cassie laid her cheek on the table and snored quietly.

Thinking Cassie had the right idea, Liz let her eyes close, just for a moment.

A cold, dry breeze swept over her. Something rough but alive leaned against her back, and it felt so natural, as if she were nestled against a wall that was breathing. But there was no wall nearby... She opened her eyes and instead of a cozy inn, she saw only open desert. Rocks and scrub and dust under a canopy of stars that were too bright. Her body felt wrong. Too large. And a wave of bitter anger washed through her, vengeful thoughts and single-minded purpose.

She was leaning against the side of some striped, sleeping reptile the size of a bus.

"Mom!"

She blinked, and Hunter was clutching her arm. Arbornelle was standing over her expectantly.

"Sorry," Liz said. "Must have fallen asleep. I was dreaming."

"Your room is ready," Arbornelle said. "Take your teacups with you."

Before Liz sat an earthenware cup of dark, steaming tea. It came to her nose with the smell of cinnamon, licorice, and cardamom.

"Drink it, Mom," Hunter said. "It's really good." His cup was already empty.

Liz took a quick sip and concurred. It was delicious, and just the right temperature to be warm but not scorching.

As Milkweed collected their teacups on a tray to bring along, up the back steps they all went to a spacious room filled with comfy-looking beds. Crystals of various colors protruding from the walls offered rainbow illumination. A pair of double doors led to a balcony overlooking a gurgling brook, runoff from the pond below the waterfall. Everything was so perfect, so pretty, so calming, it made Liz want to weep for relief. They were safe, for now.

Milkweed set the tray on a low table and said, "Will there be anything else, madam?"

They had little but the clothes on their backs, and she couldn't wait to collapse into bed.

"No, thank you."

"Then please enjoy your rest." Milkweed bowed and backed out of the room. With his hand on the doorlatch, he said, "Um, if I may be so bold, tomorrow, may I ask about your adventures?"

She smiled, "Sure thing."

Milkweed and Hunter stood about the same height. Hunter said, "We'll tell you all about it."

Milkweed clapped his hands with glee, then closed the door with a "Good night."

With no further word, Liz helped Cassie into bed. The dolls jumped up onto the mattress with her, and Cassie threw an arm over one of them, hugging it close. Liz tucked her in.

Hunter was already fading into sleep on his own bed. Liz kissed him on the forehead and stroked his hair. Then with a sigh, she took a drink of tea. It was like drinking a warm and pleasant dream, comforting, soothing, but her thoughts went back to the dream she'd had downstairs. Its vividness wouldn't leave her. When she closed her eyes, she saw the desert blanketed by night, and her breath slowed and deepened, as if she were already asleep.

And then, stranger still, she thought of Stewart, wishing he were with her, and knowing he felt the same. She yearned to feel his arms around her, his warmth, his strength.

"I miss you, baby," she whispered.

I'm still here.

His voice was as clear as if he were sitting right beside her.

Her eyes snapped open. She was still in the inn. Both the kids were sound asleep, the taste of the Sleepy Night Tea was still on her tongue, and the brook still burbled outside the balcony doors.

And it all made her unbearably sad because he was *not*, in fact, right beside her. She hugged herself and went outside.

The voice had been *her* Stewart, not the dark caricature of him she had last seen.

Beyond the stream, the wall of the cavern sparkled with tiny lights. When she looked closely, she could see that the lights were not only changing color, they were *moving*. Every single one was a tiny worm, the length of a finger bone. And the entire cavern, ceiling and walls, was filled with them, millions upon millions.

And then she was looking at the starry desert sky again. Were there constellations in the worm colonies?

She rubbed her eyes, trying to dispel the confusion.

I'm sorry, Liz. I couldn't stop it.

She flinched this time.

"Okay, that wasn't my imagination."

I'm here, with you, right now. Or I'm there.

"Stewart! Baby!" she whispered, checking to make sure she hadn't woken the kids.

The thing, it's asleep, resting. I spent a boatload of magic a little while ago. I don't have much time. I love you, Liz.

"I love you, too! We're going to do something! We're going to stop it—!"

There's nothing you can do. This is a one-way trip. It will do awful things, things I don't want you anywhere near.

"That's what you said last time."

Then around her the stars dimmed, and she felt a pressure, squeezing her smaller, too much pressure to breathe.

It's waking up. There's something you need to know. Part of me likes it, all this power. But I'm going to make things right. For you, for the kids.

The sense of his presence began to recede.

She reached out with her hands, with her mind, her will. "Stewart, no! Come back!"

And he *did.*

She felt him as surely as if he were standing before her on the balcony, smelled his hair, felt the roughness of his hand in hers.

Good one!

She felt his smile. Then his arms were around her. And she cried with relief.

And you say you can't do magic.

"What?" she said.

You brought me to you. But I have to go back now...

The sense of pressure around her increased as if she were smoke being forced into a bottle. But it wasn't her being forced into the bottle.

Stewart's presence was gone. The glow worms returned to their earlier brightness. The desert sky and the scaly behemoth were gone.

Her skin felt warm and tingly, buzzing as if with excitement.

Something had just happened. Was it magic? Was Stewart right? Was the connection between them the key somehow to power she didn't know she had?

Despite her exhaustion and the tea, sleep didn't come for a long time.

Liz was awakened by sunlight coming through the balcony doors. As she groggily rubbed her eyes, it only barely registered in her foggy mind that it couldn't be sunlight.

The children were already awake and eating pastries and milk from a tray of them resting on a low table.

"Milkweed brought us breakfast!" Cassie said, her mouth half-full of flaky confection.

"They're still warm!" Hunter said, still chewing.

Liz propped herself up on her elbows and stared at the balcony doors.

"You're a sleepy-head today," Cassie said. "But you needed rest, so we let you sleep."

Then Liz remembered. Stewart was out there somewhere charging toward something awful, and she'd been asleep. She flung herself out of bed, put her armored shirt back on almost frantically. There was no more time to waste. "You should have woken me up!"

Hunter said, "Nobody can function when they're exhausted, Mom."

She had no hairbrush, no toothbrush. She felt like she'd been trampled by horses, physically and emotionally. She had to save Stewart. She gobbled down a couple of pastries, chugged down a cup of milk—which *didn't* taste like cow's milk—and fretted until the kids were ready to go, too.

Half an hour later, she went out front, following Bob's urging, and saw what awaited them.

A wagon. But those weren't horses tied in the harnesses.

The creatures pulling the wagon resembled armadillos, she *thought,* but they were the strangest armadillos she'd ever seen, and not only because they were the size of horses. It took her a moment to remember that she was Little People-sized. Their shells were a gentle pink color, and the fur around their faces, legs, and bellies was either white or cream-colored. They had tails like armored spatulas and beady brown eyes. Aside from the pink, armored shell, their

144

front paws were their most distinctive feature, because their claws were absolutely enormous, easily as long as Liz's arms. With digging tools like those, these creatures must be able to almost swim through soil or sand.

Maybe they should be used to seeing outlandish sights by now, but... As Liz and Hunter stood agape, Cassie clapped her hands and jumped up and down.

"Mommy!" she said. "Do you know what those are?"

Liz shook her head.

"They're pink fairy armadillos! I read about them in a weird-animals book. They're from Argentina," Cassie said authoritatively.

"Wicked," Hunter said.

From the driver's seat on the wagon, Peaseblossom said, "They're not wicked at all. Well, except for Clodhopper there in the front. He likes to bite."

The fluffy, armored behemoth named Clodhopper wrinkled his pointed nose and watched them with one beady eye.

"Told ye I did that we've a conveyance for ye," Bob said, stamping his cane proudly. "We'll have ye in the City in a snap."

"All aboard!" Peaseblossom yelled with a grin.

CHAPTER FOURTEEN

Stewart wasn't in Death Valley anymore.

He never quite reached the hills on the horizon. The closer he got, the more they seemed to recede until he saw nothing except flat, empty wasteland, an endless plain of dust and thorny scrub.

The enormous crimson sun hove across the ocher-colored heavens, turning the air as hot and dry as the inside of his workshop with the forge at maximum heat.

The giant gila monster scuttled over the landscape at incredible speed, faster than a galloping thoroughbred, raising a plume of dust behind them. Its armored belly flattened clumps of cactus and vicious bramble that would have torn Stewart's flesh from the bone.

He mentally controlled the creature's movement and direction as if it were his own legs, and the abundance of Dark Source all around him allowed him to maintain the control indefinitely. As it ran, he balanced atop its undulating shoulders like a lifelong sailor on the pitching deck of a storm-tossed ship. He knew which direction to travel as surely as a moth striving to reach a single light in the darkest night. The Dark Essence that infused his form was like iron filings pointing toward the magnet of the Dark Lord.

For hours or days, the giant gila monster ran. Its weariness did not concern him. It could rest when its purpose was fulfilled.

But then he spotted another dust plume on the horizon ahead and off to the right, angling toward him.

Before long, creatures became visible at the head of the plume, then riders. The lurid sunlight glinted from polished armor and carapace. The elephant-sized beasts scuttled on segmented, chitinous legs, part centipede, part lobster. On their backs rode caricatures of knights, encased in thick metal plate. He had seen El-Mithari Garkus Riders on his last journey through the Dark Realm, but this time he did not fear them.

He brought his mount to a halt and placidly awaited their arrival.

A dozen of them circled him, a flurry of too many legs, too many eyes. He kept his sword slung on his back, kept his black wings furled. The riders circled repeatedly, their strange weapons trained on him—some sort of chrome projectile weapon—as if trying to figure out what he was.

"When you're done trying to scare me," Stewart said, "you can take me to the Master."

They halted in place. All the riders and mounts were identical, indistinguishable from one another, but one came forward. A male voice like drifting sand spoke. "Announce yourself or die."

"I'm Stewart Riley. The Master is expecting me."

Cruel laughter rippled among the riders. The alien-looking garkii held unnaturally still, even their mandibles, as if they were statues that could spring into deadly movement.

"Look," Stewart said, "I'm sure you've all lived a very long time. All the more stupid for you to waste that long life over your own arrogance. You can either choose to be my escort or food for my friend here." He had the gila monster lick its scaly lips with its great, barbed tongue.

The one who came forward said, "You are unworthy to dine upon the dung of our—"

Stewart leaped into the air, whipping out his sword. The Dark runes blazed with stored Essence. With a swing of his blade, he unleashed a fireball that blasted the rider from his mount. Blackened armor plates and chunks of carapace flew in all directions. The garkus shuddered and collapsed, and the charred, smoking body of its former rider bounced and rolled against the front feet of another chitinous steed. The garkus sniffed the motionless knight's body with spiny antennae, then snatched it up in its huge mandibles and devoured it in two gulps.

The other riders shifted nervously in their saddles.

Stewart hovered above them, wings flapping, sword trailing embers. "Anybody else want to get mouthy?"

Another rider bowed in the saddle. "We are at your service, Lord Stewart Riley."

The pink fairy armadillos could run with shocking speed. The passage walls flashed past, interspersed with patches of light and darkness. The carriage rolled along in surprising comfort, easily managing the passage's uneven floor.

Liz found the scent of the pink fairy armadillos mixed with the earth's aroma comforting, mesmerized at how fast they could travel. Her muscles were still overtaxed from yesterday; she found the movement of the carriage soothing enough to doze off, and her dreams were peaceful ones of their family.

The dolls shared one of the carriage seats, looking deceptively inert. If Liz didn't know what they were capable of, she would have thought them to be real dolls.

Bob sat beside Liz, snoring like a buzz saw, top hat lowered over his eyes. It was still strange to be the same size as him.

Along the way, they passed intersections, branching tunnels, and stone gates presumably leading to other settlements like Serenity Glen. The tunnel was illuminated in places by colonies of the glow worms, in other places by crystal lamps or torches, and other areas not at all, but the armadillos seemed quite capable of running at full speed in total darkness. The passage was wide enough to allow two carriages to pass; twice they met oncoming carriages drawn by rabbits, and a chipmunk-drawn sled.

Liz found herself trying to reach out for Stewart again—maybe she could get a clue of his wellbeing or location or plans—but without success. She attempted meditation and concentration to gather Light Source to herself like the kids had tried to teach her, but still nothing. The lack of success annoyed her. She had wondered earlier if the strength of her connection to Stewart might be the source of power for her, like Bob had said, but that annoyed her more, because it meant her powers were defined only in relation to him—and it would cost her more if she never saw him again. If she had powers, more than anything she wanted them to be hers, not dependent on anybody else.

After a few hours of travel, they passed into a near-dark section of tunnel. The light had receded behind them when Peaseblossom spoke a magical word and the carriage came to a stop.

The only light came from a patch of glow worms far behind them, and a glowing crystal hanging from a sconce above the carriage.

Peeking past Hunter, Liz saw a dark shadow across the passage floor, reaching all the way to the ceiling, a pile of rubble that spilled from a larger opening in the upper wall and ceiling of the tunnel.

"Is it a cave-in?" Bob asked.

Peaseblossom jumped down and approached the rubble. Hunter followed her.

Liz called, "Hunter! Stay away from there."

He turned back and gave her an eyebrow-raise and a *Seriously?* expression. By the time he was a teenager, his primary language would be sarcasm. She chided herself for the mom-reflex and then jumped down to follow them. Bob and the dolls and Cassie came, too.

Peaseblossom climbed halfway up the pile of stony rubble and peeked up through the opening. "It's not a cave-in. It's a new tunnel."

Bob frowned. "No one is supposed to be digging in this area."

"Can we clear it?" Liz asked.

"Not without help," Peaseblossom said. "And that would take some time."

"Can we go around? Take another route?" Liz asked.

"It will take less time to go around than to—"

Amid a sudden rumbling clatter, the distant light behind them disappeared as if extinguished.

Liz's mouth went dry, and Cassie seized her hand with a gasp.

"Another cave-in behind us," Bob said, his voice quavering.

"It wasn't a random cave-in," Liz said, her intuition screaming at her.

"Are we," Cassie gulped, "trapped?"

"I'll be but a moment," Bob said. In a flash, he raced back the way they had come.

"If that passage is blocked," Peaseblossom said, peering into the darkness of the new passage, "we have this way forward. It appears to go quite a distance." Seeing the fear on Cassie's face, she added, "Fear not, little one. There aren't any Dark creatures this close to the Light Realm. We are almost to the Border. I'm sure this is all just a misunderstanding or a coincidence." She went to the driver seat, took down the illumination crystal in its sconce, and blew on it like Arbornelle had done. The crystal brightened, becoming difficult to look at directly. The shadows in the passageway grew sharper, harsher, until nothing could hide in them.

A few heartbeats later, Bob returned. "The way back is completely blocked. So we've two options. We can wait a day or two for someone to clear one of these blockages. They'll soon be discovered, and repair crews will be on their way."

"A day or *two*?" Liz said. "Can't you use magic?"

He tapped the ground with his foot. "Pure stone. Neither I nor Peaseblossom are stone-shapers. We might summon a badger to move the rubble, but they're surly creatures and we prefer to let them go their own way..."

"What about the armadillos?" Cassie said. "They live in burrows. They could dig us out."

"Alas, my dear," Bob said, "they lack the strength of a badger."

"What's the other option?" Liz asked.

Peaseblossom pointed into the new passage that caused the cave-in. "We go this way."

"I leave it up to you, dear lady," Bob said to Liz. "We can wait for help to come, or we can press on."

Liz didn't have to turn it over in her mind. After her connection with Stewart last night, she knew he had not yet reached the Dark

Lord. But she resisted the idea of waiting an entire day, much less two, for help to come. She said, "And we have no idea where that tunnel goes? What if we get lost?"

Bob said, "We Little Folk do not get lost underground. Our sense of underground direction is flawless."

Liz glanced at Peaseblossom's look of suppressed skepticism at Bob's confidence. "You're sure we won't get lost? What if we get separated somehow?" Getting lost in total darkness was a scary thought.

"Me and Hunter can make magical light, Mommy," Cassie said. "There's Source everywhere around here, we're so close to the Light Realm."

Bob said, "If it so arises that this tunnel leads us nowhere, we return to this spot and await the repair crews. All we will have lost is a bit of time, which is the same as if we simply waited. On the other hand, we may well find a way through."

"What about the armadillos?" Cassie said.

"They might be hungry when someone eventually comes, but they'll be fine."

"All right then," Liz said. "Let's go."

The new tunnel was much narrower than the underground armadillo passageways. The stone looked like it had been *chewed* through, like a block of cheese by a mouse.

When Liz raised this observation to the group, both Bob and Peaseblossom frowned and nodded. "What kind of creature chews through solid stone?"

Bob said, "None that I know of."

The Little People glanced at each other. Peaseblossom said, "At least in these parts. This is very strange."

The tunnel was wide enough only for them to travel single file. The seven of them formed a line, with Peaseblossom in front, then the dolls on either side of Cassie, then Hunter, Liz, and finally Bob at the rear. Peaseblossom held her crystal torch high. Bob brought up the rear, holding his cane more like a weapon than a walking stick.

The tunnel curved and dipped, but it was almost an hour before they came to a branch.

"Are these tunnels new or old?" Hunter asked at one point while they paused for a sip of water. "These marks in the rock don't look fresh at all. There's this white build-up on the rock."

"I reckon you're right, lad," Bob said. "But I don't know these tunnels, and I daresay I thought I knew these tunnels like ye know the streets of yer own neighborhood."

"Some tunnels get closed off or collapsed and forgotten," Peaseblossom said. "But digging them is so much work we like to do it right, once and for all time. We seldom let that work be wasted. There are stone-shapers in the City but not in the Borderlands. These tunnels might well go back centuries."

"But then why did the tunnel collapse *now?*" Liz asked.

"If memory serves," Bob said, "that back there was new stonework. The marks were fresh. But why those were fresh, and these are not..." He shrugged at the mystery.

A few minutes later, they came upon the first fork in the tunnel, but the fork was a vertical one. An opening in the floor fell vertically into bottomless darkness, how far the light would not reach. The opening was easy enough to jump across, but as they went on, Liz couldn't help thinking about what might be able to climb those tunnel walls and come up behind them.

"How deep do the Little People tunnels go?" she asked.

"There are many levels," Bob said. "It depends much on the type of stone in the area. The gnomes delve deeper, but they prefer to live their whole lives untouched by the sun."

"Are there dwarves?" Hunter asked hopefully. "The dwarves in stories are cool."

"The dwarves all serve the Dark Lord, I'm sorry to say. Their entire race."

"But elves can switch sides, right?"

"You mean the bright elves and the dark elves, but I wouldn't exactly call it 'switching sides.' The dwarves were fashioned by the Dark Lord to mine and smith. They were made to be his slaves, perfect creations for those tasks. If ever there was one had a change of heart, I've not heard of it."

They came to another fork, this one angling upward. They had come so far, it was difficult to guess whether they had ascended or descended.

Bob pointed to the ascending tunnel. "Thataway!" he said brightly.

Soon, there was another branch. Then another. Then another, and another, until Liz strongly felt they had been lured into a maze.

The tunnels went up, down, left, right, and forward. Bob doffed his hat and scratched his head.

"We're lost, aren't we?" Liz said.

Glancing at Bob, Peaseblossom nodded solemnly.

"Um, hey, everybody?" Cassie said, eyes wide, "what's that noise?"

CHAPTER FIFTEEN

"What noise, honey?" Liz asked, dropping her voice to a whisper.

"Listen!" Cassie said.

Everyone froze. Liz held her breath and strained her ears.

It came to her then, a sound like claws on concrete, skritching and sliding, coming from every direction. Hunter knelt and quietly reached into his gym bag, pulling out his nunchucks. Blades sprang into the dolls' hands from somewhere inside their frilly dresses. Being of similar size to the two automatons, seeing the strange way they moved, still gave Liz the willies. Bob drew a slim sword from within his cane, which Liz had had no idea was there.

"Little Folk must always be ready for action!" Bob whispered with a gallant smile, flourishing his blade.

Peaseblossom rolled her eyes, but nevertheless drew a dagger that resembled a Bowie knife—at normal human scale, it would have been about two inches long—her face tense, ears cocked. She whispered, "They're all around us!"

"We can't just stand here!" Liz whispered. After all the turns in these dark tunnels, she had no idea even how to find her way back to the carriage.

Peaseblossom blew on her illumination crystal again, increasing its brilliance, which had dimmed over time as they walked.

At the edge of expanding light, two pairs of eyes the size of baseballs caught the light. Moving closer.

Liz yelped and pointed as the circle of light expanded to reveal the creatures. They looked like naked mole-rats, but the size of steers. Their skin was pale and wrinkled, translucent, and their squinty eyes peered from under bushy white eyebrows. Long, snowy whiskers made them look like kung fu masters from some cheesy Hong Kong movie. Then she spotted blades of dark, lustrous metal affixed to their forepaws with gloves or jointed frames. The blades looked like scythes.

"Kniblings!" Peaseblossom breathed with growing panic.

Bob pulled something from his coat pocket—an egg or a ping-pong ball—and flung it at the ground at the kniblings' feet. It exploded into sparks and smoke, driving them back into the pitch black. "Run!"

Peaseblossom pointed down a passageway. "This way!"

The seven of them bolted down this passageway, Peaseblossom and her light leading the way, Liz bringing up the rear at the edge of darkness. She didn't dare look back.

The sounds of pursuit erupted behind them, claws and knives skritching on stone, and a high-pitched, susurrous giggling.

Through seas of utter blackness they ran, with only Peaseblossom's crystal to keep it at bay. Liz wanted to claw through stone and earth herself to reach sunlight. The claustrophobic closeness of the air made it hard to breathe, and the impenetrable, inescapable darkness hounded every step. Her feet splashed through shallow puddles and flowing trickles. The ceiling was pale with tiny stone fingers born of slow-dripping water.

The pursuit grew nearer, and the passage narrowed, and the ceiling dropped, forcing her to bend, then stoop. If the creatures caught them...

BAM!

The crown of her head glanced off the jagged ceiling at running speed, and stars exploded in her vision. The explosive pain across her scalp and skull drove a cry out of her, staggered her, and tears blinded her. A small hand seized hers and drew her onward, steadying her. Eyes squeezed shut, she clutched the impact zone with her other hand, and her fingers came away warm and sticky. Panic lent speed to her feet, her breath turning ragged in her chest.

Closer and closer the creatures came, converging, echoing like a stampede of steel and claws in the narrow tunnel.

She could hear their pursuers' breath, smelled their foul stench like rotten fish, imagined she could feel the puff of it against her neck.

They came to another branch in the tunnel. Peaseblossom did not hesitate but took the left one that led slightly upward. The dolls clearly wanted to turn and fight, but in the confined space there was no way.

Something thumped against Liz's back, probably a stalactite, but she didn't dare slow down to look back.

Colors sparkled through her haze of tears: Hunter clutching something to his chest as he stooped along ahead. Cassie still clutched Liz's hand, dragging her along. Then he yelled back at Liz, "Mom, duck!"

Liz stopped and dropped.

"Eat this!" Hunter yelled and flung a cluster of jumping sparks like a softball over her head.

In its light, the moment before the globe exploded with sparks, she glimpsed one of those horrid, wrinkled faces. A squeal of pain and anger grated across Liz's ears.

But the sparks did not dissipate. They expanded from the point of contact and bounced from the tunnel walls, floor, and ceiling, back and forth, until the hallway was full of intertwining motes of luminous color. Through the web of light, Liz could see the creatures shying away. Black scorch lines crisscrossed the foremost one's face.

"Mommy, come on!" Cassie tugged at Liz's hand.

Liz moved as quickly as she could while stooped over, heart thundering in her ears like a booming avalanche, so loud she could hardly hear Cassie's voice. Her muscles burned with the exertion of the sustained, awkward stance. As the light of Hunter's spell behind her disappeared around a bend, she flushed with pride. Her *son* had done that! At the first opportunity, she was going to hug the pajamas out of that kid.

The only sounds in the tunnel were their heavy breaths and the scuff of fast-moving feet.

Peaseblossom yiped with surprise somewhere just ahead. There was the sound of crumbling stone, or metal striking metal. The light crystal's sconce clattered to the tunnel floor, casting wild, dancing shadows across the rough-hewn stone. The passageway filled with dust, and through it Liz could only see hunched backs...and then the flashes of blades.

"A trap!" Peaseblossom yelled.

Two side passages had been concealed by false walls, facades of soft mortar.

Bob shrank himself to the height of the passageway, then darted between Liz's knees, thrusting with his sword cane. "Get back, ye foul beastie!"

Peaseblossom fumbled for the light sconce with her left hand, blocking knibling blades with her dagger hand.

Then a third wall beside Hunter burst outward into rubble spilling at his feet. Flashing from the new opening came blades and snow-white whiskers and a wrinkled, pinkish-gray nose, lunging for Cassie, blades first. Liz tried to shout a warning, but her throat clenched shut. Jaclyn leaped between Cassie and the knibling, but the doll failed to deflect the incoming attack. The knibling's finger blades snicked through one of Jaclyn's arms, severing it, then raked her chest, shredding the once-beautiful dress and knocking her onto her back.

Jazlyn's porcelain face, seeing her sister felled, registered no emotion except for her eyes, which blazed with fury.

But before she could act, Hunter spun, whipping his nunchucks as they began to glow with a magical light, trailing glistening sparks. In a single movement, he slapped the knibling's blades down with one flail and smashed the knibling across the nose with the other. Liz caught a strange, ozone-like scent, as if the air itself were supercharged. Hunter took a step forward for another blow, but something streaked out of the darkness of the new tunnel and struck him squarely in the chest, a sharp metal projectile.

He let out an "Ooof!" and staggered backward.

"Hunter!" Liz yelled, her vision shrinking to a tunnel focused on her son. Her ears throbbed with a sound like an oncoming locomotive, deep and subsonic. Her hair stood on end. Close enough to

Hunter to see the face of the knibling that attacked him, she was also close enough to see the creature's face driven backward as if by a powerful shove.

She caught Hunter in her arms. He was gasping as if having had the wind knocked out of him, clutching his chest. A shard of dark metal as long as her forearm clattered to the passage floor.

The knibling in the passage facing her rolled away, driven back as if by a high wind until it disappeared into darkness, trailing bleats of confusion.

Silence fell.

Jazlyn fell to her knees to help her mechanical sister. Jaclyn's eyes blinked, but slowly. Jazlyn cradled her sister's head in her lap.

Peaseblossom knelt and held the light aloft, looking down the passageway now empty of any visible kniblings, then at Liz and the kids. "Who did that?"

"Who did what?" Liz asked.

Hunter said, "Mom, leggo! I'm okay."

Realizing she was squeezing him so hard her arms ached, Liz let him go. He was so strong now, almost a man.

He picked up the knibling blade, balanced for throwing, a nasty, jagged looking thing. "The armor stopped it."

Kneeling beside Jazlyn, Cassie yelled, "Jaclyn, are you okay? Everybody, Jaclyn is hurt!" She reached for the severed arm, but then drew back, her eyes brimming with tears.

"Fear not for the dolls, sweet lassie," Bob said. "She can be repaired when we reach the City."

Jazlyn helped her sister to her feet. Jaclyn picked up her arm, her eyes full of weariness that simple, colored glass could not express.

Peaseblossom said, "One of you set off a spell or a magical effect of some sort. I felt it pass through me, like a wind or an invisible bubble. It pushed the kniblings away."

Liz and the kids all traded looks, then shook their heads.

"Come now," Peaseblossom said. "It came from one of you."

Cassie said, "I think it was Mommy."

"I can't use magic, honey," Liz said.

"Maybe you're learning," Cassie said.

Liz opened her mouth to protest, but Bob cut her off. "We are still surrounded by kniblings," he said. "Shall we move along? Expeditiously perhaps?"

They hurried along the passageway again, everyone's attention focused both ahead and behind, alert for facades that concealed more traps. Jazlyn helped her sister limp along. The tunnel expanded to allow Liz to walk upright again, and Bob adjusted his height accordingly.

The sounds of pursuit had not entirely vanished. Liz often thought she could hear whispers in the dark or the scrape of metal claws on stone or the scrabble of pebbles.

As they ran, she noticed a strange sensation, like warm glitter pulsing through her veins. Could she be using magic? Could she have created that bubble that pushed the kniblings away? But she didn't know she could do such thing.

They ran until they were too winded to go on, rested until they caught their breath, and ran on again. Liz didn't know how long they did this, only that her legs became overcooked spaghetti. She had a stitch in her side, and her lungs felt full of barbecue coals.

At one of these respites, she asked, "What are those things? What did you call them, 'kniblings'?"

"They are spies for the Dark Lord," Bob said with a pained, worried expression.

"But we're so close to the Light Realm," Liz said. "What are they doing here?"

"Spying. Scheming." Bob spat. "Doing the Dark Lord's will on our very doorstep."

Peaseblossom said, "Some of those tunnels were old, others new. I daresay they've been digging their trap for a very long time. And we Little People had no notion they were so close."

"But why?" Liz asked.

"Preparing for something, no doubt," Bob said.

"But what?" Liz frowned at how she sounded like a toddler playing the Forever Questions Game.

Bob shrugged, and Peaseblossom rubbed her cheek with worry.

"Mommy, what happened to your shirt?" Cassie asked.

The question forced Liz's worries to shift gears. "I don't know, honey, I can't see it."

"The whole back of your shirt is ripped open, down to the mail," Hunter said with wonder. "They almost got you."

The hair on her arms and neck stood erect with gooseflesh.

She tried to make her voice sound less alarmed than she felt. "All hail the Queen's diamond chain mail. And for you, too, little mister."

He grinned and patted his chest, then winced. "Ow."

Cassie said, "Yeah, six inches higher and it would have gotten you in the face."

His grin faltered.

Bob stepped in. "'Tis not only luck on your side. I seen me some serious magic-slinging just now. But let us keep a lively step, shall we? The sooner we cross the Border into the Light Realm, the sooner we can see our friend Jaclyn repaired, and the sooner we needn't fret about meeting any more kniblings."

"How far is it?" Cassie asked, the voice of weariness itself.

"Oh, not far now," Bob said. "I can feel it! 'Tis...thataway." He pointed vaguely in two or three directions at once.

When night fell in the endless desert, a blood-colored moon crawled into the tarry sky.

Stewart and his escorts rested. He kept his reptilian steed away from the nasty tarantula-lobster-pedes to prevent any chance of an altercation. The beasts raised enough hostility between them that only their riders' iron control kept them from attacking each other.

The El-Mithari were not hostile toward Stewart but wary, unsure what to make of a human who could wield such power. They were used to being the meanest dogs on the block, but they recognized a meaner one when they saw it. Camped around their fire built of thorny bramble and dead cacti, they removed their helmets. They appeared to be dark elves, but of a lineage that bore different facial features than the one Stewart had met. These had pointed ears, but their noses were so small and upturned they were little more than slits, their eyes so deep-set, their brows so thick, they had an almost prehistoric look. They ate dried meat and hardtack from their saddle bags, sipped liquid that didn't smell like water from worn water-skins, and eyed Stewart askance.

Did they resent him killing their leader? From what he'd seen of Dark Realm creatures, he doubted it. It was more likely they were all scheming about how to seize the vacancy for themselves. There was ambition, strength, and determination in creatures of the Dark Realm, but little true loyalty. Their loyalty was bounded by convenience and personal ambition on one side and the threat of death on the other. How could they advance themselves without overstepping or offending Baron Tyrus or some other powerful creature? Powerful monsters were something the Dark Realm had aplenty.

Stewart slept against the side of his enormous steed, and when the crimson sun rose, a glitter on the horizon caught Stewart's eye, sunlight glinting from lofty spires of chrome and domes of bronze and catwalks of burnished steel.

"The Metropolis," he said, shielding his eyes from the sun. With two great flaps of his wings, he was high in the air for a better view.

The way between him and the Metropolis was clear and open, interspersed by clusters of machinery or buildings of nebulous purpose.

He took a deep breath, drawing a great draught of Dark Source into him, savoring the needles of pain tearing through him. He took another, and another, building up such a store of it that he began to glow, and sparks of it dripped from the ebon feathers of his wings.

Then he released it all in a great avalanche, straight toward the Metropolis, carrying with it a single message:

MASTER, I AM HERE.

The reply came moments later.

Eyes the size of dirigibles appeared in the morning sky, Baron Tyrus's malevolent orbs burning above the desolate landscape.

The voice boomed over the stones and dust: "I have been expecting you, Stewart Riley. Come to the Obsidian Tower, where all will be revealed."

CHAPTER SIXTEEN

Liz didn't know how long they had been running—it could have been hours; it was probably only several minutes. Their tiny burrow eventually expanded into a tunnel large enough to hunch only partially. She imagined she could hear the kniblings' breath behind her, the scratching of their claws, and the grate of their blades against the stone.

Then she came up hard against Cassie, knocking her down.

"Sorry, honey!" Liz yelped, helping Cassie to her feet again.

They had come up against a blank wall, the end of the tunnel. She looked back the way they'd come and tried to remember how far back the nearest branch was.

Peaseblossom scrutinized the blank wall, holding her crystal sconce close, then tapping it. "I reckon this is as false as a dark elf's affection."

On second glance, the end of the passageway did appear to be a conglomeration of stones and mortar.

Liz asked, "How do we get—"

With the butt of her crystal sconce, Peaseblossom slammed the center of it, and a rock tumbled out the other side, leaving an opening the size of a fist. Dim light filtered through the hole from the other side.

"Yay!" Cassie said, her voice echoing shockingly loud back the way they had come.

Hunter and Liz quickly shushed her.

"Sorry," she said sheepishly.

The work of a couple of minutes enlarged the hole so they could all fit through.

Beyond the wall was a cavernous, cathedral-like space, with a ceiling so high it would have been lost in shadows except for the profusion of rainbow glow worms. Millions of them formed shifting rainbows across the towering walls that disappeared in the distance. The grand, startling beauty of it, coupled with the fact there was now *light,* brought a lump into Liz's throat.

They all stopped and stared up into the vast cathedral of scintillating beads, rapt, huffing for breath. The walls reached up and up and up... Which also meant the surface must be even farther away than Liz had thought.

"Do you think they're still behind us?" she asked.

Peaseblossom cocked a large ear. "I can't hear them anymore."

Bob doffed his hat and wiped his forehead with his arm. "Scurvy devils! The Queen must hear of this. Kniblings so close to the Border."

"Fortunately, everybody is okay, right?" Liz said, checking Cassie then Hunter for injuries.

"Except for Mommy's shirt," Cassie said.

"Well, thank goodness and the Queen for these diamond mail shirts," Liz said. "They saved two of us." She hugged Hunter again. "I'm so proud of you. You really saved us with that glowing web thingie."

He said, "Thanks, Mom, but—"

"It was your magic force bubble, Mommy," Cassie said. "That's what pushed them away from us."

"*My* magic force bubble?" Liz said.

Hunter said, "I'm pretty sure it came from you, Mom. I mean, it *felt* like you."

"It smelled like you," Cassie said with a grin.

"But I can't—"

"Perhaps that has finally changed," Bob said with an appreciative smile, "because what happened back there was quite real."

"It seems," Peaseblossom said, "that your children being in mortal peril has allowed you to step beyond whatever internal blocks you possessed."

Hunter gave her a lopsided smile. "I guess we just need to be in mortal peril for your magic to work."

"Don't you dare!" Liz said, laughter bubbling out of her as she hugged him again.

Cassie said, "We're all about the peril, Mommy."

"Don't you start!" Liz hugged her, too. Liz's every limb suddenly felt like limp dishcloths, and she wanted to fall into a pile and cry until she woke up again.

"Oh! I know where we are!" Peaseblossom said.

"Indeed," Bob said, "this is Merryvale Canyon, is it not?"

Peaseblossom nodded with a relieved grin. "We'll be aboveground and over the Border in a trice."

Traversing the great cavern was like bathing in the light of millions of jewels—diamonds, sapphires, rubies, emeralds, amethyst, rose quartz. The colors were coordinated among all the worms in an area, as if they were communicating, resulting in huge hypnotic patterns shifting and swirling.

"It's so beautiful!" Cassie said.

Peaseblossom said, "We have spring equinox festivals here. Some distance ahead, there's an opening that admits a single ray of sunshine at midday. Nothing that we can reach, mind you. But the surface is near."

With that they took off through the underground canyon, less worried that kniblings still tailed them. The path they took snaked up along a ledge on one side of the canyon, wide enough for two carriages to meet safely, and worn stone showed it to be well traveled.

Liz was amazed to see the glow worms up close. They were fat and grub-like and clung to the stone in hammocks of slimy-looking webbing, as if napping, although they darkened and went out if anyone got too close.

Bob and Peaseblossom were going on about plans to send word back to Serenity Glen and other Little Folk settlements about the presence of a knibling warren on their very thresholds.

"The Little Folk'll not stand for this," Bob said. "They'll roust those kniblings like the mangy rats they are. Once they get word, that is."

But Liz's own thoughts absorbed most of her attention. If her kids had to be in danger for her magic to come out, she hoped never to use it again. It had been a completely unconscious thing, the immediate need to get her son out of harm's way, like those stories where moms picked up cars and refrigerators to save their children with adrenaline-fueled super strength.

Was she holding herself back somehow? Mentally? Emotionally? Was she too self-conscious about it? It was extra strange because she'd always enjoyed Stewart's talk of magic and looking for the wonder in everything. Or maybe it was just wishful thinking and all her mother's closed-mindedness and negativity had crawled under her skin in ways she couldn't see.

Could she do it again?

Or worse, what if the kids were in danger again and she *failed?*

She had to get a handle on this somehow.

So, as she walked, she tried to concentrate on finding Source like the kids had tried to teach her. Here, she didn't need to remember runes because in the Borderlands, magic could be used without them. Trying to focus her attention more on inner space, she felt around blindly for the sparks that would fuel her magical intentions.

Okay, Liz, she told herself, *dial back Mom's voice, and dial up Stewart's stories that he used to tell about magic. Go for that dreamy-eyed look he used to get when we were first dating, when all the world was hope and possibilities.*

She let those memories infuse her. The moment when he first opened up to her about all the magic in the world and he sounded a little crazy, but in a sweet, childlike way, how he had reminded her of all those whimsical fantasies that her mother had driven from Liz's mind the moment she hit puberty. Their first date, a simple night at the Dairy Mart over tater tots and banana splits, where she had paid and let him get by with the ruse that he'd forgotten his wallet because he didn't have any money. The first time they held hands, when he'd reached across the picnic table, enfolding her hand in his callused paw. Their first kiss, tentative, as if neither of them could believe it was happening, because up until that point he was *so* not her type. His sense of wonder at how there could be magic around every corner, and it could pop up where you least expected it. The time he had sworn to her that he'd seen a leprechaun out of the corner of his eye, so earnest that she believed him.

And then it came.

The breath of Source flowing into her like a warm rain, tingling through her limbs and up the back of her neck. It built up inside her like a ball of throbbing comfort, but also like a fully charged battery, ready to be used. Tears of joy trickled down her face.

As she walked in the rear, she quietly wiped at them with no one noticing. If she needed magic again, it would be there for her. Was this how Stewart and the kids felt all the time? It made her ache for him all the more. She would stop at nothing to get him back. Nothing.

The joy bubbled out of her. "Hey, Cassie. How about we sing a song?"

Cassie turned with wide eyes and a huge grin. "Sure! 'Touch the Sky'?"

Liz said, "Absolutely."

"Touch the Sky" was a song from the movie *Brave,* the song Cassie had sung when Liz was wounded at the mouth of the Cosmic Tortoise. It had since become their song. Mother and daughter raised their voices to the rooftops, had there been any.

The singing put a spring into everyone's step, even poor Jaclyn's, clutching her severed arm to the chest of her ruined dress.

And then the glow worms began to sing, too, not with voices but with light. In perfect time with Cassie's voice, rainbow pulses of song flowed up the canyon walls, bursting with patterns propagating into the distance.

The party could only stop and stare, giggling with wonder. And Cassie sang and sang.

In the middle of the last chorus, the profusion of rainbow glow worms began to grow sparse. A brighter glow emerged ahead, growing into a mouth filled with sunlight.

"Outside!" Hunter said.

Past the startled Little People, the humans rushed for the daylight, squinting through tears as they burst outside.

"I want to kiss the ground," Liz said, giggling with unrestrained glee, wiping her eyes.

"'Tis certain the ground would be most appreciative," Bob said.

As their vision adjusted to the stabbing brightness, they saw they had emerged on the side of a verdant river valley. It stretched for miles in both directions, one leading up into forested mountains, the other sprawling down toward a plain, where the river's fingers stretched out through lush orchards and fields of grain.

"I reckon ye're ready to go back to yer normal size?" Bob asked.

"It'll be so weird!" Cassie said.

Hunter added, "I'm kinda used to being the same size as you."

"Kniblings are a sight less frightening when you're human size," Bob said with a wink.

He tapped each of them with his cane, and there was a sensation like touching oneself with a vacuum cleaner hose, and then *pop!* Bob and Peaseblossom were back to being knee-high, and the cave entrance too small to fit through.

"Ah! Giants! Flee for your lives!" Peaseblossom said with mock terror.

They all laughed and set out down the river valley. Somehow Liz knew the direction of the City, like a compass needle. The breeze was warm and the sunshine more welcome than at any time she could remember. Her veins pumped life through her, and every breath got sweeter and sweeter, every step lighter, her exhaustion seeping away.

They were crossing the Border into the Light Realm. And the City was waiting for them. Unlike the last time, when they had had to travel across the Light Realm for some time, the City stood visible through the misty distance.

Part III

CHAPTER SEVENTEEN

Their return to the City felt like coming home.

Bigger in the sky here than in the Penumbra, the sun warmed Liz's face and arms, casting a dazzling array of coins across the surface of the Lake. The Lake only looked like water, however. It was actually a recirculating reservoir of magical Source, projected in her perceptions to look like water, because that's what her human mind could comprehend.

As they traversed the paths between fields and orchards, swarms of rainbow-colored pixies burst into the air, their dragonfly wings glittering in the sun, warbling in gibberish that sounded like coherent speech, but Bob assured them wasn't. The pungency of fruit blossoms and the earthiness of grain predominated the tapestry of scents.

Like the last time, entering the Light Realm was like stepping from a black-and-white movie into a Technicolor one, but for every sense, so vibrant, the colors exploding, the scents unfolding, the breeze like a friend's kind hand. Music in the distance, the smells of baking bread and roasting vegetables, the sky a cerulean blue streaked with orange and red clouds of sunset.

The grandeur of the City's ancient trees, formed still living into dwellings and crafting halls and theaters, could not easily be encompassed by coherent thoughts. Jewels gleamed in resplendent mosaics embedded in living tree trunks half a mile high, fifty yards thick. Great boughs stretched back and forth between the trunks, forming walkways with pristine white balustrades just visible in the hazy, blue distance.

Some of the structures were also of stone, but without the use of cut blocks, as if the stone had been shaped like clay and then re-hardened into the most whimsical and elegant shapes, filled with figures, faces, bas-reliefs and painted frescoes so intricate they told the stories of entire universes.

Being this close to it rejuvenated her, erased her exhaustion, making her feel as if she wouldn't need to sleep for a week. Seeing all these mind-blowing spectacles again made her wonder what Stewart was seeing right now. Had he reached the Dark Lord? Was it already too late to save him?

She couldn't help but feel motherly pride at how Cassie, now that she was normal-sized, picked up Jaclyn and carried her like a baby.

As Peaseblossom had said, Liz and the kids were already the stuff of song and sonnet, so whenever anyone spotted them, recognition spread. Some of them even waved in greeting. Children of many colors and shapes cavorted alongside as if Liz and the kids were heroes of legend.

The ogre children, often called the Big People, were about human size, and they bounced along with their friends and did somersaults and backflips, sending streams of drool in all directions from their flabby lips. Their eyes were so bright and innocent that Liz couldn't even be annoyed about the drool.

Happy denizens filled the streets and parks, pausing their conversations and laughter to tip their hats at the human passersby. Many of the inhabitants looked mostly human, but with variations that didn't exist in the Penumbra. Skin and facial features were a myriad of types, a pleasant lavender color or sage green, sometimes with pointed ears, sometimes great rounded ones, sometimes no ears at all but only little round holes. To Liz's eye, they were a spectrum of beautiful and not-so-beautiful, just like back home, but all of them had a ready smile and a twinkle in their eyes.

By the time they reached the Queen's mansion, night had fallen. The stars were so bright and scintillating, however, the night could hardly be called dark. The last broad thoroughfare rose into a twirling series of bridges and walkways reaching into the highest reaches of the great trees. The bare wood of the balustrades looked pale as ivory, shaped and polished into motifs of interwoven vines. A moist breeze wafted up from the Lake, brushing Liz's skin and carrying the scent of flowers and cinnamon. The last bridge leading up to the Queen's great entrance hall was hundreds of feet above the ground.

The mansion's walls were fashioned of the same kind of intricate bas-reliefs as elsewhere, filled with stories of gods and epics and everyday heroes. An art scholar could spend years studying them— even if the images weren't moving, as if the stories being told were still underway.

As before, their approach to this grand mansion made Liz feel like a very exposed bug with many eyes upon her.

Standing at the mansion's gate was a familiar, rotund figure with bushy eyebrows like white caterpillars and a horizontal ring of white hair circling a bald pate. He wore plaid trousers, a starched white shirt, and clashing suspenders of garish colors.

"Claude!" the kids yelled, and ran toward him. The dolls limped along toward the man who had once "sold" them to Stewart.

The strangely hunched, rounded man hugged them, beaming with a smile, the dolls close behind. "Welcome! Welcome!"

When he saw Jaclyn's sad state, he clucked his tongue and said, "Oh, dear." He reached down and took them both in his arms. "We must find Lady Jocinda, mustn't we. No doubt she'll have you good as new before morning. Would you like that?"

Jaclyn nodded despondently.

He turned to Liz and the others. "And welcome to you as well."

Liz hugged Claude. "It's so good to see you again after all this time."

"It's hardly but an eyeblink," he said. But his expression darkened. "No doubt you're here to see the Queen."

Liz nodded. "You've heard about Stewart then."

He nodded grimly. "I'm so sorry, my dear. You must be heartbroken."

Her eyes teared up at that, and she gave a sniffling nod.

"We must see what can be done, yes?" Claude said. "Come."

He led them through the thirty-foot-high double doors, into a vaulted hall several stories higher, filled with floating lights and grand staircases. The floors and staircases of polished wood were somehow still alive, their woodgrain shifting and changing like the City outside. Paintings, murals, sculptures in wood and stone, mosaics, bas-reliefs, tapestries. Some depicted epic stories, others simple abstracts that grabbed her subconscious attention and wormed deeper, lodging half-guessed impressions in her psyche. The floor was a polished parquet of many colors, depicting...a human couple and two children, standing before the mouth of the Cosmic Tortoise in a heroic pose.

Liz stopped and stared. "It's—"

"Us!" Hunter and Cassie said, pointing.

"Quite lovely, is it not?" Claude said.

"Fetching indeed," Bob said, scratching his bushy sideburns in appreciation.

Peaseblossom just stared and stared, up, down, and all around, rapt, at the immense grandeur of the hall, probably even more so for one of her size. "I've never been here before," she breathed. She hugged Cassie's knee. "Oh, my stars, it's..." But she couldn't find a word to finish her sentence.

But Liz was already feeling impatient. Every moment wasted brought Stewart closer to the Dark Lord. Before she could open her mouth to inquire about the Queen, however, a light like a sunrise emerged in the hall, and the Queen materialized in the center, amid a burgeoning chorus of light and sparkles.

The Queen of the Light Realm moved like liquid sunbeams, so graceful her movements were difficult to comprehend, all nine feet of her, all the ageless feminine beauty in the universe bound into a single form. A flowing cascade of hair caught the light from many angles, with a different color in every direction, hanging to her waist. Even now, after previously being in the Queen's presence, Liz couldn't tell if she brought the light with her or emitted it herself. She wore a gown embedded with precious gems of every imaginable color. Rubies, emeralds, sapphires, diamonds, aquamarines, garnets, opals, all so bright she was difficult to look at directly. Luminous motes orbited her head in irregular patterns. Her eyes glimmered yellow-white in an alabaster face, and in them resided the mysteries of the cosmos itself.

"Welcome to you all," the Queen said in a voice booming with the chorus of galaxies and nebulae, surf and cataract, playgrounds and birthday parties. "We are pleased to see you again."

Everyone in the hall knelt before her. The sheer, cosmic majesty of this creature made Liz shudder with awe.

Then beside her stood the Princess. She looked about Cassie's size, still an incredibly beautiful child, with eyes so full of wisdom it was unnerving to meet them. Maybe she had grown in the two years since Liz had seen her, but it was difficult to tell with a child who was already centuries old.

The Princess came forward and hugged each of them in a warm embrace, for all the world feeling like a normal child of flesh and bone, even though she was a magical being rather than a biological one. Like the Lake, she was more of a projection that resembled a child than an actual child. But there was sadness in her eyes, too, at Stewart's absence. She glanced at her mother with some trepidation, and a hint of stubbornness, as if Liz and the kids' arrival had landed amidst a disagreement.

Appearing from one of the hall's many entrances was a familiar figure in armor that made him look like a small samurai. The commander of the Royal Guard, the bright elf Wyn Ar-Chaheris, came forward to greet them with a smile that was no less pleased for its subtlety. The sharp ears stuck out from his head, poking through hair tightly bound in a dark ponytail. He was handsome in a narrow, big-eyed sort of way, his features too sharp, too smooth, to mistake him for a human, even if he hadn't stood only to Liz's shoulder. "The

Riley family has been away from these halls for too long, my friends." He bowed deeply. "But, alas, your purpose for coming is not a happy one."

Liz sighed. "Unfortunately, you're right. It's not. As much as we'd love to enjoy this reunion with all of you for a while, we're here because we need your help."

The Queen nodded, "And it saddens me like you cannot know, that we are unable to offer it."

Liz and the kids gaped at her, and before they could finish processing what she had said, the Queen faded away like a fast sunset.

"Mommy!" Cassie said, staring quizzically into the space the Queen had just occupied. "What did she mean?"

"She's not going to help?" Hunter said incredulously.

Liz turned to the Princess, who stood frowning, lips scrunched. "So, is that what she meant? You're not going to help save Stewart?"

The Princess's voice rang like precisely tuned bells. "Mother and I have been...discussing this since we first learned of the umbral's escape. Or its release, whatever the case may be."

Liz gaped. "Someone let that thing *go*?"

"Regrettably, yes," chimed in Wyn Ar-Chaheris, his expression darkening. "One of my brethren was apparently subverted by the Dark Lord's magic. He turned traitor, ventured into the City's deepest vaults, and released the foul thing. And regrettably we cannot ask him why, as he ended his own life." He failed to control fully the bitterness and shame in his voice.

"The Dark Lord can bring down even the most exalted among us," Claude said. "I'm sure the Queen has her reasons."

"Yeah, well, whatever they are," Liz said, "they're not good enough! Princess, we need to talk about this."

"If it were up to me," the Princess said, "we would not hesitate. I owe him my life after all."

"Can't you help us save Dad?" Hunter asked.

"Unless Mother approves of our plan, she would likely negate whatever help I tried to offer. And I could not hide it from her. We are...connected."

"Can you bring her back?" Liz asked. "I want her to tell me her reasons for abandoning my husband to..." Her voice cracked.

The request hung in the silence. The denizens of the Light Realm all hung their heads and sighed.

Cassie's voice was small. "We came all this way."

The Princess nodded. "I will go and entreat her for an explanation. Meanwhile, please refresh yourselves." She gestured toward a table laden with food that had not been there before. Then she disappeared like a mist.

"Thanks, but I'm not hungry," Liz said.

"I'm starving!" Hunter said and charged the pile of fresh bread, cheese, and fruit.

Cassie looked uncertain. "My tummy is not happy."

Liz hugged her. "Me, too, honey. And don't you worry. We're not giving up."

Cassie sniffled against Liz's side. "Okay."

Bob and Claude walked away together, talking in hushed tones. Peaseblossom followed Hunter, jumped onto the table, and yanked a dewy, green grape from a bunch with both hands.

Wyn Ar-Chaheris bowed to Liz. "If the Queen wills it, I shall gladly escort you to the Dark Lord's very throne."

The hall blazed with light again, and the Queen reappeared, her face resolved. The Princess appeared next to her, her expression unreadable.

Liz addressed the Queen. "Have you changed your mind?"

"I understand your disappointment and hurt, Liz Riley," the Queen said, "but the magical realms are a vast place, dependent upon the very rules of the universe to exist. These rules are woven into the fabric of space-time as intricately as the force of gravity. They are the foundation of reality itself, all the realms, not just yours. If we go against them, subvert them, the fabric of reality will unravel. Thus, we of the Light Realm cannot intervene directly in the lives of Penumbral mortals, only offer assistance, guidance. I fear I overstepped when I extracted the umbral from him in the first place. Nevertheless, for the sake of the debt we owe Stewart, I did consider it." She glanced at the Princess. "I explored a vast number of possible futures based upon such a course of action, and nearly all of them were catastrophic. The word 'Armageddon' might be appropriate." She met Liz's gaze, and Liz had to look away or else fall into those cosmic abysses. "Is a single human life worth the fate of every individual, every form of life everywhere?"

Liz wanted to say *Yes, to me he is!* But it sounded so incredibly selfish. Then she grasped something the Queen had said. "You said, 'nearly all.'"

"Indeed, there are possibilities we might call 'Armageddon lite.'"

"Oh."

"What concerns me most, however, is that there are paths that I cannot see. You must understand, I experience all of time, all possibilities, as happening to me simultaneously. But there is a portion of it that is somehow beyond my sight, like a blackboard that has been erased. The path into that patch of possibilities is fraught with too much chaos. Breaking the rules to save Stewart might be what ends the universe itself, all the realms. Everything."

The Princess's voice rose like wind chimes. "Mother, Liz is right. Perhaps there are real chances to save Stewart and avert catastrophe. I have experienced the same glimpses of possible horrors that you have. The end of everything. Every life in every universe snuffed as if it never existed. But the Light Realm is built upon compassion, kindness, the creation of life, the nurturing of life. If the balance of saving Stewart gives life to thousands more, in ways that our simple actions in this moment ripple outward with after-effects, then we owe it to everyone to take the chance. Stewart risked everything to save me, and you have told me yourself that his chances of success were slim. In plenty of other realities, he failed, and the Dark Lord became ascendant. Perhaps there is something about Stewart, about this family, that is a force for Light, a force the universe needs."

"But to balance the fates of so many on one human..."

Liz stepped in. "A being like yourself must find uncertainty to be the scariest thing ever. I mean, you're used to knowing everything, right? You've already experienced it all."

The Queen spoke slowly. "It is most disconcerting. Leaving the fate of every living thing, every tree, every human, every animal, to a roll of the dice is a choice I find unconscionable."

"My Queen," Claude said, raising a finger, "if I may interject a point for consideration, beyond whether saving Stewart is the just and moral thing to do. Whatever Stewart is planning, he seems to be bent on destroying the Dark Lord all by himself. We all know that this is simply the umbral feeding him delusions, for the simple purpose of driving him toward irrevocable, irredeemable immersion in the Dark Realm. We also know that there is no way for a human, no matter how powerful, to destroy a creature as powerful as Baron Tyrus. Despite Stewart's best intentions, it is far more likely that the Dark Lord will subvert Stewart to the Dark, thus acquiring the most powerful ally anyone has seen in ages. How can we allow this? The Dark Lord simply does not care that conquering the Light Realm will doom his existence, too. He too much enjoys the act and spectacle of destruction. He might gladly spark the destruction of every universe if he got to enjoy the ride."

Bob stepped up before the Queen, doffed his hat, and bowed deeply. "Your Infinitude, I have always believed it is our solemn duty to save people and cipher out the consequences afterward."

The Queen's gaze focused somewhere into unknown cosmic vastness.

The Princess said, "Mother, we must have faith that love will overcome whatever unpleasantness comes after."

Another long, agonizing moment, during which Liz's stomach flopped around like a moth the size of a trashcan lid.

The Queen said, "Very well. It is not often that I am wrong, but I let uncertainty cloud my judgment. Saving Stewart is the right thing to do. But there is only one path forward. You must leave immediately."

CHAPTER EIGHTEEN

"I'm ready," Liz said to the Queen, "but I don't know what to do. I'm running on faith and intuition. Could you please give us some guidance?"

"Those possibilities are outside of my awareness," the Queen said.

"Will you protect Hunter and Cassie while I'm gone?" Liz asked.

"Mom!" Hunter said. "No way you're leaving me here. We talked about this. *We* have to save Dad."

"I'm sorry, kiddo," Liz said. "I'm the mom. I can*not* take my babies into the Dark Realm. It was bad enough getting you this far." It was as unthinkable as throwing her children to starving wolves.

Cassie looked up at her with a stern expression. "Hunter's right. We talked about this. You need us to help save Daddy."

"Until you get your magic to work when you need it to, you need us," Hunter said.

"We can't lose you, too, Mommy," Cassie said.

The look on her little girl's face broke Liz's heart, and thus, her resistance. She clutched a hand over her mouth and choked back tears. They were right. If she went on her own, it would be a suicide mission, and her children would be left as orphans. But they would be alive! What mother wouldn't give her life for her children? Well, maybe she could think of one. But not going would consign Stewart to certain death.

It was an impossible situation. The horrors they might encounter in the Dark Realm had to be the vile flip side of the wonders of the Light Realm. Stewart had refused to talk about the things he'd seen and done in the Dark Realm. Surely there had to be worse things than goblins, even worse than dark elves.

As much as she loved Stewart, as much as the kids loved their father, how could they go on what was likely a suicide mission?

In this moment, everything felt like it was falling apart around her.

The Princess approached Liz with an expression of profound compassion and hugged her.

In the embrace of this beautiful celestial being, Liz's breakdown was complete. She sobbed in the Princess's embrace.

"I can't do it. We came all this way, and I can't do it. I should have left the kids with Alice and come all this way alone. I should be locked up for dragging them all this way to the brink of danger. I'm such a failure!"

Hunter and Cassie tried to hug her, too, but she couldn't look them in the eye.

"No," the Princess said, shaking her head gently. "That voice is not yours. It belongs to someone else. Deep in your heart, you have faith in your children to be strong and brave. What you lack is faith in yourself."

"But I'm a good mom! How can I take them into what might as well be Hell?"

"Mom, you have to let us be who we are," Hunter said.

"We're wizards, Mommy. And the only way to save Daddy is together," Cassie said.

Hunter said, "It's our choice."

"Well, you're not old enough to make those kinds of choices!" Liz snapped.

Hunter's earnestness turned into an angry frown tinged with hurt.

"Mom, you said we could go!"

"I changed my mind!"

Hunter crossed his arms. "So, you're either going to give Dad to the Dark side or take yourself on a suicide mission. All because you lost your nerve."

"You watch your mouth, little man!" Liz snapped, pointing a finger. But as the words came out of her mouth, they sounded exactly like her mother. That realization formed a sick knot in her gut.

His face gaped with shock, and he flinched as if she'd just struck him.

Cassie stared at her.

Liz could count the times she'd spoken that sharply to her children on one hand.

Hunter turned half away from her, tightening his arms. "It's true."

The Princess's voice was like a wind chime. "I have something that may help." She held out her hand, from which a cluster of oval lockets dangled on silver chains. On the face of each locket was the likeness of the Princess's profile. "Inside each is a special spell fueled by pure Source. It will make you invisible to the magical perceptions of Dark Realm creatures. They will still be able to see you if they are close enough. But they will not be able to magically sense your presence. Nor will Stewart."

Liz wiped her eyes.

Claude stepped forward. "I will accompany you."

She blinked at him. "Are you sure you can make that kind of trip?"

"Some spryness remains in these fat, old bones," he said.

Bob thrust out his chest. "And I as well, dear lady."

"But you're a creature of Light," Liz said. "I didn't think you could exist there."

Claude said, "We have studied the technique the dark elf used on himself and the goblins, a magical war paint that anchored them here, made from the Princess's blood. We think we can replicate the effect—but without the use of blood."

The dolls stepped forward and hugged Cassie's legs, Jaclyn with her severed arm tucked under the other.

Peaseblossom looked up at Liz. "May I have a word?"

Liz nodded, and Peaseblossom whisked faster than sight to sit on Liz's shoulder.

Peaseblossom spoke low in Liz's ear. "The Princess is right. Talk to me, girlfriend."

Liz sighed, walking a few steps away from the kids, Peaseblossom clinging to her shirt. The way the little woman had said it made Liz wish Alice were here, but Peaseblossom had centuries more wisdom to draw upon. "Yeah, you're right. I sound like every harsh helicopter mom I've ever heard. Worst of all, my own. But how can I knowingly take my kids into danger?"

"Because I'm fairly certain you don't have a choice. You'd never forgive yourself for giving Stewart over to the Dark Lord. Eventually, you'd wither and turn into your mother. Your little giants wouldn't want you to become that. Cassie and Hunter often plot and scheme to avoid 'going to Grandma's house.'"

Liz snickered at that. "How often?"

Peaseblossom's eyes widened. "A *lot*. And if you force them to stay behind now, after everything you've already been through, they'll feel like failures, like you've no faith in them, so then, why should they have any faith in themselves? By trying to protect them, you might well turn them into the kind of people for whom magic doesn't work at all. Magic thrives in a childlike heart, or have you forgotten that? Forgive me for saying so, but hasn't that always been the hub of the bond between you and Stewart?" She waited for Liz to respond.

Liz nodded sullenly, her heart aching.

"Protect them too much, and you might squash their beautiful little souls."

At that, Liz's eyes burst with fresh tears. The truth of it hit her like an anvil.

Peaseblossom went on. "We're all in this together. For me, it's because I love your wee giants, but also the wider concern. If the Dark Lord has Stewart as an ally, a weapon, that's *bad*, that is. I'm just a regular person, and a little one at that, compared to you, nothing special about me. But I cannot sit this out. Neither, I suspect, can you."

Liz swallowed hard. Peaseblossom was making far too much sense.

The little woman turned to face Liz. She felt like a kitten sitting on Liz's shoulder. "We're going in there like magical commandos. They won't see us coming. Neither will Stewart. We'll take him by the scruff and shuffle him out of there before the Dark Lord is any the wiser. And to escape, all you must do is remove whatever spell is keeping you there and you'll fall right out to safety."

That last hadn't occurred to Liz. They had an escape plan.

She turned back to everyone, drew a deep breath, and steeled herself against the emotional tumult inside her. "Sorry for the mom spasm, kids. We need to get this show on the road."

The kids beamed and ran to hug her. The Princess's smile was as bright as headlights on a dark, lonely road.

Claude said to the dolls, "You two run along and find your mother. See about getting your arm repaired, and perhaps some clothes better suited for stealth." Their frilly dresses were long since ruined anyway.

Jaclyn and Jazlyn hesitated.

"Don't worry, we won't leave without you," Claude said.

They looked at each other, and then ran off so quickly they could have raised a dust plume.

The Princess said, "I must caution you about using magic in the Dark Realm. Each of your lockets has been infused with a small supply of Light Source so that you might use magic without having to absorb Dark Source. But when it is spent..." The Princess shook her head. "The faster you use it, the sooner you lose your magical concealment. Any creature with the ability to sense magic will know of your presence like a searchlight on a dark night. This and the Source you've gathered into yourself are all the Light magic you can take with you. If you collect any Dark Source, you risk the same thing happening to you as happened to Stewart. Darkness will take root in you."

"But how do we get Stewart home?" Liz asked.

"That is the lockets' final power," the Princess said. "If you open one while wearing it, you will return to this room immediately."

"So I put one on him and open it?"

The Princess nodded. "There is an extra one for him." She distributed them.

Liz tucked Stewart's locket into her jeans pocket. Knowing the kids could be saved in a desperate moment eased Liz's fears—but only a little.

"And this is how you will be able to exist in the Dark Realm." The Princess held out a glass bottle filled with shadow. "The Dark Ink. I shall not tell you how it is made, but it will hold you in the Dark Realm until it is removed or its magic runs out. You must refresh it once a day at sunset. This was all we could make with the...materials we had." The distaste on the Princess's face made Liz wonder what they had used instead of blood, but on the other hand, Liz didn't want to know. Just looking at the bottle made her queasy. She edged away from it, reminded of how Stewart's umbral looked when it was trapped inside its crystal prison, swirling, churning, too black for the eye to grasp.

Several bright elf Royal Guards came forward, carrying backpacks filled with provisions.

"We are preparing everything we will need," Wyn Ar-Chaheris said. "Food, water, weapons, equipment, elixirs for healing."

Hunter said, "Won't the Dark creatures be able to sense things made in the Light Realm?"

"We believe the lockets will dampen their perceptions for our things as well as our bodies."

"You *believe*?" Liz said, raising an eyebrow.

"We are...fairly certain." Wyn Ar-Chaheris looked away. "If we were not, there would be no point in my accompanying you."

"With you along," Hunter said, grinning, "I feel safer already. I've seen you fight. Maybe you can show me some cool moves."

"I would be honored, young Riley," the bright elf said. "Perhaps you can show me some of yours as well. I hear you've become quite a martial artist."

Hunter's face flushed. "Sure!"

"Mommy, I wish we could stay here for a while," Cassie said.

"Me, too, honey," Liz said, "but we can't waste any time."

"I know, but it's just so beautiful. If we come back, I never want to leave again. I want to stay here and sing for people."

"What about school?" Liz asked.

"You think I could go back to Ms. Hackett's class after all this and not be bored out of my mind?"

Hunter said, "This whole place is more school than we'd ever get back in Mesa Roja."

Liz chuckled, in spite of the fact that Cassie had said *If we come back*. "Well, we'll worry about that some other time."

Claude was shrugging into a shirt of diamond mail like Liz's, but the size of a small tent. Catching Liz's gaze upon him, he said, "No one will mistake us for Dark Realm creatures. So it will be best not to be seen at all."

Ar-Chaheris said, "If we require subterfuge, I might be able to impersonate a dark elf, if only temporarily. You could be my prisoners. I will wear armor taken from dark elves."

Thinking about contingencies was a dark spiral that knotted Liz's gut. Best to focus on the now, this moment when the entire Light Realm seemed to be focused on making their journey a success. No pressure at all.

A blaze of light heralded the reappearance of the Queen. "You have everything you need for the journey, Captain Ar-Chaheris?"

"We do, Your Infinitude," Ar-Chaheris said. "Our preparations have been thorough."

"So, you did not believe my initial refusal?" the Queen said, arching an eyebrow.

Ar-Chaheris cleared his throat and bowed. "We had faith you would change your mind, Your Infinitude."

The hint of a smile curled her majestic lips. Then she turned to Liz and the kids, gesturing toward the bountifully laden table of food and drink. "Eat and drink your fill. Muster your strength. You are going to the most desolate place in existence."

Hunter burped. "We already did, Your Amazingness."

Liz hadn't, but when her stomach, knotted tighter than a fist, might be willing to accept food again was an open question.

The Queen said, "Very well, then. Stay hidden. Use your magic carefully—"

Just then quick-scuttling footsteps zipped closer. Jaclyn and Jazlyn skidded to a halt next to Cassie, dressed in elastic garments that hugged their limbs like Lycra, colors shifting through the dark end of visibility, not unlike Pooh's coat, the giant, chameleon Kodiak bear. The garments made the dolls look even more alien, highlighting the unnatural shape of the dolls' limbs and joints. The illusion of life had been stripped away, leaving only the uncanny resemblance of humanity. They were automatons, and deadly ones at that, suggested by the sheaths strapped to their limbs and torsos, containing blades and projectiles of many types. All topped by blank, porcelain faces and cerulean blue eyes, where their personalities lived. These had to be the scariest dolls anywhere, ever.

They all made quite a crew. Three humans, one former human, a bright elf, two Little People, and two miniature robotic assassins. Was nine a lucky number?

As if reading her thoughts, Hunter said, "Hey, how many were in the Lord of the Rings fellowship?"

"Nine," Claude said.

They all looked at each other, counting. Then they burst into laughter.

"Who gets to be who?" Hunter asked.

Cassie crossed her arms and sniffed. "Yeah, well, Tolkien didn't have any *girls* in his stories. *This* fellowship is all about girl power."

Peaseblossom laughed, and Cassie reached down to knuckle-bump her.

A laugh rose from Liz's throat, a brittle one covering her pulsating terror at what they were about to do.

Just then, a dry, chill wind blasted through the hall, carrying a dusty smell of desiccation and decay.

A curtain seemed to hang in midair depicting a rugged, wind-swept desert lit by ruddy starlight. Wind whistled from the curtain.

"The Borderlands, just outside the Dark Realm," the Queen said. "This is as far as my magic can reach."

A sick feeling washed over Liz. "How do we find Stewart in all that emptiness?"

The Queen said, "It was your intuition that brought you here. Keep faith with yourself. Trust your heart. Trust each other. Those are the best tools you can take with you."

Claude stood at the portal and gestured through. "Shall we?"

Liz looked at the kids. "All right, kids, anybody need a potty stop before we go on this trip?"

They rolled their eyes. "Mom!"

Liz and Claude laughed. The Light Realm beings didn't get the joke.

CHAPTER NINETEEN

The chill of a desert night raised gooseflesh on Liz's arms. The desolate landscape stretched in all directions, wafting scents of dust and sage tinged with decay, as if there were a carcass upwind. The disorientation of stepping from the Queen's hall directly into this open, windswept place made her knees wobbly. To her spirit, it was like the difference between birthday cake and sunbaked roadkill. The weight of the new backpack on her shoulders, however, made it all feel more real, more concrete. A light sword was slung alongside her sleeping roll. She paused to buckle the sword belt around her hips. It did her no good if she couldn't reach it. She had little skill with a finely wrought weapon like this sword, but it was superior to bare hands.

While they waited for everyone to step through the portal, she found herself trying to hug her children close, but Hunter shrugged her off, perhaps still upset by her earlier refusal. She couldn't be offended by the emergence of his quest for manly self-reliance, but it still caused her a wistful sigh. Her baby was growing up.

When all nine of them had stepped through, they looked back into the hall, where the Queen and the Princess waved to them, limned in sparkling brilliance.

Then the portal shrank into nothingness, closing them into solitude, very far from help.

Liz rubbed her arms against the night chill.

"It's cold, Mommy," Cassie said.

"Just like back home in the desert," Liz said.

The landscape did indeed resemble the desert they knew so well. Hills and mesas formed the horizon, and the in-between bristled with sagebrush, cacti, and Joshua trees.

Then she realized that everyone else was looking at her.

"Oh, fudgesicles," she said, "am I in charge?"

Captain Ar-Chaheris said, "You have a mystical connection with your husband, do you not? We must trust in that in order to find him."

She nodded solemnly. "Well, where would Stewart go?" she said, more to herself than to anyone, as a way of kicking off the thought process.

"To wherever the Dark Lord is?" Hunter said.

"And where does the Dark Lord keep himself?" she asked.

Claude said, "The heart of the Dark Realm is the Metropolis, the Dark analog to the City. No doubt he has other haunts, but that is where Baron Tyrus resides."

"But how do we find it in all this emptiness?" she said. But she already knew the answer. Somehow, she could sense the direction of the Dark Realm, like the heat of Stewart's forge when the workshop door was open. The night gave no indication of cardinal directions, but there was enough reddish starlight to see by. She steeled herself and faced the distant horizon. Beyond the nearer hills, jagged mountain peaks formed darker shadows against the celestial canopy.

Where are you, Stewart? she thought. *Give me a sign. We're here. We're coming for you. Throw us a bone.* She listened for a long moment, then added *Just not a* fresh *bone.*

A niggling urge drove her finger to point in a particular direction. "It's that way. But before we go, we need a plan. Just blundering into the Dark Realm feels like a terrible idea. Captain?"

"Indeed, milady," Ar-Chaheris said. "We must balance swiftness with economizing our resources. Use no magic unless absolutely necessary. Remember the Princess's warning. Using Dark Source will have a permanent effect on your spirit. Use too much and you will become a creature of the Dark Realm."

"I get all that," Liz said, "but what do we do? What if we're caught?" She just felt so helpless. "I've never been in the military, never been interested in it, and this feels like a very military kind of situation, if you know what I mean. Like we should have plans within plans, right? All sorts of tactical, if-then stuff."

Bob said, "I should think the captain's keen tactical mind will carry us in good stead. And your intuitive connection will guide us to Stewart."

Captain Ar-Chaheris said, "If you would permit me, milady, I can serve as strategist and tactician. We will avoid any conflicts we can. But there may come a time when we are forced to fight. In that event, my sole aim will be to ensure the success of our mission. That means you and your children must survive. At *any* cost." His expression was grim, solemn, but matter of fact.

Peaseblossom said, "We're here because we believe in you. I'm not keen on the idea of a one-way mission—I suspect none of us are—but this is the dance we've chosen. Let me say it again. We believe in you."

Liz teared up and her chest swelled at the earnestness in the little woman's small, high-pitched voice. "Thank you, all." She hoped she was worthy of it.

"Let's get moving, shall we?" Claude said. "But before we reach the Border..." He pulled out a glass bottle. The Dark Ink. "We must apply this first. It should last until the next sunset." He removed the stopper, took a quick sniff, then wrinkled his nose and grimaced. "At least we'll all smell equally repugnant."

He shook some of the tarry liquid into his palm and proceeded to paint his face with two fingers.

When the stench reached her, Liz clamped a hand over her nose and mouth to keep from gagging. "We have to put that stuff *on our faces?*"

"Alas, yes," Claude said, his pale countenance now resembling an Army Ranger's.

"The bad guys will smell us coming," Liz said.

"And we shall smell just like them," Captain Ar-Chaheris said as he grabbed a gobbet of the stuff from Claude's palm with two fingers and started smearing.

With a stoic expression, Hunter followed suit.

"It's like the outhouse where we hid from the goblins," Cassie said, swallowing hard. "But worse."

Liz swallowed hard, too. "Let's just get it over with. The sooner we get used to it..." She took a dose for herself. Having it on her skin was even worse than the smell, like an oily mud-mask. She clenched her teeth against a tide of rising disgust. When they found Stewart, she was going to smother him with hugs and kisses—and then kick his lily-white behind.

"Yuck!" Cassie said, now sporting dark streaks across her petal-soft cheeks.

"You look like a grease monkey," Liz said with a grin.

"Yeah, and you smell like a real monkey!" Hunter said.

Cassie slugged him on the arm. "Shut up. You smell like a dead gorilla."

"Enough, kids," Liz said. "Let's all be a little extra nice. You two don't normally talk to each other that way, so we're not going to start now. The Dark Side is going to be crawling into us. There's no need to make it worse."

"Okay," the kids said, looking at each other with narrowed eyes.

They set off across the dark desert.

As they walked, Liz found herself searching the sky for familiar constellations. The Big Dipper. Orion. But there were no familiar shapes in this sky. The Milky Way's streak across the sky seemed closer somehow, filled more of the star-scape than she remembered.

The invigoration she'd felt back in the City drained away, and the exhaustion resurfaced. She checked in with the kids often—probably too often to suit them—asking how they were doing. The responses she got were variations of "I'm fine" that became more and more untrue, but they had their father's stubbornness, tramping along until Cassie looked like she was about to keel over with every step.

Liz also worried for Claude. His rotund figure trundled steadily along, but his breath often sounded labored, and the weariness already showed in his face.

The terrain they traversed slowly shifted from otherwise normal-looking Arizona-Nevada desert to something else. Instead of saguaro and Joshua trees came dense thickets of nasty-looking black brambles that clung to the landscape like clumps of tangled spiders. The air became thicker, drier, with a bitter tinge.

"We've crossed over into the Dark Realm," Captain Ar-Chaheris said.

When her thoughts weren't on the children, they turned to things the Queen had said. Liz would do anything for Stewart, but was it fair to ask others to do the same? To put all the living creatures in all the magical worlds in jeopardy for the fate of one human? Was it wrong to ask children to sacrifice themselves to save their father? Shouldn't it be the other way around? How could she expect her companions to sacrifice themselves for this quest? All were here by their own free will, but still it gnawed at her. Peaseblossom and Bob took turns riding on Liz's and Claude's shoulders, but her weariness was such that Peaseblossom now felt like an anvil, not a kitten. These thoughts cycled through her mind with the beat of her footsteps.

Cassie stopped, interrupting their forward motion and Liz's reverie. "Hey, did you all feel that?"

Bob said, "I had hoped 'twas just me."

Hunter said, "Like somebody opened a shook-up soda bottle, but the universe, not a bottle."

Cassie nodded, and they all looked around at the landscape and the sky.

Baron Tyrus, Lord of the Dark Realm, eased back into the shadows of his Blood Throne, a monolithic block of blood-red copper. He was alone in his cavernous throne room, having sent away his dark elf lackeys to allow himself solitude to think and plan. Only a single globule of ruddy light offered illumination, suspended in midair by his will alone.

The throne's prehensile, metal vines, studded with finger-length thorns, twitched of their own volition, swirling around him in a nimbus of lethal, shredding arms.

He toyed absently with his long, waxed beard and mustache, feeling the metallic coldness of his jeweled rings.

No onlooker would recognize his glee, but that's what it was.

Moments ago, it had begun, just as he had planned.

A tiny rip. Smaller than an atom.

A tear in the barrier between the Dark Realm and the Light.

For thousands of years, he had planned for this moment. In her endless quest for altruism, the Queen had bent the rules just enough to rupture the boundaries between worlds. She had given in to the Riley family's demand to try to save Stewart. She must have known she was taking that chance, but the Dark Lord had predicted that outcome. The Queen's forces must be near the Dark Realm now, if they had not already entered. The human game called chess, with its sixty-four squares and thirty-two pieces, contained more combinations than atoms in the Penumbral universe. Baron Tyrus was playing a game with thousands of pieces on a board that measured two entire magical realms. The pawns had been in place for a long time, and now the more powerful pieces were coming out.

It was all a win-win for him, as Penumbral humans liked to say.

He had successfully subverted Stewart Riley to embracing his Dark nature, turning him into the most powerful Dark wizard in a millennium. The Queen had strained the laws of the universe, which were woven into the very fabric of existence itself, as fundamental as gravity or the bonds between atoms, when she gouged the umbral out of Stewart Riley's spirit, in effect, separating him from himself.

All that Baron Tyrus had to do now was await the arrival of his new and powerful ally. And if somehow, the Light Realm managed to stop him, they would either have to destroy him, which would most likely turn the rest of the powerful Riley family to the Dark Realm, or attempt to save him, which would expand the tiny rupture into a giant rip, allowing the Dark Lord to attack the Light Realm directly. Since the beginning of time, the battleground between the Light and Dark Realms had been the Penumbra. The two magical realms were constrained by the laws of existence to never come into direct conflict, or the result would be not unlike the mutual annihilation that occurred when matter and antimatter came into contact. But the Dark Lord had foreseen victory in that event as well. If the rip opened sufficiently, he could take the fight directly into the Light Realm and claim its power for himself. The Queen and the Princess would become his slaves. And such beautiful slaves they would be.

The Light Realm would not be able to help itself. It would continue to save whatever hapless fools crossed its path, and doing so would contribute to the rift's inevitable expansion.

It was all coming along nicely.

The celestial being known as the Queen of the Light Realm reposed within her verdant bower, tears brighter than diamonds or stars trickling down her flawless cheeks. On the lush thousands of leaves and the flower petals surrounding her of any imaginable hue, dew formed and dripped as if the plants were weeping, too.

As the embodiment of the entire Light Realm itself, she was not an entity accustomed to fear, but now... She feared she had made a mistake of cataclysmic proportions.

She had felt the rupture appear between the Light and Dark Realms, just as, no doubt, Baron Tyrus had. It had been like tearing a hole in her very flesh, and now, she was bleeding into the Dark Realm, just as Darkness was now seeping into her like a cancer, a poison.

The tears continued to flow. There was nothing she could do now. They had entered the gray void of uncertainty in which she could not see the consequences of their actions. Too much chaos, even in the simplest of events.

Have faith, the Princess had said.

That was all that was left. She could offer no more interference, no more aid. She had already done too much and jeopardized the existence of all the magical worlds. Now, she must have faith in the strength of the Riley family.

CHAPTER TWENTY

"Mommy, I'm so tired," Cassie said. "Can you carry me before I fall over?"

"Sure, honey," Liz said. "C'mere."

Cassie climbed up into Liz's arms and clung to her like a baby koala, at least for a minute or so until her arms and legs started to go slack. Liz squeezed her little body as tight as she could until fatigue began to take its toll.

The desert night encircling them was unending. She had driven through Death Valley before, but this place was like Death Valley if it were actively malevolent. She felt as if eyes were always on them, even though the lockets were supposed to shield them from magical sensing, even though the only living things to be seen were strange, twisted cacti and the nasty-looking clumps of razor-sharp thickets. Sometimes in the distance, she would hear an eerie cry of what she hoped was only some sort of night bird, not a warning sent ahead to the Dark Lord.

As the night passed, they stopped every hour or so to rest and have a sip of water. She wondered if she would ever get used to the place's acrid stench, like an oil refinery or a chemical plant gone terribly wrong. But then why would she want to? The weariness crushing them all wasn't just physical. It was mentally stifling, crushing her emotions like a blanket made of cactus needles and lead.

On a rest break, Captain Ar-Chaheris gave Liz a glance fraught with meaning, then pointedly looked at the children and Claude, whose every breath now was a ragged wheeze. The determination on his face was iron-hard, but even that wasn't enough to keep his body moving forever.

Liz took a moment to search her intuition for the connection to Stewart. She wanted to believe that if he were really in trouble at this moment, she would know. She nodded at the captain's deference to her. "All right, everyone, I think it's past time we camp and rest for a few hours. Get some sleep."

"What about Dad?" Hunter said.

"Once we settle down for some rest, I'll try to reach him," she said.

"Won't that warn the bad guys, too?" Hunter asked. "What if he's on their side now?"

"Your dad will *never* be all the way on their side," Liz said, laying a hand on his shoulder. "We have to have faith that he knows what he's doing. We all want to save him. We have to believe that we still *can*. If he knows we're here, he might come to *us*."

Claude's weariness couldn't hold back the questions in his eyes. "Liz, may I have a word?"

Liz shrugged. "Sure." She and Claude walked off a distance, out of earshot from the others.

He said, "Having dealt with the struggle between the realms for a good long while now, I do not share your certainty that Stewart cannot be corrupted. So, I must question your gamble. You're right, he might come to us. But he also might bring the Dark Lord with him."

She bristled slightly. "Never say that in front of the kids."

"I understand," he said. "Stewart's integrity and force of will are formidable. But I've studied the Dark Realm and its minions for much longer than any of you have existed. We all saw the creature that used to be Stewart when he rescued the Princess. He's all of that now, and more, because he's had time and practice to come into his full power."

"Then what are we supposed to do? Give up?"

"If I thought it was hopeless, I would have spoken up long ago. But I, too, believe there's a chance, or else I would not have come. But attempting to contact him is a gamble. We could reveal ourselves somehow."

"That's what the lockets are for, right? To magically conceal us."

"Well, yes—"

"And I don't think my connection with Stewart is a Source-based magical ability. It feels more like a back door or maybe a psychic bridge. Maybe one that magic has built but it's not required anymore."

"Very well," Claude said. "I don't know about you, but I could do with some rest."

"We all could," she said.

Captain Ar-Chaheris nominated a rock outcropping flanked by a thicket of black razor thorns to set up camp. From his pack he withdrew a fine, textured net of a clever design that served as both tent and camouflage, securing it to the nearby stones or staking its corners into the ground. It was under this net they unrolled their sleeping mats and blankets, munched quietly on berry-and-apple fruit leather and some dry crusty bread. In Liz's overexerted state, it might have been one of the most delicious meals she'd ever had, and when sleep came, it came like an avalanche.

"Awaken, milady!" came a whisper in her ear like the wind, along with a small hand on her shoulder.

Daylight stabbed her eyes, even in the shade under the camouflage netting. She opened her mouth to speak, but the finger of a leather glove fell across her lips.

Captain Ar-Chaheris's breath brushed her ear. "Something is coming."

Her frantic mind scratched away the fog of sleep in record time, and that's when she felt the subsonic throb of the ground under her, like a subwoofer thudding nearer.

A shadow fell across the outside of the net like a cloud moving over the sun, and there was a vibrating in her bones that was more like dragging a rasp over rusty sheet metal. But it wasn't physical, more like a dental drill digging into her soul.

It moved so slowly, like a sloth, but enormous, with legs like sequoias sixty, eighty feet high, tipped by spiny claws, and a crustacean body like some sort of deep-sea crab that blotted out the sun. A comparatively tiny head—only about the size of a panel van—swept back and forth above the ground as if searching for food. Through the netting, Liz could see dozens of shiny, black orbs covering the head—eyes pointing in all directions. Whiskers or feelers twenty or thirty feet long stretched out over its path. Chitinous spines covered its titanic legs, which carried it forward like pile drivers—straight toward their camp. Could it see them? Had it sensed them?

The dolls stood stock-still, facing the creature with useless little blades in their hands.

Bob and Peaseblossom crouched in the cracks of some rocks, trying to make themselves even smaller.

Claude stood frozen like a statue, a look of gobsmacked terror on his face, his mouth working, but nothing coming out.

"We have to get out of here!" Liz whispered.

"If we flee, it will surely see us," Captain Ar-Chaheris said.

"We can't use our magic, can we?" Hunter said, gaping in terror. He clutched the sword Captain Ar-Chaheris had given him the night before, and Liz almost laughed at how feeble a weapon it looked against the beast of this size. He might as well try using it to chop down a hill.

The thing was maybe a hundred yards away. How fast could it run? It looked so slow, so ponderous, but each step brought it twenty yards closer.

With each of its steps, the dental drill digging into her mind and soul got louder, harsher, like millions of demented, bloodthirsty hornets stoked into fury, bringing tears to her eyes. This thing was *hungry*, and nothing escaped its ravenousness. Could it sense them like they could sense it, or did their lockets shield them from its perception?

Its mouth parts worked constantly, clicking, clacking, scraping, smacking, while smaller tentacles, each a few feet long, swept up everything they could grasp into the churning maw. It paused to devour a large clump of razor thorns, slurping up the deadly bramble like wiry noodles, then masticating them with its bizarre mouth parts.

There was nowhere to run, no shelter to crawl into.

The stark terror on Cassie's face, the kind that erased all reason and volition, made Liz reach out and clutch her daughter close, but as she did, she felt like someone had just hit her with ten big, fluffy pillows all at once. Her ears went silent. The relentless grating of the titanic thing's hunger ceased. Suddenly she felt herself growing, expanding, ballooning over the landscape even as she clutched Cassie to her and remained the same physical size. Her will became an invisible shockwave, and she felt it pass over the enormous creature.

The leviathan paused as if it had just been struck a blow, a great shudder going through its limbs, a shudder that propagated through the ground itself, and it staggered, as if a mountain could stagger.

A thrill shot through her. Had she done that? Had she just used magic somehow?

As the thing steadied itself, the movement of its head suggested its multitude of eyes were scanning the area for signs of what had happened.

How sentient was it? With a head that size, its brain might be the size of a Volkswagen Beetle, which might make it incredibly intelligent. How acute was its vision? Could it spot the net? What spectrum could it perceive? Could it see their infrared signatures *through* the net?

Her invisible bubble surrounded them, throbbing, whispering *Go away! There's nothing for you here!* into its mind.

Bright crucibles of energy were all around her, a web of quiet power, feeding her bubble. The lockets! When she closed her eyes, she could see their glow like splashes of color, connected by glittering chains, a hidden web of Light magic.

The awful, grating vibration of the creature's hunger was hardly noticeable now, perhaps deflected by the bubble.

This was real. It was happening. And *she* was doing it.

The leviathan looked off in a different direction, as if hearing something, its feelers sweeping and reaching. Then in a series of ponderous, pounding strides, the thing changed direction, angling away, and resumed its slow, thumping stride.

No one dared to speak, but with every one of the creature's steps, Liz found it easier to breathe. Cassie trembled in her arms with the kind of stark terror that left trauma burned into one's very soul. Liz kissed her forehead and whispered over and over, "It's going away, we're okay, we're safe."

When the beast had moved maybe a quarter-mile away, Bob wiped a sheen of sweat from his brow. "I reckoned we were goners."

They all nodded fervently.

Cassie's voice was a barely audible whisper. "Mommy did it."

All eyes turned to her.

"I felt it in my brain," she said, shuddering, her voice thick. "I still do. I think I always will."

Hunter tried for wry levity. "Yay, PTSD for everybody."

Cassie turned to look up at her mother with growing wonder, her big eyes aglow. "Mommy, you saved us again!"

All eyes were on Liz now, with several nods of agreement.

"I guess I did," Liz said. "It wasn't intentional, or conscious, but I felt it happening. And I let it happen, and then I...pushed." That had been the bubble expanding. The wonder of success was growing in her heart, too. She had *done it.*

Her children hugged her, and she found herself blushing at the gratitude and admiration of the others. "Well, let's not wait around until it comes back."

They waited until the titanic creature was out of sight before they packed up and moved out. Fortunately, their own course lay perpendicular to the beast's.

It was midmorning, and the desert heat had already reached blast-furnace levels. Being an Arizona native, she was used to that kind of heat. Lots of precautions had been instilled in her from a young age, such as carrying water all the time, everywhere she went, and never leaving anything plastic inside your car. But as the day progressed and the miles passed underfoot, the heat grew so oppressive they began to discuss only traveling at night. Her armored shirt felt like a hundred pounds of lead, soaked with sweat, wadding into sodden clumps, slowly baking her. If she'd been thinking ahead, she'd have brought sunglasses and a hat—she found herself wishing for them—but her mind had been too clouded by fear and urgency for that kind of preparation.

The sun was a lurid, punishing orb, casting a glow that was more reddish than she was accustomed to. It made everything look *wrong*.

"For this being the Dark Realm," Hunter grumbled, "it's not very dark at all."

As the miles passed, the terrain grew rougher, rockier, crumpling into rock formations and mesas. There was no sign of any arroyos or other creek beds. Apparently, no water existed here. All the water they would have was what they carried.

It was noon when they called off their trek. They were already sun-baked and going through water so quickly they wouldn't get far before it was gone. Claude was obviously suffering, even though no sound of complaint passed his lips. From his backpack, he had produced a pith helmet with a neck curtain, which gave him an explorer look.

The sun and heat sapped their strength as well as their moisture. They would rest in the shade of their net and a rock outcropping until nightfall, then set out again. They clung to the coolness of the rocks' shadows, sipped their vanishing water supplies, and catnapped.

In the quietude, Liz closed her eyes and thought about Stewart. Where was he? Would she ever see him again? How long could they all keep going across this blasted landscape populated by things like they had seen this morning? How many things like that had Stewart encountered when he'd first entered the Dark Realm? If she knew anything about nature, it was that there was always a bigger predator, unless it was the apex predator. But even apex predators could be hunted.

She tried to reach out to Stewart like she had done at the Thirsty Chipmunk, but it felt like reaching into an empty cave. Nothing there. She would try again tonight, before they set out.

The interminable hours until the sun finally touched the horizon felt like days all by themselves. There was no cheerful banter, or even empty chatter. They all sat alone with their personal suffering.

The diminishing heat brought such relief that Liz wanted to cry, but instead she roused the kids for more travel with gentle touches, her heart breaking at their expressions of dread mixed with determination. They were their father's children.

She still felt the internal compass needle, a consistent pull toward wherever they were headed. There could be no doubt they were headed in the right direction.

Among the rocky outcroppings and undulations appeared dark clusters of artificial, industrial-looking installations. They resembled dwellings as much as half-buried machinery or foundries or mines or chemical plants, varying in size from telephone booth to auditorium. But places where things had been built meant the possibility of encountering denizens of the Dark Realm, so they steered their path as far from them as they could.

No one had brought a binoculars or spyglass, but Captain Ar-Chaheris's elfin eyes were sharp, so Liz believed him when he said he saw no activity among the industrial clusters. They weren't dwellings or villages.

"But what are they?" she asked him.

"I cannot say precisely, but I suspect they are part of the inner workings of the Dark Realm itself. This is a place of exploitation and greed, industry without restraint. Those clusters of strange machinery might represent this place's 'blood vessels,' so to speak, regulating the flow of Source. They might also be conduits for information and surveillance, so we must be wary. As with the Queen, little happens in the Dark Realm to which Baron Tyrus is not privy. Perhaps these are part of a vast, underground intelligence network. And he is the giant spider at the center of the web."

Claude chimed in, "They might even be the exterior parts of a transportation system. Perhaps Dark Realm dwellers are smart enough to travel underground, out of the heat."

"If we could find a way underground," Liz said, "we might be able to travel faster, and out of the sun."

Then Peaseblossom's small, high voice broke into the conversation. "Prick up your ears and peel your eyes, folks." She was standing atop a boulder pointing toward the north, the direction they were heading.

The last remnants of daylight revealed a shadow clinging to the horizon, a cloud.

"'Tis a dust cloud," Peaseblossom said.

Bouncing up beside her, Bob peered long enough to add, "And them that's making it are comin' this way."

CHAPTER TWENTY-ONE

Just as with the titanic crustacean, there was nowhere to hide. At the head of the clouds of dust emerged bizarre, scuttling creatures with some sort of knight upon their backs.

"El-Mithari Garkus Riders," said Captain Ar-Chaheris with desperation in his voice. "They must have been drawn to our use of magic. They are the worst of the Dark Lord's minions, dark elf knights riding deadly beasts that are nearly indestructible. I count thirteen of them. We cannot fight them. We can only hide and hope they haven't seen us. Everyone, gather together near these boulders. With my netting, we shall pretend to be a sand dune."

Liz's heart was in her throat, almost hammering against her chin, pounding in her ears, as she clutched the children to her against the base of the boulder. Captain Ar-Chaheris threw the netting over them, then scooped handfuls of choking sand over them to obscure the netting. As he worked, she could hear the raspy scuttling of the giant mounts as they neared. Then the bright elf gingerly crawled under the netting with them. Through its ingenious weave, they could clearly see great distances. The strange creatures—elephant-sized abominations that blended spider with centipede and lobster—and their riders angled off toward the southwest in the direction from which the Light Realm party had come.

When the garkus riders had moved off about two hundred yards, Hunter breathed a sigh of relief and whispered, "They didn't see us."

But Captain Ar-Chaheris still looked worried. "Not this time, but we foolishly left a clear trail across the sand. If they spot it, they could follow it and be upon us like lightning."

"Okay, then how do we not leave a trail?" Liz asked.

Hunter said, "We could go single file and drag the net behind us to erase our tracks."

"Excellent idea," the elf said.

Claude said, "I have a somewhat uncomfortable proposition. We could attempt to go underground. My surmise is that the underground passageways all ultimately lead to the Metropolis."

"But we don't know what's under there," Liz said, tension growing. "There could be, I dunno, whole towns of goblins or other creepy-crawlies. I mean, we couldn't even travel underground on our side of the Realms without running into kniblings."

"It might be worth a look," Claude said.

"One of us could check it out down there and come back and report," Hunter said. "I could do it."

"Uh-uhn, no way, kiddo," Liz said.

"Mo-om!"

Claude said, "Let us table this debate until we come to a potential access point. Until then, we're stuck aboveground in any case."

"As soon as they are out of sight," Captain Ar-Chaheris said, "we move, and quickly."

The minutes ticked past as the garkus riders shrank with distance and finally disappeared over the horizon.

At that very moment, Captain Ar-Chaheris jumped up. "Let us go. Now." His voice brooked no hesitation.

Liz said, "I'll drag the netting to wipe out our tracks."

"Very well," the captain said. "Remember, single file. And we must move quickly. When we come upon one of those strange clusters of construction, I will turn us toward it."

Then he set off at a brisk jog, aiming for the horizon. As Liz hurriedly tied the netting around her waist to drag behind her, her heart fell into her shoes. Claude had a look of frightened resignation mixed with intrepid determination. There was no way he was in the condition to maintain that pace. Nevertheless, he set off at his trundling gait.

Liz brought up the rear of the column, unable to stop herself from looking over her shoulder in the direction of possible pursuit. The sun bludgeoned them with its heat and turned their mouths to deserts, their lips to sandpaper. Claude ran out of gas after about two hundred yards. There was no way he could maintain the elf captain's pace.

They stopped and waited for him to catch his breath. He said, "I'm terribly sorry, everyone. Perhaps I shouldn't have come at all. This old, fat body is not up to the demands upon it. You should all go on and leave me behind. I will go off in another direction, mislead them if I can—"

"No!" Liz said. "We're not leaving you behind."

Claude gave her a weary smile. "Remember, all I have to do is open the locket and I return to the Light Realm. I'll be fine. It will be all of you who are still in danger."

His reasoning was sound, but Liz's intuition was still screaming that this was a bad idea. Something didn't feel right. Claude still had a part to play, and the look of regret on his face made her heart hurt.

"We stay together," she said.

"I must regrettably disagree," he said. "I'm becoming a burden." It was not the desire to end his own suffering that motivated him, but a desire to ensure the mission succeeded. But there was too much that he knew, things she did not.

"Claude, we need you," she said. "I need your help. You're like the encyclopedia that helps me understand what's going on. I don't think I can do this without you." What frightened her more was that she might need all the help she could get to subdue Stewart long enough to put the locket on him.

He gave her a kind smile. "You're kind to say so. Captain?"

"As you say, the lockets are our escape route. You are free to use it at any time. But perhaps my pace was a bit too brisk."

Cassie gave an exaggerated nod. "Yeah, that was way too fast for me, too." She took Claude's hand. "We should go slower."

Liz suppressed a smile at Cassie's ploy, transparent to everyone but her.

Claude sighed, "Well, it's decided then. I've caught my breath. Shall we proceed?"

So, they moved on at a fast walk. Claude was able to maintain that pace with a lot of heavy breathing and sweating, but at least he kept up. Sometimes the ground underfoot was gritty, dusty hardpan, other times drifting sand dunes that sucked at their feet and slowed them down. They had traveled several miles before they spotted a clump of machinery in the distance, toward which the captain angled their course. Exhaustion had siphoned off their speed until they could only walk. The sun had peaked and now slid toward the horizon.

They were still a couple of hundred yards from the cluster of machinery when her ears caught the mass scuttling sound of the garkus knights. She spun and there they were, less than a quarter-mile distant, following her obscured trail like ants on sugar. The eyes of elves were as sharp as those of raptors. There could be no doubt the dark elves could see them. She yelled a warning, and they broke into a run.

Captain Ar-Chaheris spun to face their pursuers. "Keep running!"

Shards of glimmering Source—the Light kind—emerged from his body and coalesced in the air around him, and he gathered it into a ball between his hands, his brow furrowed in concentration. Then he released it in a thunderous wave.

A wall of dust and grit exploded from the desert floor and into the air in an instantaneous, swirling wall, obscuring the oncoming enemies.

"Run!" he shouted.

Liz's breath came in gasps, and she quickly overtook Cassie's shorter legs. She snatched Cassie's hand and dragged her along. Fleet-footed Hunter kept pace with Peaseblossom, who somehow ran as fast as a rabbit. Bob ran and blinked from rock to rock every time Liz looked away from him. And poor Claude huffed along, his cheeks beet-red and his eyes full of desperation. The dolls' little legs raised dust plumes as they scuttled along on either side of Cassie.

Ten seconds. Twenty seconds. None of them were competitive sprinters. But they finally reached the cluster of strange, metal pipes and enclosures, which was about the size of two city buses and looked much older than she expected, probably predating the Industrial Revolution on Earth.

His magical impediment launched, Captain Ar-Chaheris turned to follow them, leaping across the terrain like a gazelle.

The dust storm rose into the sky like a rusty-brown wall hundreds of yards long, sweeping toward their pursuers.

"Find a way in!" Liz yelled, losing sight of the pursuers behind the sandstorm. Hunter and Cassie started searching, and the Little Folk started jumping all over the installation.

Liz and Claude ducked behind one of the three-foot-thick pipes and watched the captain's approach. The dolls faced their pursuers, prepared for battle.

A hundred yards behind Captain Ar-Chaheris, however, several massive scuttling shapes burst from the dust cloud. Two of them were missing riders, but the rest of the knights clung to saddles and carapace. The gritty blast had only slowed them down, and as they emerged the creatures put on a burst of frightening speed. The first rider to recover raised some sort of weapon and fired it at the captain, who was only fifty yards away now.

"No! Look out!" Liz called.

But a splinter of light lanced from the weapon and clipped Captain Ar-Chaheris on the shoulder. The shot spun him half around and he fell hard onto his side. He scrambled back to his feet and tried to run.

Hunter's voice was yelling something behind her, but all she could focus on was the captain and the oncoming pursuers. The creatures' eyes glinted with hunger, and the knights wore dark, spiky armor that made them look like crustaceans themselves.

Something tugged at her hand. Cassie. "Mommy! Come on!"

But Liz could only watch transfixed as one of the riderless beasts plunged forward, blurred with speed, and caught Captain

Ar-Chaheris in one of its pincers, and then everything went into a horrific slow motion. Like a tide-pool crab sweeping detritus into its maw, the creature stuffed Captain Ar-Chaheris into its mouth. But then it came on, looking for the next morsel.

Liz's ears suddenly felt full of cotton, and she felt herself expanding with a sharp cry on her lips. "*No!*"

Her expanding bubble of magic struck the creature so hard it flopped onto its side. Its awful legs scrabbled at sky and dirt. The same effect struck the riders and other steeds, bringing them to an abrupt halt in clouds of grit, one rider tumbling headfirst over his mount's head onto the earth. The riders waved sharp metal prods, striking their mounts about the head and in the cracks of their shell segments to regain control of them.

"Mommy! Hunter found a door!" Cassie yanked hard on Liz's hand.

Together they ducked into the conglomeration of pipes and metal framework.

Liz and Cassie soon found the rest of them frantically trying to pull open a thick metal hatch, but its wheel was so old and corroded it looked like it had become one with the door.

The sounds of the scuttling monsters surrounded the cluster of machinery. The air filled with a stench not unlike an aquarium full of Madagascar hissing cockroaches she had seen once at a museum, insectoid, unnatural. Sharp commands echoed from the riders' helmets as they struggled to control their steeds. Liz's knees felt wobbly, her grip weak on Cassie's small hand. Launching this repulsion bubble had left her all but depleted.

Hunter tugged futilely on the hatch wheel. "I can't get it open."

Together with Claude and Hunter, they all applied themselves to the hatch wheel, but it did not budge.

Then a shadow fell over them. One of the creatures loomed directly above as it crawled over the structure to where they hid and peered down at them with its terrible eyes.

One of the dolls launched herself upward, bouncing from one surface to the next, ever higher, then straight at the rider, blades in both hands. With his incredible elfin speed, the rider swung his riding prod and with a burst of sparks swatted the doll out of midair. Jaclyn smacked the air with a *thud*, arcs of what looked like electricity crackling over her body. Jazlyn gathered herself to leap.

Atop the saddle, its rider gathered a wad of netting that snapped with scarlet energy and flung it toward them. The net expanded in midair, headed straight for Liz. It all happened too fast. The net engulfed her, and the moment it touched her flesh, everything went black.

From five thousand feet above the desert pan, Baron Tyrus looked out over his realm. He stood atop the roof of the Obsidian Tower, this dark needle that served as an observation deck when he needed to observe the heavens. The sun was sinking toward the horizon on what had been a day for the ages. All his meticulous plans with schemes within contingencies were coming to fruition.

Somewhere out there, Stewart Riley was traveling with a company of garkus riders, coming here to the Obsidian Tower. When Riley arrived, Baron Tyrus would gain the most powerful ally he had known in centuries. And how would he control this human wizard? With his family, of course. Because who else but Stewart's family would be foolhardy enough to come to the Dark Realm to "save" him? They were out there. It was just a matter of finding them.

He sensed a throb of magic behind him and turned toward the Onyx Orb, a swirling stone ball floating upon a glittering crimson column of Dark Source springing from the center of the tower's lofty platform. Turning toward the orb, he saw its dark, smoky surface lighten into an image of several human figures ensnared in nets made of grimspider silk, as sticky as they were difficult to break.

A dark elf's voice emanated from the stone. "Your Magnificence, we have captured the intruders you described. Three Penumbral humans, a Light Realm human, two automatons, and two leprechaun vermin. A bright elf with them was slain." The dark elf was no doubt speaking to a similar orb, but much smaller and embedded in a bracer, and mystically bound to the Onyx Orb.

Baron Tyrus's withered breast swelled with dark glee. "Most excellently done, Captain El-Mithari. You have done great honor to your house and brought glory to your name."

The dark elf's voice choked up. "It was my pleasure, Your Magnificence. What is to be done with them?"

"Bring them to the Obsidian Tower immediately, with all possible speed. And if you allow them to escape, your promotion will be the most short-lived in a millennium."

"Yes, Your Magnificence."

"And do not underestimate them. Their skills with magic have brought them this far."

"How far may we go, Your Magnificence, to prevent their escape?"

"Do not kill the mother and children. You may dispose of the others as you wish."

"Must they be in good condition, Your Magnificence?"

"They must be alive and unspoiled. If you must lame them to prevent escape, you may consider that among your acceptable options."

"Yes, Your Magnificence. It shall be done."

The Onyx Orb went dark again, and Baron Tyrus laughed and laughed, his voice's booming echoes passing over the endless, empty leagues.

CHAPTER TWENTY-TWO

Stewart and his cohort of garkus knights had paused to rest their mounts when the leader approached him with interesting news.

"Some of our brethren have apprehended a group of enemy spies," said the band's dark elf captain. "Perhaps you know them?" He swept his arm in a circle that drew puffs of sand and dust up into a little dust devil, and in the dust devil appeared faces Stewart knew better than his own.

His teeth clamped together like a vise, his fists clenched, and his great, black wings quivered.

Smug amusement exuded from the expressionless faceplate of the knight's helmet.

How would the Dark Lord respond if Stewart left his escort behind in the desert, dead? Perhaps the dark elf sensed Stewart's thoughts and in the interest of self-preservation, dismissed the magical image.

Stewart's mouth was full of sandpaper, his voice a husky rasp. "Where are they?"

"On the way to the Dark Lord, in custody," said the dark elf.

Stewart nodded. "Good."

The dark elf seemed to expect something, more reaction perhaps, a clue about Stewart's loyalties, but Stewart turned away, using his wings to block any view of his face. Inside him, a war was raging.

He had known on some level that Liz would try to help him, but he hadn't expected her to get this far. And worse, she had brought the kids, which angered him. By what right had she purposefully put his children in dire jeopardy? The Dark Realm was not a playground or a place for kids from anywhere, especially his kids. Liz should have known better. And now, it was possible they would get in his way. Under no circumstances could he see his family come to harm, especially not with what he had planned. Furthermore, the thought of them seeing what he had become made him queasy and filled his mouth with bitterness. He could not become what he needed to become if they were anywhere nearby to see it. He still remembered the looks of horror on their faces at the sight of him when he returned from the Dark Realm with the Princess. Their weakness might weaken him at a critical moment.

The war between his dark, twisted nature and the absolute, diamond-hard kernel that sustained him—the love and protectiveness for his wife and children—turned him into a statue, even as the eyes of the garkus knights held upon him.

Moments ticking by became minutes as his body quivered and his mind roiled. On one hand, he would let *nothing* stand in his way. On the other, he would let no harm come to his family. And the Dark Lord would not hesitate to use Stewart's family against him. They would become either human shields or bargaining chips, levers for coercion. What would happen when an unstoppable force slammed into an immovable object?

He didn't want to find out, but something told him he soon would. He had less time than he thought.

Turning back toward his giant, reptilian steed, he said to the dark elves, "Let's go."

Liz awakened to dim, reddish light from a harsh pinpoint floating above. Nevertheless, its brightness stabbed her eyes, making her blink. Her back and head lay against rough, unyielding bars. Warm softness lay limply across her, one of Cassie's legs. Hunter's foot lay against her ribs. Claude's balding head rested against her shoulder. A lattice of stark shadows fell over them, cast by the crude metal bars of their cage.

Something cold and hard and heavy encircled her wrists. Shackles. And not plain metal shackles. She could feel the Dark Source pulsing through them like the flow of blood, like tiny fishhooks brushing her wrists.

She sat up and looked around. The source of the light was too bright for her to distinguish, just a blinding pinhole in surrounding blackness. Their cage sat in a huge cavern that stretched into blackness in two directions. The cavern floor was worn smooth, and a set of what resembled railroad tracks ran along the floor and followed the cavern in both directions. Here and there, other pinpoints of illumination along the cavern ceiling gave a sense of great distance. On the opposite wall, orange light emanated from a hatchway, with shifting shadows made by things she couldn't see. The familiar stench of hot metal mixed with a strange, organic mustiness filled the air.

Movement a few feet away startled her, an armored knight, still as a statue the size of an elf. A dark elf in an insect-like steel carapace. His malevolent glance froze her in place like a rabbit before a rattlesnake. This was not casual badness, but active menace. This creature *wanted* to hurt them.

Nearby sat a smaller cage with bars much more closely set, in which rested two small shapes. The shadow of a small hand told her they were Bob and Peaseblossom. But where were the dolls?

This was it. This was too much. She had to get the kids out of here. Maybe she could stay and somehow reach Stewart. Maybe there was a chance she could see him again. Some sliver of hope remained for her, but she had to get the kids out of here. Better they be orphans than dead. She had to open the kids' lockets without the dark elf seeing what she was doing. But how?

Claude's eyes were open, watching her with a mournful look. He held up his wrists and the manacles that bound him and shook his head. Then she understood.

The manacles were holding them in the Dark Realm, anchoring them. As long as the manacles bound their wrists, they could not escape back to the Light, even with the power of the lockets. She clamped a hand over her own mouth to stifle her cry of desperation. That "escape hatch" had been the only thing that allowed her to overcome her maternal resistance to bringing her kids into danger. Stewart had mentioned similar chains when he had described how he rescued the Princess. The forces of the Dark Realm had perfected ways to imprison Light creatures in the Dark Realm, without them disappearing back to their natural place.

Cassie sat up, wiping her face with her sleeve. "Where are we?"

Claude said, "I suspect we are somewhere below where we were captured, in some underground transportation system."

"Creepy," Cassie said, her voice a husky whisper. Then she spotted the nearby dark elf and yelped in surprise.

Liz could sense his malevolent smirk behind his expressionless faceplate.

Hunter rolled onto one elbow and levered himself to sit, rubbing his eyes. He felt around himself for his weapons, but everything was gone. They still wore their armored shirts, however, and Liz could feel the locket hiding underneath. Would the locket still work, even if they were bound by the shackles? It might be their last hope to escape. And with the guard standing right there, they couldn't very well discuss options.

Cassie looked around. "Hey, where are Jac and Jaz?"

Liz said, "I don't know, honey."

Undaunted, Cassie turned to the dark elf. "Hey, you! What did you do with my dolls?"

The dark elf ignored her, inhumanly still.

Liz said to him, "What are you going to do with us?"

The dark elf's voice came hollow and metallic from inside the helmet. "The Dark Lord wishes very much to meet all of you."

"What a surprise," Liz said.

"The feeling is *not mutual!*" Cassie snorted. "Where's my Daddy?"

The dark elf turned his back.

Just then a short, stumpy shape, very muscular, emerged from the nearby opening in the cavern wall, the orange light casting an extended shadow. The creature stood about Cassie's height, clomping toward the cage wearing a rough-spun shirt and a thick leather apron. His arms looked like knotty ironwood branches, thick and scarred and smudged with soot. His hair was a tangle of rusty steel wool, and his beady eyes were like polished eight-balls. His pocked, ruddy cheeks and scabrous lips bore a malicious smirk.

Behind him came two small figures, marching in lockstep with each other in that unnatural automaton motion.

The dwarf said, "I've yer new helpers, Captain." He gestured to the automatons.

"Excellent, Master Dar-Chakkum," the dark elf said. "They will be most helpful on our journey."

Their clothing had been removed, revealing the porcelain limbs and metallic joints, and their embedded sheaths full of dark blades. Their pretty hair had been burned away, leaving only patches of blackened stubble. Their porcelain and metal skulls were freshly scored with burn marks, as if they'd just been opened, tinkered with, and welded shut again. Their beautiful faces remained the same— except for the awfulness that had become their eyes. Their beautiful blue eyes were gone, replaced by empty pits of yellow-orange flame.

"Oh, no!" Liz whispered.

Cassie screamed and clutched the bars. Tears burst out and streamed down her smudged cheeks.

"What did you do to them?" Liz yelled.

The dwarf gave her a snaggle-toothed grin. "Just a few adjustments, really. Their brains are much less complex than say, a dragon's or a rail-weevil." He turned to the dark elf. "They'll serve you well, my lord."

Cassie started calling the dolls' names, but they didn't respond, except to rotate their heads together to regard her with cold curiosity, as if she were a moth they might have to pin to an examination board. She descended into a fit of sobbing, and Liz hugged her close. "Why did they have to do that? Why? Why?"

Liz kissed her head, trying to comfort her, stroking her hair.

Just then, over the sound of her daughter's sobbing came a sound like an approaching subway train. Whooshing air, screeching wheels on rails, and an unfamiliar growling noise. Down one of the tunnels, a light appeared far away, growing brighter, then spreading until it resolved into nine lights arranged in a horizontal line that became a set of glowing eyes in a beetle-like face. Below the row of eyes, resembling the cowcatcher on an old steam locomotive, was an armored proboscis twenty feet long.

Long sheets of metal had been riveted to the creature's carapace, which stood a full twenty feet high, and its legs had been replaced by steel wheels as tall as Liz. Behind it trailed five segments like the cars of a subway, but they were fashioned of the same horrid conglomeration of metal and carapace as the "locomotive." The train rumbled to a stop, letting the squealing brakes come to a halt. The strange growling noise persisted, however, then Liz realized it was coming from the locomotive. She'd never heard anything like it, a constant growling, grating noise that ebbed and rose like a conversation heard through a wall. A burst of that strange musty organic smell came with it. The entire construct settled closer to the ground, and a gout of thick, steaming liquid squirted out the locomotive's side and splashed across the cavern floor.

The stench of it smashed all of them in the nose moments later, evoking a chorus of disgusted cries.

"Ugh! What is that?" Hunter said.

The dwarf said, "Overheated lubricant."

"What does it use for lubricant?" Hunter asked.

"I suppose you could call it blood," the dwarf said, "but it's not really. Its blood is replaced when it's built."

"Eww!" Cassie said. "Gross!"

"A wee snippet like you wouldn't understand," the dwarf said with some pride.

"I'm taller than you are!" Cassie said.

The dwarf gave her one of the nastiest grins Liz had ever seen. "Not for long." Then he chuckled and strutted back toward what was probably his workshop. "Have a nice trip, snippet."

Liz clutched the bars, seething with anger.

From the small cage, Peaseblossom yelled, "Don't listen to him, Cassie!"

The dark elf approached the locomotive and uttered a bizarre, metallic chittering sound. The lights of the creature's eyes flickered in a rhythmic pattern, then one of the "cars" popped open like a beetle opening its carapace.

Trundling out of the car came a smaller, single-segmented version of the train, this one the size of a minivan. Instead of horns made of carapace, like a rhinoceros beetle, this one's horns had been replaced by three segmented, metal tentacles. It rolled toward the cages on treads like those of a tank.

There was nothing they could do but watch it come. Its tentacles snaked through the bars of their cage and hoisted it into the air, throwing its contents against the lowest wall with a painful lurch. Then it hooked the small cage, spun with a squealing grate of its treads, and returned to the train.

The lift-bug rolled up a low ramp into an interior cargo bay. The bay's walls looked like what Liz imagined a giant, hollowed-out insect would look like, but augmented by metal structures, pipes, and wires. The interior stank worse than the outside, dimly lit by rows of lights that looked bioluminescent.

Cassie clutched Liz in small, vise-like hands. "Mommy, what are we going to do?"

As the shell closed like a door, Liz kissed her daughter, held tightly to Hunter and Claude, and bit back tears. She had no idea what to do, except rely on the strength their family shared to be stronger than ever. And hope, hope for any sort of opportunity...

CHAPTER TWENTY-THREE

As the shell-hatch closed them into darkness in the belly of the beetle train, the clang felt like the slam of a cell block door.

Liz hugged the kids closer, whispering, "It's going to be okay. We'll figure this out."

A pool of orange-yellow light shone through a forward window, but it was opaque, allowing no view of what might be in the next car. The chamber was about double the width of a normal train car, an ovoid dome that was unmistakably biological, the interior of a beetle's carapace, even though it was also augmented with metal supports and bundles of pipes and cabling. Two parallel rows of bioluminescent globules crossed the ceiling from front to back. The forklift beetle that had carried their cages sat quiescent in the corner, all eyes dark.

The floor of their cage was a lattice of bars, uncomfortable to sit or kneel on. She could stand but had to bend into a right angle. The shackles on her ankles were heavy, clunky, and allowed only tiny steps.

Their cages shared space in the chamber with containers of various sizes and types, cylinders and crates and bags—and three shapes moving in the dimness. The dark elf and the two dolls.

The dolls approached the cage, their burning eyes floating in their smudged faces like bits of malevolence. They stopped an arm's length from the bars and fell as still as statues. The way they moved—or didn't—sent the screaming creeps up and down Liz's skin.

Cassie started to reach out a hand toward one of them. "Jaz?"

Liz grabbed it and pulled it back. "Don't, honey."

The doll remained so still, but its eyes were open, glowing like coals. The glint of the blades nestled along its naked porcelain limbs reminded her of how fast and dangerous they were—and it was impossible to know what changes the dwarf had made to how the dolls' brains worked, whatever strange brains the dolls had.

From the small cage a few paces away came Bob's voice, shaky, fluttery, "Is everyone hale and hearty?"

"We're okay," Liz said, "but not hale or hearty."

"Alas, we Little Folk are not well," Bob said. "These arcane bonds do not sit well against us."

"I want to throw up," Peaseblossom said, high-pitched and queasy.

"Silence!" the dark elf said, stepping between the cages, hand on his hilt. "The next one to speak gets a taste of my steel."

"That's crap," Hunter said. "You're not going to hurt us."

Before the boy could draw another breath, the dark elf's sword flashed with orange-yellow glimmer and thrust through the cage bars, straight into Hunter's chest. The strength of the thrust slammed Hunter back against Liz with an expulsion of breath.

Just as fast, the dark elf withdrew his weapon, leaving Hunter rubbing the spot in his chest where his diamond armor had stopped the sword point.

"Next time," the dark elf said, "it shall be your eye, not your armor. The Dark Lord wishes you alive but cares not whether your limbs are intact or your faces unspoiled. Do you understand?"

They all nodded.

Liz seethed with a hatred she had never experienced before, her body trembling with the urge to act, to do something, to attack this creature that had threatened her child, to fall upon him like a lioness.

The dark elf chuckled. "This shall be an interesting trip." He turned to the small cage, where four tiny eyes caught the light like animals in headlights. He pointed his sword toward the Little Folk.

"Leave them alone!" Liz said.

The dark elf slid the point between the bars, sending Bob and Peaseblossom scrambling back against the far side. "Perhaps I shall spit one and send it to the chef for preparation."

Liz joined a chorus of disgusted, horrified sounds.

The dark elf laughed. "They are not 'folk' at all, just sub-creatures really." He peered into the cage, his point hovering before them. "Which should it be, do you think? Not much meat on the female..."

"Ye vile blackguard!" Bob snarled, shoving Peaseblossom behind him. "Those dolls were more truly people than ye'll ever be!"

Just then, the train lurched into movement, accelerating so hard that everyone went tumbling against the rear wall of their cages—except for the dark elf, who stood stock-still, unperturbed by the violent movement. Even the dolls slammed against the cage wall before righting themselves, but the dark elf held his stance rock steady.

The sound of hissing wind rose outside the shell of the car, and the rumble of metal wheels came up through the floor.

"Underway at last," the dark elf said. "Now, which shall we—"

A shimmering golden cloud coalesced in midair in Liz's cage and became a razor-tipped projectile like a crossbow bolt or a small spear. Hunter was glaring at the dark elf with anger and determination.

Even as Liz recognized what was happening, the missile shot toward the dark elf.

It exploded against the interior wall of the cage, erupting into a shower of sparks.

The dark elf half-turned, his blank metal faceplate betraying no emotion. "Admirable grit, youngling, but Light magic cannot pass those bars any more than you can escape your shackles. It is a perfect shell." He circled their cage, sheathing his sword. "No doubt the Dark Lord will enjoy molding you to his will, just as he did your father."

"Shut up!" Hunter yelled, sniffling.

"Leave us alone!" Cassie yelled, clutching the bars.

The tilt of the helmet might have indicated a smirk. He turned to the dolls. "Watch them." Then he headed toward the forward hatch, his armor silent, unlike how plate armor should be, as if it were part of him.

As he disappeared through the hatchway, the dolls remained stock-still, exuding vigilant menace.

The thought of these two beings, as dangerous as they were beautiful, these two who had protected Cassie with steadfast courage and conviction, who were now subverted and turned against them apparently irrevocably, twisted Liz's insides into bleeding knots.

As Cassie looked at them, tears streamed down her cheeks. They had been her friends, her toys, her protectors, for two years, one-fifth of the child's life. It felt like a monumentally tragic betrayal. The dolls had had no choice. They were simply machines that had been reprogrammed. Or were they?

Liz noticed Claude curled up in the corner farthest from the dolls, legs crossed, quietly weeping. Catching her glance, voice crumbling, he said, "They were like my own children. I kept them in my shop for years and years, waiting for the right moment, the right person."

Liz reached out and squeezed his hand, letting her own warm tears flow.

Hunter whispered toward the small cage, "Are you two all right?"

"We are uninjured, dear boy," Bob said, with a quaver in his own voice.

"Do dark elves really eat Little People?" Hunter asked.

"We know precious little about the habits of dark elves, only rumors," Peaseblossom said. "When all sense of decency and empathy is abandoned, when all that remains are selfishness and purblind loyalty and devotion to the most depraved being in all the realms, how can it be beyond possibility for them to kill and eat other sentient beings?"

Bob added, "Especially when they don't see us as 'people' at all."

The dolls didn't seem to be reacting to the ongoing conversation. The dark elf had said *Watch them*, not *Keep them silent*. Nevertheless, Liz knew them to be highly intelligent in their own rote, literal way. What behavior would they allow? The trouble with attempting to find the boundaries was the dolls' possible reaction upon reaching the limits.

To Claude, Liz said, "How much do you know about how they work?"

He said, "Their minds are an amalgam of magic and machine, Source conduits and clockwork. I might be able to repair a broken limb, but the workings of their minds are far beyond me. There is

247

no way I could undo what the dwarf did. What's worse, the dolls are now Dark Realm creatures, so there is no way to bring them back to the Light Realm to be restored."

Cassie's voice filled with tears, shrilling higher. "So they're like this *forever*?" Liz tried to hug her again, but Cassie shrugged off the comfort, her eyes flaring with righteous anger. "That's. So. *Mean!*" She went to the bars again. "Jac and Jaz, if you're still in there, I will find a way to take you back to your mommy so you can be yourselves again. I promise."

The dolls didn't move even a hair's breadth.

Then Cassie leaned back into the curve of her mother's arm with a suppressed sob. "This place sucks."

"It's like everyone here is dead inside," Hunter said.

"That is the essence of the Dark Realm itself, Hunter," Claude said. "Cruelty. Selfishness. Beings bereft of feeling for others."

The cage bars dug into Liz's backside and shoulders as she leaned against them. A blast of profound weariness swept over her in this moment of quiet, turning her limbs into lead again and hanging anvils on her eyelids. They had no idea how long before they reached the end of the line. Maybe it would be better to get some rest, so they could face whatever was coming.

As she let herself drift off, part of her mind was still furiously at work, churning through disparate ideas and bits of information, tossing them out as quickly as they came. Her consciousness swam in a sea of random thoughts, drifting toward dreams. How much of their dwindling stores of Light Source had Hunter used in his failed attack on the dark elf? How desperate would they have to become to use Dark Source? How much Dark Source could they use and still escape back to the Light Realm? Could they use any at all? And what about her own powers? Was there something she could do but was too mired in her own ingrained limitations to see it?

Bubbling up from this morass of mental detritus came a series of images.

A hollow eggshell.

A soda bottle.

A steam engine with a gleaming, red-hot boiler.

Kniblings tumbling away down dark passages, shoved away by the front of a magical wave of repulsion.

A wave that *she* had created.

She was *inside* a perfect shell, a closed magical shell.

An egg in the microwave.

A heavily shaken soda bottle in the Arizona sun.

A boiler stoked too high.

Closed systems under enough pressure *exploded.*

It came to her, what to do.

But could she do it *consciously*?

The return of the dark elf at the side of their cage roused her from these half-dreamed thoughts. His hand toyed with his sword hilt. Where had he come from?

Half-dreamed or not, her ideas were still crystal clear in her mind. Maybe she could do it consciously, but it couldn't hinder her to arrange some motivation.

She slid up to the bars and faced him. "So, what do you get for all this anyway? What do you get for being so awful to everyone else in the universe?"

"Humans are such fools. Do go on, continue to entertain me with your simian antics."

That gave her an idea, recalling one time near a monkey cage where the monkeys had flung a certain something at a nearby pair of pubescent boys who were taunting them.

She said, "If you don't care about anybody else in the universe, how can anyone trust you? Why don't you all just stab each other in the back and the last one standing gets to go bow before the Master, so that he can eat you, or throw you aside, or do whatever it is he does?"

"We are the Master's children—"

She guffawed in his face, piling up all the contempt she could muster. "You're a joke! That's what you don't get! None of you do, apparently. You're too stupid and short-sighted to—"

He struck at her fingers with his gauntleted fist, sending her jerking away from the bars.

"Oh, look!" she said. "Who's acting like a monkey now?"

He squared on her.

She started scratching and making monkey noises, hooting and squawking.

The three other humans stared at her.

"Look, kids!" she said. "The mindless toady thinks he's better than us monkeys." She winked at them, encouraging them to join her.

"What a loser!" Cassie said.

"Yeah, you're afraid of us!" Hunter laughed.

The dark elf chuckled. "One of us is *outside* the cage."

"You had to put us in here to feel safe," Claude said. "What a loathsome, despicable, pitiful creature you are."

"The only difference is that *our* cage is visible," Liz said. "And when we're not in it, we're *free!*"

Hunter hooted and bent over, showing his backside to the dark elf. "And you're too stupid to even see yours!"

The dark elf whipped out his sword and thrust it through the bars, straight at Hunter's unprotected backside.

In that moment of flashing movement, Liz's instincts boiled out of her, and a great rush filled her ears. Seizing her children's hands, she drew a deep draught of Source from each of them, and Claude, too, without having to touch him. This great influx of Source funneled through her and burst outward in an expanding bubble, like the top of a mushroom cloud. The bubble instantly crowded against the interior of the cage and its magical shell, but its force would not be restrained. The cage burst open with tremendous force. One heavy, spinning wall of riveted metal slammed into the elf, snapping his sword in half, sending him spinning across the chamber. He smacked the wall, limbs outspread, with a great clang and clatter, and slid to the floor.

The same force bubble had flung the dolls like chaff across the chamber, but they righted themselves instantly.

But then Liz somehow *felt* them, as if the bubble were part of her own skin. She directed the force, shaped into something like a huge, invisible hand, and slammed the dolls against the wall again. They struggled against it, but she held them fast.

"Mom, you did it!" Hunter yelled.

The dolls reached for their blades.

"Oh, no you don't!" Liz said, and refined the shape of the force hand into smaller pseudopods that immobilized the dolls' limbs.

251

How long she could hold them like this she did not know, but her force bubble was much stronger than they were, and now that it was up, she found she could control it almost as easily as her own body, like a toddler figuring out simple movements for the first time.

She said, "I've got these two. You all find something to tie up that dark elf."

Hunter, Cassie, and Claude found a wealth of materials in this cargo bay—netting, ropes, loose bundles of wire, cables—and soon they had cocooned the dark elf so completely, arms tight against his sides, he looked like a chrysalis with a spiky helmet. And just in time, because he awoke as they finished. As soon as he realized what they had done, he began to squirm and curse.

"We need to silence him before he brings any undesired attention," Claude said.

Hunter yanked off the dark elf's helmet, revealing a pallid, waxen face with sharp, gaunt features, so steeped in rage and hatred it made him draw back. The dark elf opened his mouth to shout, drawing in a deep breath, but quick as a striking rattler, Liz sent an invisible tongue of force bubble into the open mouth, stopping it like a cork.

"Hurry! Find something to gag him," Liz said.

Claude whipped out a handkerchief and stuffed it in his mouth. Then he set about tying it in place by wrapping several loops of thin cord around the elf's head and mouth, tying a secure knot.

"Was that handkerchief dirty?" Hunter asked with an impish grin.

"Oh, quite," said Claude. "I've been using it for days."

"Eww!" Cassie yelled with glee.

The dark elf's expression turned queasy, but no less hostile.

Claude said, "We've no idea who or what else is aboard this train, or whether the train itself is sentient enough to stop us." He glanced toward the forklift beetle with its prehensile metal tentacles, still sitting quiet and dark in the rear of the cargo bay.

Liz said to Cassie, "I'm really sorry, but we need to get rid of the dolls. I don't know how long I'll be able to hold them, and if they get loose..."

"I know," Cassie said. "The real Jaz and Jac wouldn't want to be used this way. But I don't want to hurt them."

Hunter suggested, "We could throw them off the train."

"Great idea!" Liz said.

Hunter was already looking for a latch or handle for the car's side door. Finding one near the floor, he hooted in triumph and made monkey faces at the dark elf, then he tugged on the handle. There came a metallic clank, and he lifted the shell hatch like a garage door. But it took all his effort, and he could lift it only to chest level. "Is this high enough, Mom?" he said through gritted teeth. The rumble of the train and the whoosh of air poured into the cargo bay. Outside, dark cavern walls flashed past at high speed, at least sixty miles an hour.

Liz could feel her invisible hand starting to expire like the exhalation of a breath. Just another couple of seconds...

Snaking invisible fingers around the dolls' bodies, clutching them tight, she dragged them across the room with her mind, and with a silent apology flung them through the opening. They disappeared into the darkness.

As an afterthought, Liz grabbed the dark elf and threw him through the opening, too.

Hunter let the door slide closed and stepped back, breathing heavily.

Cassie clapped. "Yay!"

Liz ran to her son, hugged him close, and kissed his forehead. Clutching his face in both hands, she said, "That. Was. Awesome!"

"That was all you, Mom," Hunter said with a sheepish grin.

"Indeed," Claude said with a grin. "Good show, Liz."

The sound of small hands clapping came from the small cage. "Well done!" Bob and Peaseblossom called.

Not knowing what else to do, her face heating, Liz took a small bow. She felt like a magician about to say, *And now, for my next trick...*

"Let us out?" Peaseblossom said plaintively.

"Maybe there's something in our stuff we can use to get you out," she said.

Hunter found their packs among the cargo nets, complete with weapons, equipment, food, and water. They used one of Stewart's stout-bladed daggers to pry open the cage's lock. It broke open with a snap, and the Little People burst forth with arms raised, still shackled, but exultant.

Cassie lifted Peaseblossom to her shoulder, and the little woman hugged the child's head.

Liz's mouth was powerfully dry, so she pulled out her water skin and took a long drink. Then she pulled out some rations. "We need to keep our strength up for wherever we arrive. There's no way we're jumping off this train ourselves."

They all nodded agreement.

"But where are we going?" Bob asked. "That is the golden question."

"And what do we do when we get there?" Hunter asked, looking expectantly at his mother.

CHAPTER TWENTY-FOUR

"Before we worry about that," Peaseblossom said, "might I suggest we remove these shackles?"

"How?" Liz said. "I, uh, threw the guy with the key overboard."

The little woman winked and headed toward Cassie's backpack, her feet doing a quick shackle-shuffle. She unzipped the backpack and dove inside, flinging out various things as she dug.

"Hey!" Cassie said. "My stuff!"

Peaseblossom emerged triumphant, holding up a paper clip, which looked half the length of her arm. With a series of determined grunts, she unwound the paper clip's bends, then re-bent the end of the paper clip to have a ninety-degree angle.

"You're going to pick the locks?" Hunter asked.

"Blessings of a misspent youth," Peaseblossom said with a grin. "Oh, I never stole anything, but it was fun knowing I could."

"Why can't Bob just shrink us out of the shackles?" Hunter said. "You can shapeshift, right, Bob? You shrank us before."

"Our dashed cunning adversary seems to have thought of that," Bob said regretfully. "It was the first thing I tried. There's a permanent spell on the manacles that they will shrink with ye."

Peaseblossom waved Hunter nearer, jumped onto his forearm and wrapped her legs around it, then set about trying to pick the lock on his manacles, tongue poking from the corner of her mouth.

"Wait!" Liz said. Their backpacks still contained the Dark Ink, which must have long since worn off. She dug out a vial of the stuff and quickly reapplied it to everyone.

"We look like Army Rangers," Hunter said.

Claude made a face. "And no doubt smell like them after a month in the field without a shower."

Cassie gave a fervent nod of agreement, holding her nose.

To Liz the stench of it somehow fit this place, as if it were the Dark Realm's version of a breath of wildflowers and fresh air.

Moments later, Peaseblossom had Hunter's hands free, and he rubbed his wrists while she set to work on his ankles. Peaseblossom continued her work quickly and methodically.

When Liz was free, she explored the confines of the train car, giving the motionless forklift beetle a wide berth, having no idea how intelligent or aware it might be. Would it harm them?

What interested her more was what or who else might be on the train. The door with the opaque window at the front of the car led somewhere, and she remembered that along the side of the forward car there had been windows like those of a passenger train. Would someone or something be coming to check on the missing dark elf?

Second thoughts plagued her. Had the dark elf survived being thrown from the train? What if throwing him off the train had broken his bonds but left him otherwise uninjured? How resilient was a dark elf? They were practically immortal, after all. Could he raise an alarm? And what happened when they arrived at their destination and were discovered?

Could they somehow get off the train before it arrived at the station without killing themselves, and remain unseen?

Liz was pretty sure they were headed to wherever the Dark Lord was. She could only hope Stewart would be there, too, and she could intercept him before he carried through with his plan, whatever it was. She knew Stewart had a plan that involved the Dark Lord, but was it to join him or destroy him? Even if he somehow succeeded in destroying the Dark Lord, how could he ever be her Stewart again? She tried to settle her mind to contact him, but whatever conduit had been opened that night in the inn, she could not find it again. Stewart remained closed off to her. Or was he dead? Or so far gone that she wouldn't recognize him as her husband? She still remembered the horrible, black-winged thing that had returned with the Princess. The thought stabbed her in the heart.

At the forward door, she paused to listen, but the noise of the beetle train was too great to hear anything beyond. She poked a soft membrane, and the door slid open quickly, like a flinch of pain. Beyond was a conglomeration of connective tissue, augmented by metal struts, and then another door into the next car. Encircling the space between cars were interlocking scales of ridged carapace. She didn't want to open that door, because if it opened as quickly as the first, she would be caught standing in full view of whoever might be over there. She wanted only a peek, not to reveal herself.

But then the train car gave a small lurch as power was reduced. The train began to coast.

She hurried back to the others. "We're slowing down!"

257

"What do we do?" Hunter said.

She looked around at her ragtag, beleaguered band. "We jump."

The words began to sink in, and they all traded looks.

Cassie said, "That's gonna hurt, Mommy."

"We wait until the train slows down," Liz said. "This isn't like a subway or a light rail that runs on electricity. There's no third rail."

"Yeah, just rocks," Hunter said with a grimace, but he wasn't protesting, only anticipating pain.

"And we shouldn't use magic," Liz said. "We've already used too much. It might show up to them like a flare."

"It would, yes," Bob said, scratching his head. "Your escape method probably already did."

"We'll jump off before the train gets to the station," Liz said, kneeling before the door. "It'll be like jumping out of a swing. And maybe we'll get some bumps and bruises, but—"

"It'll be better than getting caught again," Cassie said.

"Right," Liz said. "Okay, let's get the door open. We'll prop it up with some of those crates."

They could all feel the deceleration, and it lent speed to their work. They managed to prop open the heavy carapace door to about chest height, and Liz leaned as far out as she could, to see what was coming.

Maybe three hundred yards ahead lay a patch of orange light and a series of loading platforms. Even this close to the station, the ground was moving past at frightening speed, a rough-hewn expanse of stone floor and stalagmites. Yep, this was going to hurt. If they managed it without any broken bones, it would be a miracle.

Time to remember some cheerleading and tumbling practice. "Keep your chins tucked, and when you hit the ground, roll with it."

The station was coming fast.

"Grab your backpack and go! Now!"

Claude gave her a terrified look, but he jumped anyway. As he struck, he loosed a sharp cry of pain, then bounced and rolled. Hunter took a deep breath and jumped with the fearlessness only kids possess. He hit the ground and rolled like a paratrooper.

Cassie took Liz's hand. "Together?"

"Together," Liz said.

Liz took a deep breath and stepped off.

The hardness of the ground shocked her, slammed her teeth together, drove the breath out of her, sent a flash of red-hot pain through her shoulder and stars through her vision. Fire seared her skull as she rolled, losing Cassie's hand. Pain like jamming her head against the corner of an open cupboard door, but her body remembered instinctively how to roll to break her fall. She came to a halt on her back, lying on rough, gritty stone. Warmth flowed over one ear, into it. Road-rash seared her arms and knees.

But she was alive. And nothing felt broken.

Nearby, Cassie made a tiny sound. "Owie..."

Liz flipped over and scrambled toward Cassie, despite the pain. "Honey, are you okay?"

But Cassie wasn't crying, only staring at the ceiling, eyes wide, a little teary, a little breathless, but in control. "Yep, that hurt, all right." She looked at Liz. "But I'm okay."

Relief turned Liz's limbs to water, and she kissed her daughter, suppressing a sob.

As the train's brakes screeched and brought it to a stop at the station about 150 yards away, Liz scanned the nearby dimness for

Claude, Hunter, and the leprechauns. Claude was a motionless white mound with limbs splayed. Hunter was levering himself onto his hands and knees. She ran toward Claude and found his chest rising and falling, his face scrunched in pain.

"Is anything broken?" she asked.

"Something in my arm popped when I struck the ground," he said in a husky voice. "So, maybe..." He was cradling his right arm with his left. It wasn't obviously broken, but that didn't mean it wasn't fractured.

"Can I touch it?" she asked.

"If you must," he said.

She felt along the length of his forearm, then his elbow, and he winced.

"I'll be all right," he said. "I can walk, but these old bones have suffered a blow."

She helped him to his feet. As he steadied himself, he cradled his arm against his body.

An agonized peep like Peaseblossom's voice sounded somewhere nearby.

"I got ye, lassie," came Bob's voice.

The two of them emerged from behind a stalagmite, Peaseblossom limping, an arm draped over Bob's shoulders.

The beetle train rolled to a stop at the station, and Liz could just see figures getting on and off the train. She'd been right not to open that forward door. She caught the glint of armor among the figures, denoting more dark elves. They would be looking for their brother.

"We don't have much time," Liz said. "We have to hide."

"Aye, they'll puzzle it out in a trice. Let's get away from the station, into the dark," Bob suggested. "Our eyes will lead, but you have to trust us, and we have to hurry. Dark elves can see in the underground just like Little Folk. Come!"

"And they have ears like foxes," Peaseblossom said.

It would be so easy to lose someone in this darkness. "Everybody hold hands!" Liz whispered.

The humans all joined hands and followed Bob, Claude limping along painfully. They crept away from the station, trying to balance speed with stealth. Liz hoped the noise of the beetle train masked their movement. Armored dark elves climbed into the cargo car. The lights of the station offered enough illumination to see their way— until they rounded a bend, and all fell into blackness. Then all they could do was follow Bob's whispering voice.

Liz tripped over a railroad track and sprawled in the gravel, gouging her palms with fresh road rash. Small hands patted over her, trying to help her up. "I'm okay, just annoyed."

"There's a side passage just ahead," Bob whispered. "It will get us out of this cavern and out of sight."

Liz's intuition seemed to agree with him. Yes, they needed to get out of this cavern and hide. The dark elves would be searching it.

She heaved back to her feet, and they hurried onward. Then the timber of small footsteps changed ahead of her, shuffling quietly in a smaller space. She bumped into a wall and into a narrow passage, just wide enough for one. The walls themselves seemed to hiss and sigh. Her outstretched hand brushed over pipes and conduits, some of them uncomfortably warm. The air warmed and thickened. The darkness was absolute.

Time passed. Their feet shuffled along with occasional whispers of encouragement or warning from Bob. "This way. That's right. Watch this corner. Keep yer heads down. Some stairs here." The rumbling roar of another beetle train came and went, its deafening echo shaking them to their bones.

How far they had come Liz couldn't guess. It felt like a mile but could have been a hundred yards. The pitch blackness was too disorienting.

Then Bob said, "Looks like a stairwell upward. Might be our chance to get back to the surface."

Their tunnel hadn't branched as far as she knew. If this were some sort of maintenance tunnel, where would it emerge above? They would certainly be fugitives by now.

"Let's rest a minute," she said.

Sighs of relief sounded all around her. The kids sat on the tunnel floor. Claude leaned against a wall. "Claude," she said, "how's your arm?"

"It is either broken or a very bad sprain," Claude said, the pain evident in his voice.

"Why don't we send you home?" she said. "You've done enough."

"I have come this far," he said. "I may yet be of use."

She heard Hunter rummaging in his backpack. A white light suddenly stabbed her eyes. "Sorry," Hunter said, suppressing the small flashlight against his body. He held out what looked like a thick roll of bandage. "Let's make Claude a sling for his arm."

"Oh, that would be lovely!" Claude said with breathless relief.

Hunter set himself to the task, forcing Liz to suppress another surge of proud tears. So grown up, her little man. A couple of minutes later, Claude's injured arm hung in a sling.

In the dancing light of Hunter's flashlight, Liz caught sight of Peaseblossom leaning against the bottom step, silently weeping into her hands.

Liz called out to her, "Are you all right?"

Peaseblossom sniffled and shook her head, wiping her eyes. "These wee bones are all right, but I know not how much longer I can bear to be in this place. 'Tis like there's a rat gnawing at my very soul, or a noose choking me. 'Tis difficult to breathe."

"Aye," Bob said, "folk such as us are not meant to exist here, Dark Ink or no."

Peaseblossom groaned. "I feel like if I stay much longer..."

"We won't be able to go home ever again," Bob said.

"Then we have to hurry," Liz said. While she was sure the Little Folk felt the Dark influence most acutely, she did not doubt that the same influence was at work on everyone. It was time to finish this. She offered Peaseblossom a hand, and the little woman crawled onto it. Liz hoisted her onto one shoulder. "It looks like we have a climb."

Part IV

CHAPTER TWENTY-FIVE

Endless flights of stone steps rose above them, and of those below, Liz had lost count somewhere in the seventies. Her thigh muscles howled as they turned to Play-Doh. On their way up, they passed several doors that opened into long, empty tunnels stretching into blackness. They paused at these to listen for signs of pursuit or accidental encounter, but they found themselves blissfully alone.

With every step, she wondered where Stewart was. She tried to open her awareness to him, to feel him like a compass needle feeling its pull toward magnetic north.

Suddenly, his presence was there in her mind, looming like an immense, winged shadow, spreading raven-black feathers across her mental landscape. Power crackled from him like scarlet lightning. He had fully embraced the Dark Source. It infused him, flowed through him like his own blood.

She heard herself say, "Oh, Stewart..."

"What is it, Mommy?" Cassie said, puffing with the exertion of the climb. "Are you talking to Daddy? Where is he?"

Liz paused to clear her throat and wipe a tear. "He's close, I think. We're in the right place."

"Yay!" Cassie whispered.

Liz sighed. At war within her were the urge to be hopeful and the need to be realistic. "We have to be careful. I can't tell how much of him is Daddy anymore. What I can see is that he's all Dark magic now, and he has a plan." She felt that purpose now more strongly than ever, his mind becoming a battering ram. She knew that resolve in him, could even picture his face when it had hold of him. Had her touch alerted him to their presence? "He has the wings again."

"We have to find him before he reaches the Dark Lord," Bob said. "Whatever he's up to, if he meets the Dark Lord, there'll be no turning back for him."

These worries lent fresh speed to their feet long enough to reach the end of the stairwell, a featureless metal door with a robust-looking latch.

Suppressed groans tinged Claude's ragged, gasping breaths. The smell of his sweat-drenched shirt filled the space. She had to admire his grit, and she was thankful for it.

As everyone paused on the landing, huffing, shaking out their burning legs, Liz touched the door, and it was uncomfortably warm to the touch. A strange, arrhythmic vibration thrummed under her fingertips. She listened at the door and caught the sound of wheels rolling over gritty earth, the distant, throaty cry of some unknown creature, and the whisper of hot wind.

She put a finger to her lips, then worked the latch handle. It resisted at first, but then moved with a raucous, echoing screech. She cringed at the noise, but there was no helping it now. A puff of wind pushed the door inward, blinding them all with a sudden frame of blazing sunlight. She allowed the door to open just far enough to peer through the crack.

Outside lay a broad thoroughfare paved in dull black flagstones. Wheeled vehicles trundled along, some with visible drivers like carriages, others like miniature variations of the beetle train that had brought them here and the tentacled lifter.

As she peered around, she saw the street was not a straight line but a ringed plaza around a colossal, roughly cylindrical tower that rose so high she couldn't see the top. The tower was fluted, covered in haphazard spines and protrusions of metal and black glass that could have impaled a dragon or a jet airliner. The lack of symmetry or pleasing lines grated across her eyes. Just looking at the thing, trying to focus on its black ridges and textures made her head swim for reasons she couldn't grasp, as if the shape of it could not exist in a mind that understood geometry.

She shuddered and let the door ease shut, trying to catch her breath.

Hunter touched her arm with a silent question.

She said, "We're here. This has to be the place."

"Is this the Metropolis?" Claude said.

"It's a tower that looks like nasty black glass," she said, "huge, unbelievable. Lots of vehicles and machines outside."

"Any dark elves?" Bob asked.

"I didn't see any, or those monsters they were riding."

In her mind, Stewart's presence lingered like the shadow in the corner of her childhood bedroom, always at the corner of her mind, always unclear whether its movement was real.

She peeked outside again. The sun was high in the sky, painting stark shadows of the surrounding buildings, but she didn't know if it was morning or afternoon. Outdoors felt wildly impersonal, as if all the denizens were robots, so absorbed in their own business they weren't paying attention to anything beyond themselves.

Maybe they could use that to their advantage. If everyone outside was so self-absorbed, would anyone even care about four humans? Their Light magic was shielded from the perception of Dark creatures. Would the denizens of this place pay any attention at all?

But then a sharp, winged shadow drifted across the ground. It was too big to be Stewart, and it had a long, serpentine tail, but it was too high for her to see. Whatever it was, it was huge. The thought of getting *that* thing's attention sent a shiver down her spine.

The tower itself was about a hundred yards in diameter, situated atop a circular dais that rose three or four dozen steps up from the surrounding street. Somehow, she knew the dais did not support the tower, but the other way around. The tower's roots reached deep into the ground.

Then a hard skittering noise caught her ear, as sharp as iron-shod horses' hooves on the flagstones. Two of the gigantic crustaceans, ridden by plate-armored dark elves, scuttled into view around the curve of the street and paused before what appeared to be the tower entrance. A pair of metal doors, pitted and weathered by eons, stretched thirty feet high. She could scarcely imagine how heavy such doors were.

Then around the crustaceans came a different creature, just as big, just as ugly, but reptilian. It had the thick body, frog-like mouth, and beady eyes of a gila monster but was the size of a city bus. And there on its back...

"Stewart!" she whispered. Relief that he was alive flooded her, followed immediately by—

"Do you see Daddy?" Cassie yelped, stifling herself to a squeak in mid-sentence.

She nodded, a sick dread settling into her belly. She fought it back with the kernel of belief that enough of the man she loved remained that he could be saved, salvaged.

He stood astride the giant gila monster, with great raven wings folded. The nearby dark elves seemed to be watching him with uneasy deference, perhaps fear, as if unsure what to do with him.

Bob moved to the crack beneath Liz and peered out.

"'Tis Stewart, it is," Bob said. "It appears he's going into the tower."

Stewart jumped down from the monster's back, a flick of his wings gliding him to land on the third step. On his back were a backpack and the great, two-handed sword with the wavy blade.

"Might we be in need of some reconnoitering?" Bob said. "I might be of service there."

Stewart climbed the steps toward the massive double doors. The dark elves remained on their hideous mounts.

Liz said, "We need to get in there with him."

The tower's double doors swung inward to receive Stewart.

Before Liz could protest, Bob blinked into the shape of a mouse wearing a little, emerald-green waistcoat. He wobbled dizzily for a moment and made a distressed squeak, but then righted himself and darted outside. With incredible speed, he scurried out of sight.

Outside on the steps, Stewart paused halfway up, turned, and looked around. His gaze swept toward Liz like a sleet of flint shards. She shut the door, her heart hammering in her chest. Had he seen her peering out the cracked door?

She felt like such an idiot. What was she doing here? This was all so far beyond her, monsters everywhere, evil minions, the entire place poisonous to her very soul. She loved Stewart, but that wasn't the only reason she was here. Something had happened on the journey to this point, something had been revealed in her, something unearthed.

With magic, she could protect herself. She had uncovered the home of her magic inside. She could protect her children. And when push came to shove—as it had to, she knew—she could say goodbye to this creature who wore her husband's body and return to the Light Realm to begin her mourning. She would do everything in her power for that not to happen, but she knew she could do it.

Should she open the door and call out to him? If she marched out there right now, hands on hips, and called him out, what would he do? Would he protect her from the dark elves and their monsters? She needed to *talk* to him, alone, to look into his eyes. She needed him to look into hers. Maybe that would give him pause enough for her to put a locket around his neck. That was the only way to save him. Once in the Light Realm, it would be up to the Queen and the Princess to drag him back from the abyss one last time.

A booming, metallic screech echoed down into the street, and a heavy shadow fell over the ground, growing quickly. A massive shape the size of an airliner alit in the street between her and Stewart, and a blast of wind and stench blew Liz's door wide open, knocking her back a step and exposing them all in the flood of sunlight. She scrambled to shut the door again, hoping they hadn't been seen, but left enough cracked for her to see. She couldn't bear to look away, even though her mind could hardly encompass what she saw.

It was a dragon, but its flesh and bones had been augment-ed with metal and machinery, inside and out, just like the beetle train. It was some kind of *Terminator*-dragon; that movie had ter-rified her, and still gave her the willies. The stench of it was like a machine shop, a reptile cage, and a cauldron of rancid blood all thrown together.

The great beast folded its leathery wings and squared itself on its haunches toward Stewart, shuffling its gigantic, three-toed feet. Its head was twice the size of the T-rex's she had seen in a museum, a nightmare of horns, teeth, and armor plating.

Stewart flew into sight, wings outstretched, his hands gleaming like crimson suns. His voice boomed over the plaza, "You remember me, do you?"

The dragon's smaller front feet hit the flagstones, claws plunging deep into the rock and earth and squeezing like a cat, and roared again, a sound like a sonic boom and screeching freight train that drowned out Cassie's scream of terror and pain.

"Your master is here, isn't he?" Stewart said. "I intend to see him, and you will not stop me!"

The dragon loosed a deep-throated hiss, its thick chest and long neck swelling with rage and flame poised to be set free.

"Hold your flame, dragon, or I'll give the Master your head!" Stewart roared. He seized the hilt of the flamberge from his back and drew it, hovering there forty feet above the ground, a nimbus of Dark magic coalescing around him. It was the most beautiful and horrific thing Liz had ever seen, sending her heart slamming into the bottom of her throat.

The dragon snorted and backed away from Stewart.

273

Then it gathered itself and bounded into the air again. Liz was ready for this wind blast and slammed the door just in time. She leaned against it, trembling like dry leaves ready to fall, trying to gather her scattered wits and courage. "Oh, cheese and rice, what are we doing?"

Hunter's voice was plaintive, tremulous. "That was a dragon, wasn't it?" He had been peering around her through the crack.

Liz nodded.

"Dad just faced down a *dragon*," he said, as if struggling to wrap his mind around it.

Then another voice from just down the steps made them all jump. "I found our way in!" Bob hooted, wearing the shape of a small owl, an elf owl, complete with emerald waistcoat, on the landing below, his great eyes glimmering in the light of the flashlight. Elf owls are so small they could fit in your palm.

After a moment to process what she was seeing, Liz said, "Then let's go." The quicker they got moving, the less she would have to think about what she had just witnessed.

Stewart settled back to the tower steps, watching the dragon's terrible shape diminish in the slate-colored sky. He hadn't been sure that would work. That dragon was a beast of such tremendous power, the outcome would have been a coin-flip. What was worse, he hated for Liz to see it.

He had spotted her there across the plaza, peeking through a cracked door, but more, he had felt her presence, like feeling the warmth of the sun on a closed door. Following him had been an incredibly foolish thing to do, but he was oddly proud of her for getting this far. The kids were with her, he knew, and he was proud of them, too.

A pang of shame lodged in his gut at what he must look like to them. But there was no helping it now. He had a job to do, and he would complete it, no matter what.

Baron Tyrus, Lord of the Dark Realm, was about to meet his end at Stewart's hand.

He folded his wings and turned to the nearby El-Mithari garkus knights. "Remain out here. My business is with the Master alone."

Then he faced the cavernous mouth of the tower entrance, put away his flamberge, and strode up the steps.

CHAPTER TWENTY-SIX

B ob hopped back into the air, spread his wings, and glided down into the dark.

"Come on, everybody!" Liz said. She scooped up Peaseblossom and deposited her atop her backpack, then hurried after Bob.

"Onward!" Claude said, as sprightly as he could manage.

Bob led them to one of the branching hallways below, and they followed him down a tunnel for about a hundred yards. The tunnel ended in another metal door.

Bob resumed his normal appearance. "I'll warn ye, it ain't pleasant on the other side, but if ye hold yer nose, ye can get through it."

Liz already caught the scent like a half-full dumpster baking in the sun. "It's a trash chute or something, isn't it."

"Something like that," Bob said apologetically, "but it takes us exactly where we must go." He popped back into his elf owl shape to lead the way.

She opened the door and stepped into the cavernous space.

The kids made disgusted groans and cupped their shirts over their faces. On Liz's back, Peaseblossom peeped in disgust.

Beyond the door was a ledge about two feet wide carved from stone and covered in a sticky gunk a quarter-inch thick. Every footstep raised a fresh squelch of horrid stench. The rough-hewn stone wall was covered in a similar film, and touching it made Liz shudder from head to toe.

"Don't think about what it is!" she gasped, clamping her shirt over her nose and mouth.

"Thanks, Mom," Hunter said. "*That* helps."

Bob circled out into the dark and back. The opposite side of the cavern was lost to darkness. In his small owl's voice, he said, "Pipes from all the surrounding structures empty into here—"

"It's a *sewer?*" Hunter said. "For *what?*"

Bob came around again. "Well, yes, I suppose it is, in a sense."

It didn't smell exactly like sewage. There was a quality about it Liz couldn't place; the closest thing she could come up with was a kind of antiquity.

"Eww!" Cassie yelled. "It's *warm!*"

"Just don't think about it," Liz said. "Imagine it's toy slime or something." Cassie was right, the stuff was warm to the touch, but not a comforting warmth.

Closing her eyes, Cassie said, "Imagine *really hard!*"

After a couple of minutes of steeling themselves to overcome their disgust, Bob led them along the ledge, which was its own kind of terror. Liz's heart flew into her throat, and her mouth went dry as desert dust. The ledge's lip was way too close, and beyond it lay...nothing. There were no loose stones to drop—everything was covered in muck—but she doubted there was actually a bottom. Strangely, their voices and squelching footsteps made no echo at all, as if the cavern were acoustically dead.

Behind her came Cassie, then Hunter, then Claude. The big man's girth put him much closer to the edge than her and the children.

Bob the elf owl circled and circled, appearing and disappearing in the vast blackness. "This way! Be careful but step lively."

The four humans edged along the ledge with their backs to the wall. Even though it was sticky, Liz had no illusions it would hold her if she slipped.

The cavern appeared to be cylindrical, and judging by the radius, Liz thought it might be roughly the same diameter as the great tower above, as if the structure of the tower somehow reached down into the earth.

"Mom!" Hunter said, pointing down into the blackness. "Those look like stars down there."

Liz peeked down into the endless pit and thought Hunter might be right. The depths of the pit resembled the night sky, glimmering with tiny reddish pinpricks and sparkles. She called out to Bob, hoping his sharp eyes might be able to see. "What is that down there?" No matter what it was, it looked impossibly far away.

"I know not," Bob called as his course veered and wobbled. "Just looking at it makes me head spin."

A vertigo effect took hold the harder she tried to focus on it, and she quickly turned her attention ahead of them along the ledge.

"Just don't look at it," Liz said. "Bob, how much farther?"

"Not far, only another fifty feet or so," Bob said. "There's an opening that slants upward, leading to a rubbish chute."

"So we're *reverse* garbage," Cassie said, trying hard to lighten the mood. "Sorry, that wasn't as funny as it sounded in my head."

Liz chuckled despite the situation. "Just be careful, pay attention to where you're stepping." It was all she could do to steady her breath. *Breathe, scootch-step, breathe, scootch-step.* Inch by inch. *Don't look down.*

279

Finally, the opening came into view, a yawning mouth in the wall at their back, angling upward, also covered with the stinky muck.

Feeling the pressure of time, she took two steps upward—and discovered in the most horrible fashion that the muck was not sticky *enough*. Both feet slipped out from under her, and she went front-first into it. She caught herself on her forearms, keeping her face out of it, but then she was sliding feet-first toward the lip of the abyss. She yelped and flailed for a handhold but found none. Her toes slipped over the edge, her shins, her knees. Then a strong hand seized the back of her shirt and held her fast.

No one moved.

The kids stared in horror at what had almost happened. Liz struggled to control her breathing.

Claude hovered over her, then pulled her back onto the ledge. "That almost went poorly," he said. He helped her to her feet.

She almost said a few words her mother would definitely disapprove of as she tried to get control of her panic. The awful muck now covered the front of her from chest to feet.

"So gross, Mom," Hunter said, "but at least you didn't..." He couldn't finish the sentence.

Liz still couldn't speak, her breath caught in her throat, but she had to reassure the kids that she was all right. She mustered enough strength to gasp, "Sorry to scare everyone. Thanks, Claude." She flashed a wan smile.

He nodded in acknowledgment, then said, "Now we must find a way to get up there."

Bob lit on Claude's shoulder. "I may know a way."

Claude's eyes bulged with pain. "Arrest your grip, Bob!"

"Apologies," Bob said, furling his wings, "sometimes I forget the strength of me talons."

Claude relaxed and held still so Bob could balance without clamping too tightly.

Bob said, "Have we any sort of rope?"

Hunter said, "Yeah, I have a roll of cord left over from when we tied up the dark elf."

"I could take one end, fly up there, and tie it to something."

"What if it's too short?" Hunter asked.

"Then we shall burn that bridge when we come to it, as they say," Bob said.

"Anybody have any more?" Hunter asked.

Liz was thankful for something concrete to focus on to help drive back the pounding terror at having almost died. She fumbled through her backpack, hands trembling so badly she could barely work her fingers, but found no rope, nor did Cassie or Claude.

"This is it then," Bob said before he took one end in his beak and leaped into the air. He swooped up into the diagonal tunnel and disappeared, trailing the thin cord as Hunter unspooled it as fast as he could.

Liz watched the coil shrinking rapidly, nearing its end. The angle of the tunnel was simply too steep to climb up without help, and none of them had any climbing equipment. Every moment they wasted was a moment she couldn't reach Stewart and try to stop him from doing whatever it was he had in mind.

The cord stopped moving, and a sliver of hope bloomed.

Bob's voice trickled down from above, as if from an even greater distance. "Our rope is secure, but let's not overtax it. One at a time!"

"I'll go first," Liz said, "then I can help pull you all up."

"Careful, Mommy," Cassie breathed.

Liz tugged on the cord to test it. It seemed secure.

With a lopsided grin, Hunter said, "You want me to wait at the bottom with my catcher's mitt?"

"Shush!" Liz said, gripping the cord and trying to concentrate, stoke her courage.

Cassie looked at him quizzically. "Why did you bring a catcher's mitt?"

Liz began to climb into blackness, steadying herself with the rope, and finding it was easiest to go on her knees. Her shins and knees were soon killing her, grinding into stone beneath the muck, but then she saw two small eyes reflecting the flashlight glow from below. Bob's leprechaun form stood on a narrow lip, his back to the wall, beside which the cord was tied securely around a strange metal fixture emerging from the stone. The upward sloping tunnel simply ended. Seeing the end of her climb renewed her hope and sped her pace. Relief flooded her as she reached the fixture and pulled herself up onto the lip.

"Well done!" Bob said.

Liz called down. "I made it! Cassie, you come next. Tie yourself to the rope. I'll pull you up."

A faint, tremulous, "Okay!" came back.

A couple of minutes later, Liz had pulled up both kids, Peaseblossom riding on Hunter's back. There was only barely enough room on the lip for the three humans.

Liz had never shamed anyone for being overweight but pulling Claude up the tunnel was like dragging a recalcitrant steer. He

climbed as best he could, but whatever sprightliness he'd once possessed was long since spent. Having one arm in a sling made it all the
slower and more painful. Liz could hear the pain in his breathing.
She pulled until her arms and shoulders and back burned with exertion and her hands were raw. With excruciating slowness, his bald
dome and thick shoulders inched up the tunnel.

Gasping, his face pale with overexertion, he reached the top looking abashed, and Liz seized his hand and hauled him up. "Thank you
for giving an old man this opportunity."

It seemed an odd way to phrase it, but Liz answered, "You're welcome. Now where to, Bob?"

Claude said, "Allow me a moment to unkink my limbs." He
seized the metal fixture and hauled himself to his feet with grunts
and groans of discomfort.

Liz chafed at further delay.

Bob pointed at a small metal grate on the wall above him, like a
vent cover just large enough to crawl through. "Through there, and
we are in the tower."

Inside the entrance doors of the Obsidian Tower, Stewart paused
to gaze upward. Its hollow core reached high into misty distance.
Ruddy sunlight slanted through irregularly spaced window slits,
casting random spears through the mist and splashes of searing light
on the opposite wall. The faceted, glass-like interior of the Obsidian
Tower turned the splashes into glittering shards. The way the interior
wall scattered the light reminded him of the Princess's former prison,

a dome of black, glass-like substance resembling obsidian with thousands of polished facets. Those facets had nearly been his death, because looking into them, he had seen distorted, twisted snippets of his life, relived his failures, and almost fell into despair on the cusp of success, nearly allowing the Dark Lord's cyber-dragon to kill him.

This entire tower looked made from the same substance. Best not to touch the wall, or even look at it. He didn't want to see what it would show him now.

On opposite sides of the interior, two spiral staircases ten feet wide crawled upward, disappearing into the heights. Structures like catwalks or heavy beams stretched across the core like the steps of a DNA spiral. The tower's construction was a wonder of vastness and mind-bending geometry.

But the most wondrous thing was what appeared to his magical senses. The tower's interior seethed with crimson motes like untold millions of tiny fireflies, more Dark Source than he had ever seen, like red pinpricks in the fabric of the universe itself. Could this be the analog to the great Lake of Light Source beside which the City rested in the Light Realm?

He stood for a moment in awe of it. Inside this tower, with unlimited Dark Source at his disposal, his powers would be nearly infinite.

But so would the power of Baron Tyrus.

The feathers of Stewart's wings ruffled in anticipation. The Dark Lord no doubt expected Stewart was coming to join him, to bend his knee in obeisance. But this moment was everything Stewart had planned for. With the sword he had made, infused with both Light and Dark magic and amplifying his powers, he would destroy the

Dark Lord once and for all and bring balance to the magical realms. And if he failed, well, he had tried. He owed his family that much.

By sundown, either Stewart or Baron Tyrus would be no more.

Stewart began climbing the stairs. It was a long way to the top, a mile or more. He considered flying for a moment, but something about the way the interior of the tower skewed his vision, shifting with shadows and half-seen shapes, told him that something was different about space-time in here, perhaps similar to his journey down the gullet of Chukwa, the Cosmic Tortoise. Trying to fly straight up the core might take him somewhere he didn't wish to go. All was not what it seemed. His mostly human eyes might well deceive him.

Would the Dark Realm have a new master by nightfall?

In the vast chamber atop the Obsidian Tower, the Dark Lord waited with great anticipation. The Onyx Orb hovered in the air, a spherical repulsion to the eye.

Stewart Riley was powerful indeed, but foolish beyond measure. How could he, a mere human, with almost no real experience wielding his powers, hope to stand against the very personification of the Dark Realm? Untold millennia ago, Baron Tyrus had been some sort of mortal creature, but almost no memories remained of that life, buried like a few grains of sand in an ocean of experience, nor could he more than dimly remember how he had risen to be something more. His ascendance came when he discovered magic, mastered it, destroyed anyone who stood in his way, and rose through the ranks of powerful ambitious beings known as the Lords of the Dark, and fought them until only he remained supreme. Survival of the more worthy, more ruthless, more committed, a simple equation. The powerful survived by climbing upon the backs of the weak, exploiting them, feeding upon them. Baron Tyrus had left mountains of the dead behind him in his climb to the pinnacle.

If Stewart Riley had the patience to take a few centuries to master his powers, he might become a formidable opponent, but Baron Tyrus would have long since turned him into an "ally," a polite word for "minion." Stewart's foolish impatience would brook no such delay.

The truth was that the Dark Lord had foreseen every possible outcome and considered them.

The Obsidian Tower was a nexus of time and space. Its interior reached into the past and the future, touching all areas of the Dark Realm simultaneously and forever. From here, with the Onyx Orb, he could examine the past and the future, following the infinite threads of choice and chance to arrive at the outcomes he desired. The Tower's second purpose was to collect Source, and it did so more efficiently than anything in any realm, even the Light Realm, because it was gathering Source from both the past and the future. All Source that had ever existed was available to him whenever he wanted it, in whatever quantity he could channel. It was the ultimate reservoir of power in all the Realms, and it was why he had had the advantage over the Queen for a very long time. The Light Realm had no such means of collecting Source. He had heard a grand lake of it was gathered near the City that was home to the Queen, but she had no way of gathering and focusing it in such vast quantity.

And that was why the Dark Realm would soon be victorious.

The microscopic rupture in the fabric of the multiverse had grown from smaller than the size of an electron to the size of a water molecule, orders of magnitude larger. When it had expanded to sufficient size, he would charge through it with his army and attack the Light Realm directly. He would destroy the Queen and claim all the Source in all the Realms for himself, and he would remake all in his image, rewrite the very laws of existence.

Stewart Riley would help him do that, one way or another.

CHAPTER TWENTY-SEVEN

Liz boosted Bob up to the grate so he could push it open and peek out. "All clear!" he whispered.

They took turns helping each other through and emerged into the interior of the tower, a vast, quiet, strangely empty space.

While he waited for them to climb up, he said, "I'm a wee bit frettish that me Source is almost spent. I've perhaps one transformation left. I fear trying to use Dark Source would destroy me. Or turn me into something unfit for company."

With all of them now inside, Liz took in the vastness of the tower's dim interior. Two staircases on opposite interior walls spiraled upward. High catwalks crossed the empty space between the staircases at various levels in a pattern that reminded her of a DNA strand. About a hundred feet away, the massive entrance doors stood open, allowing a harsh splash of light across the dark, polished floor. Liz still remembered the dark elf knights gathered in the street out front.

And there, several stories above, so very far away yet so close, climbed a figure with great raven wings.

"I see him!" she whispered to everyone.

Her heart reached out to him, yearning to hug him, kiss him, talk sense into him like she always did.

He paused his ascent and looked back.

His voice echoed in her head as if across a vast chasm. *You shouldn't have come, and you brought the kids to* this place! His wave of anger washed over her, something he always kept restrained, seldom let her see, but now, it was off the leash. Even in his Darkened state, he was still fiercely protective. Maybe she could use that.

She sent her thoughts back to him. *Before you do whatever it is you're planning, just talk to me. Just for a moment.*

No. Go home. It's too dangerous here for you and the kids.

But you can protect us.

A long moment passed.

You can't help me. Way up there, poised on the stairway, he looked like some sort of dark angel climbing to Heaven to meet his maker.

Come down here and tell me that! she thought back at him.

He seemed to consider this, then resumed his climb.

Claude's urgent whisper rose somewhere behind her. "We must lock out the dark elves!"

He and Hunter ran for the front entrance.

Claude's voice came faintly, "These are locking bolts, my boy! Crank that wheel!"

"Yeah, but then aren't we locked in here?" Hunter whispered.

"The only way we leave this building is with our lockets!" Claude puffed as he cranked on a capstan, which operated a series of bolts, each of them as thick as Liz's arm. Hunter threw his whole body into cranking the other, and the clank and grind of metal echoed strangely through the space, almost like the sounds of a theremin, as if they were changing tone with each reflection. The entrance doors were sealed.

"Stewart!" Liz called out. But could he hear her at this distance? He kept climbing. She yelled to the kids, "We have to catch him! Come on!"

"Right behind you, Mommy!" Cassie called, grunting with the effort of acceleration. The Little People scampered along behind.

Hunter and Claude waited for them near the foot of a staircase.

"What's the plan, Mom?" Hunter asked.

"We catch your dad, put a locket on him, and go home." She felt for the locket the Princess had given her for Stewart, a hard lump in the front pocket of her jeans.

"I want to go home," Cassie said. Then she cupped her hands around her mouth and shouted up the tower, "Daaaddddeeeeee!" Her voice echoed strangely, like the locking bolts had. Maybe there was something about this place that prevented sound from carrying.

"We have to catch him," Liz said. "Come on!"

"Wait a moment," Claude said, with an apologetic look on his face. He slipped the chain of his locket over his head. "You may need this."

"No, I have..." She felt for the locket at her throat, but it was gone. Her stomach plummeted. Had her dark elf captor taken it from her? Had she lost it in the tunnels somewhere? When she jumped from the train? When Claude had grabbed her by the collar? "Oh, no..."

"Take this for Stewart," Claude said.

"But—"

He raised a hand. "Don't worry. My Dark Ink will wear off at sunset, and then I'll be back in the Light Realm, right as rain." He gave her a wan smile. "But Stewart needs this to return. Take it."

She took it, and it seemed to weigh more than any locket should.

"Now you must catch him," Claude said.

There were tears in her eyes as she turned to climb the stairs, stuffing the second locket into her pocket.

Stewart was climbing at a normal walking speed, as if contemplating what he might find at the top. If she ran, she could catch him. Anger rose in her chest and made her teeth clench. After everything she had been through, he would *not* walk away from her. Was that guy going to get a talking to!

She threw the last of her flagging reserves into her legs. Her overtaxed muscles protested, but she had no choice. The others fell in behind her as she pelted for the nearby foot of the stairway and then took the steps two at a time. The higher she climbed, a hundred feet above the floor, two hundred, the more the wall changed, becoming more faceted, so polished she could see herself in the facets, but in no recognizable geometric pattern.

She was physically fit, but no marathon runner. Her legs were burning, aching. At this height, the staircase was about six feet wide. The heights and distance alone would have made her queasy, but the quality of the space and the way sounds traveled—or didn't—sent her into stomach flip-flops. It was incredible to her that the interior helix of the tower resembled a strand of DNA. There had to be some significance to it.

Amid the emptiness inside the tower, the air itself was like a series of funhouse mirrors, full of vague, shifting distortions, and among those distortions, moving shapes. Glimpses of leathery wings and gnarled limbs and beady eyes full of amused malevolence peeking out of nowhere. But, like the umbral looking out from its crystal prison, could they see her from their half-existence? Were they real? Did the word "real" mean anything in this place?

She looked over her shoulder to see her party straggling along behind, with Claude and the Little People bringing up the rear. Claude looked beyond exhausted, like he might keel over from a heart attack at any moment. The Little People had to drag themselves up steps that were half again as tall as they were. Everyone's magic was all but spent. This was the end of the line. She either had to catch Stewart now and stop him or admit defeat and go home.

It took all her concentration to keep her burning legs pumping, staring at her path. If she stumbled and fell, there was nothing to stop her from tumbling back down or going straight over the side. How many stories' worth of steps had she climbed? Fifteen? Twenty?

The strange wall pulled at her eyes, but she focused on the steps. One false step and she was done for, and the wearier she became, the more likely that outcome.

She couldn't see the kids anymore, but she had to trust they were okay. Claude and the kids and Bob and Peaseblossom would take care of each other. Liz had to go on, catch Stewart. She looked up the stairs for him. There he was, still climbing, much closer than before—she had gained on him tremendously. He continued up the stairs like a robot, gazing steadily forward. She called to him again, and her voice reflected back as if she were standing in an empty closet. "This place is like a fun house from down under!" But she didn't mean Australia.

She kept after him, taking steps two or three at a time. The higher she climbed, the more her skin tingled and stung, as if she were bathed in a shower of invisible sparks. The unpleasant sensation reminded her of passing in front of Stewart's grinding wheel when it was throwing out a rooster-tail of sparks from whatever he was grinding. But she felt stronger, reinvigorated, and ran faster. Stewart was only fifty yards ahead of her.

Then she realized what the sensation was: pure, concentrated Dark Source, flowing into her like radiation from a nuclear test site.

"No," she said. "I don't want it!"

Unlike with radioactivity, she had a say in what she absorbed. It would only become part of her if she *used it*, at least she hoped so. It was a good fiction to tell herself.

She took a deep breath, closed her eyes—that's when she could see how much of it bathed her, covered her like hot dust—and expelled it from her body like she was blowing her nose.

Immediately, the weakness returned, but somehow she felt better, more herself, and realized how oblivious she had been to the degradation of her state of mind. Expelling it from her was like whacking the dust out of a rug. It was insidious, quietly making things seem easier, smoothing the path. Was that what it had been like for Stewart on his journey through the Dark Realm? Losing himself by inches and he hadn't even noticed? Or making a series of impossible choices that led him inexorably to absorb more Dark Source than he could withstand?

Somewhere Cassie's voice drifted to Liz's ear, calling, "Mommeeeeee!"

Liz looked across one of the catwalks that reached across to the other side of the tower like the rung of a DNA ladder—and had to fight back a spike of vertigo. Claude and the kids were directly across from her, climbing an Escher-like staircase *in the wrong direction*. *Climbing* upward, but *going* downward, as if gravity itself were out of joint. Her head spun as she looked back in the direction she had come, tracing her path down. Claude and the kids were no longer on that path. Fighting back dizziness, back pressed against the glassy black wall, she told herself, "Settle down, Elizabeth. Settle down." Maybe this place was like traveling to the City, where what was happening externally was just a representation of an inner journey.

In this moment of touching the surface of the wall, she thought she heard her name. Alice's voice? "Liz..."

The wall's facets were mirror polished. Her wide-eyed, curious face looked back at her.

But then her reflection turned away and sat down at a table outside Caffeine Dreams, with Alice. A few days ago, a lifetime ago. And the handsome stranger who came up to speak to her, and the stranger being so charming that she let him take her hand and lift her to feet and look deep into her eyes and she wanted so badly for him to kiss her because he smelled so good and she *wanted him*, and then they left together and... She got dizzy. The image shifted to a day in a department store where she had come upon her mother haranguing her father, and him just putting his hands in his pockets and taking it, soaking it in as if he deserved every cruel word and Liz had walked up to her mother and slapped her across the face. But it hadn't happened that way. Had it? It was so real. Liz remembered the sting of the slap across her palm. How could she have done such a thing? And there was the time she had started dating Stewart, but then decided to get back with her ex-boyfriend Bill for one last fling, and made sure Stewart saw them making out in the school parking lot, and how his heart had been so utterly crushed it had broken him forever and that was how she knew he really loved her, and...

"No—"

The word came out of her like a ragged gasp as she pressed her hands against the polished facets for support.

Those things hadn't happened.

And then she was back with the handsome stranger from the mall, in a motel room, and she had never wanted anything more in her whole life, and she saw the darkness emerge from behind his eyes, turning them into black pits of malicious lust, and she realized he'd been *sent*, but in that moment, she didn't care and...

"No!"

She couldn't tear her eyes away, couldn't peel her hands away. The wall held her fast.

All the times she had berated her children in her mother's voice and made them feel small and useless and degraded.

The abortion she'd had and not told Stewart.

The time she'd been arrested on a narcotics charge and laughed in her father's face when he came to bail her out.

"No, no, *no!*"

She tried to look away, tried to peel her hands away, tugging and tugging, but a million tiny hooks held her skin to the stone.

Her third DUI arrest with Cassie in the back seat.

Locking three-year-old Hunter in the closet for a week.

"It's not real!" she yelled, hoping everyone would hear her. "Don't look at the walls!" Was anyone close enough to hear?

With a ragged scream of rage, she braced her foot against the wall and pulled. Tears of rage and shame and grief poured down her face.

Peeling her fingers away felt like ripping away the outer layers of super-glued skin. As her flesh came away, so could her eyes. Tearing her gaze away felt like her corneas had been ripped off.

Her momentum carried her over the edge of the stairs.

She was falling.

CHAPTER TWENTY-EIGHT

L iz couldn't even scream, because her mind was too full of the horrible images she couldn't shake. They felt like real memories. In those memories, she was not just an awful person—she had reveled in it. Those terrible things had felt natural, normal, reasonable, the tip of the iceberg.

Her arms and legs flailed as she tumbled. That very hard floor was coming up at her very quickly. There was nothing she could do, and worse, nothing she wanted to do, except despair at who she was.

But then the flap of wings sounded far away. And two powerful arms hooked under hers from behind, squeezing her ribs, turning her descent into a spiraling swoop, with a sickening plunge like the bottom of a rollercoaster. Black wings flapped and twisted, and the scent of dusty feathers filled her nose, and the scent of something else she recognized. Stewart's scent. Sweaty and grimy, for sure, but his. She clung to his strong arms.

Stewart's stubbled cheek rasped against her temple. Back upward they swept like a rocket, losing momentum with peculiar irregularity as they passed through areas of malleable space-time in the tower's center, where everything looked as distorted as in a fun-house mirror.

It was all over in a shocking scantness of seconds. Stewart and Liz lit upon a high terrace at the summit of the tower's interior, maybe thirty feet wide and thousands of feet above the ground. Dying crimson sunlight slanted through narrow windows across the stone floor. The ceiling hung about twenty feet above. Another stone staircase led up through the ceiling to the next level.

Stewart's rough hands spun her around, squeezing her shoulders like vises, his arms like knots of bridge cable. His great wings flexed and furled, but it was his face that seized her gaze.

Streaked with grime, eye sockets hollowed out and filled with eyes that weren't Stewart's eyes. His teeth looked longer, sharper, and his breath was like a desert wind.

"Is this what you wanted to see?" he said angrily. "Is this what you came all this way for?" His inhuman eyes bored into hers.

"Well, yes." She had come this far to see him as he was. Raw truth. No deceit.

"Why?" His voice was filled with anger, frustration, incredulity, a final way to ask *Why would you want* this?

"Because I love you," she said. "How could I not try?"

It was like a switch was thrown. His eyes became Stewart's again, looking out from those inhuman sockets with a steady gaze she knew so well. His grip softened. The spirit looking out at her was the one she had inadvertently touched that night in Serenity Glen—the man who had remained steadfastly good despite the horrific hand life had dealt him, the man she had fallen in love with. He'd been cemented inside thick layers of blackness, but he was still in there.

Then he hugged her, and she kissed him, and he kissed her back with the tenderness and fervor he'd always had. In that kiss, she felt the shape of his face change, become more Stewart.

"Where are the kids?" he asked.

"They were right behind me, then they weren't and…then I touched the wall and everything got really weird and…"

A flapping of leathery wings filled the air, approaching from below the terrace's lip.

"Do not fear," said a voice like malevolent thunder. The swish of robes brushed over the stone steps coming down from the level above, robes of black and crimson that just kept coming, until they became a figure impossibly tall. An ashen face, long thin mustache, and eyes that seemed to devour the light.

Liz's core turned to ice.

"It is time to reunite you all." The figure's chuckle was so bereft of humor it was almost painful, a grating rasp across her soul. The thing moved with a kind of smooth, effortless alacrity that reminded her of a tarantula—an eight-foot-tall spider—but measured, precise. The face was human-like if viewed through a nightmare looking-glass. He, it, she couldn't decide. If he had ever been a mortal human, any semblance of that was long since twisted out of existence.

Her voice was a tremulous whisper, "Is that—?"

"Baron Tyrus," Stewart said, stepping around to interpose himself between the Dark Lord and Liz.

Four winged shapes hove into view from below—emaciated, mummified things like sentient leather—and tossed their burdens onto the terrace. Claude, the kids, and the Little Folk sprawled at the Dark Lord's feet.

All of them stared, transfixed, sheet-white, like mice before a cobra. Cassie emitted a tiny peep.

The Dark Lord's hand snatched Claude's shirt, faster than a striking snake, and yanked him into the air, holding him suspended as if he weighed no more than a doll. Claude struggled and cried out, but he might as well have been struggling against a girder.

"So, you're the shopkeeper who thought he could thwart my plans with *dolls*," the Dark Lord said.

Claude gasped and fought, choking for breath.

"Perhaps you'd like them back."

From the level above, Jaclyn and Jazlyn tumbled down the steps like mechanical circus acrobats and came to rest on either side of their new master.

Cassie began to cry.

The Dark Lord dropped Claude into a pile.

The dolls moved in on him with cold menace.

Liz's breath caught, and a fist of doom clutched her heart. She whispered, "Stewart! Help him!"

Claude entreated the dolls, "Please don't! I love you." He held out his arms.

Little black blades appeared in their hands.

"Stewart!" Liz said. "Do something! He's your friend!"

"I don't have any friends," Stewart said, but he drew his flamberge. Liz could see the runes engraved upon it, feel their magical throb. It was a stunning work of sword-smithing, a weapon of kings and princes. It belonged in a different century, or in a museum.

All eyes, even the Dark Lord's, watched as one of the dolls circled behind Claude, the other stood before him.

"Please, lovelies," Claude said, "I know you're still in there. Please." He was crying not with fear, but with grief for what had been done to them. "Let me take you home."

The Dark Lord grinned with pleasure, entwining his fingers like a knot of bony worms.

Liz couldn't tear her gaze away from the sheer menace glowing in the dolls' orange eyes. They edged toward Claude as if considering. Liz could almost imagine their little magical clockwork brains spinning, pausing, spinning, their little mechanical limbs as still as statues.

Until the one behind Claude darted in.

Claude convulsed and cried out in pain.

Liz screamed, "No!"

The doll in front of Claude darted in, its blade glinting and licking.

Stewart's form turned hazy, indistinct. A wave of furnace-like heat boiled from his flamberge, but it was a wave of magic, too, gushing through her, both Light and Dark imbued in the blade's runes, Dark for Power, Light for Purity. His wings gave one mighty flap that propelled him across the distance with the speed of a swooping raptor.

The dolls' tiny blades were like sewing machine needles.

But they were not Stewart's target. They were the distraction. *Claude* was the distraction.

Stewart's blade arced like a bolt of lightning and cleaved into the Dark Lord's back with a sound like a sonic boom. The shock wave sent Liz sprawling, her ears gone dead. The kids and Little Folk bounced and rolled toward the lip of the terrace.

Liz was screaming, but there was no sound, only a muffled ringing in her ears. Hunter grabbed onto Cassie's arm, and they came to a halt together, inches from the edge. Bob went over the side. Peaseblossom caught herself by her fingertips.

301

Baron Tyrus staggered under Stewart's blow. Stewart's enhanced strength swung the heavy blade as if it were a broom stick and landed another thunderous blow. The Dark Lord's robes were too thick to see how effective the blows were. Stewart's third strike flung Baron Tyrus onto his side, scarlet sparks springing from his eyes, obscuring whatever emotion might be in them.

Liz scrambled on all fours toward the kids, seized their shirts, dragging them back from the edge. Peaseblossom pulled herself up and over to safety.

Baron Tyrus raised a hand to ward off Stewart's onslaught, but the flamberge, like a six-foot serrated steak knife, severed the arm near the elbow, without sign of any blood. An elemental shriek filled her head—her ears still felt stuffed full of foam earplugs—a sound that wasn't a sound, from no throat at all, as if the entire Dark Realm had screamed. But not in pain.

Rage.

For Baron Tyrus, this just got *real.*

A spray of red-hot metal slivers blasted from the Dark Lord's good hand, sleeting over Stewart, through him. The air filled with the smell of ozone, hot steel, and burned flesh.

But even as the attack tore through Stewart, his flesh knitted again just as quickly, and with Liz's new magical senses, she could see the scarlet motes of Dark Source weaving him back together. No doubt the same was happening to Baron Tyrus.

The interior of this tower was an endless, bottomless well of Dark Source. How long could these titans go toe-to-toe with endless power at their disposal? How much Dark Source could Stewart absorb and use before he could never be Stewart again? He had

302

power and purpose, but the Dark Lord had cunning and experience. Had Stewart been a boxer, he would not have been a finesse fighter.

Baron Tyrus moved with such speed it was like he teleported, or took a single, thirty-foot step without crossing the intervening space. But he was on his feet now, across the terrace. His severed hand disappeared into a puff of ashen powder.

The kids huddled together, gasping, their faces frozen into masks of horror at everything happening around them. Liz couldn't bring herself to look at Claude and the dolls. All she saw was...blood. Liz dragged the kids farther from the edge. Peaseblossom clung to Hunter's pants leg, eyes empty and shellshocked. She checked them for injuries. And then...

Hunter's locket dangled into view.

This was it, and a momentary wave of pride overwhelmed her for this boy's courage, for his kind, pure heart. But there was nothing else for him to do here at the end of all things.

She opened his locket.

In a burst of white light, Hunter disappeared.

She met Peaseblossom's eyes and said, "Go."

A look of relief tinged with regret flashed across the little woman's face as Peaseblossom opened her locket and disappeared.

Cassie looked confused, her mouth making words Liz couldn't hear. *Mommy! Wait!*

Liz cupped her daughter's cheek, hugged her close, then opened Cassie's locket. The sensation of Cassie's disappearance was like squeezing laundry fresh from a dryer, a burst of collapsing warmth, dissipating scent. Gone.

Then Baron Tyrus's gaze fixed on her, squarely and with supreme malevolence.

She scrambled to her feet to face him, but he was already within reach of her, pallid hands—two of them again—and black talons coming at her.

A roar of defiance echoed through her magical senses, not her deafened ears, and Stewart was coming at them like a black comet, the runes on his blade glaring with power.

With that incredible speed, as if he could move between the beats of time itself, Baron Tyrus slapped the incoming blade aside with the back of one hand, sending it spinning away and over the edge of the terrace. He slashed Stewart across the face with the claws of his other, knocking Stewart sprawling back, upended by his heels striking Claude's inert form. The shockwave of the blow sent the dolls tumbling as well.

Stewart crashed into a wall, snapping one of his wings.

Liz yanked the lockets out of her pocket and put one on, feeling the passage of eons against the Dark Lord's incredible speed.

Then she ran for Stewart. Would this work? More troubling was the question: *should* this work? She took one glance at Claude, and his empty, staring eyes implanted a nightmare that would plague her the rest of her life.

Suddenly the dolls stood between her and Stewart, their porcelain faces stained, their glowing-coal eyes fixed on her, considering, considering...

"Get away!" she yelled, but she couldn't hear her own voice over the ringing still in her ears.

But the last of her magic rushed up and blasted out of her in an expanding bubble of force, blowing the dolls into the air and away.

With her increasing deftness, she sculpted the bubble's outer surface and flung the dolls over the edge of the terrace.

But then what felt like a mountain struck her bubble, a volcano of malignant hate, a thing of endless hunger and greed. The Dark Lord had thrown himself against the bubble. Through the magical membrane, she could feel his essence in her very bones, in her blood, in her soul, in her mouth like the sickly bitter taste of rotten meat. An image flashed in her mind of being strapped into some horrific machine that would drain her blood and her lifeforce together, a machine she was bound to perish in, to be devoured by this *thing*. The Dark Lord's presence, touching the membrane of her magic, held at bay, struggling to reach her—and very soon, Baron Tyrus *would* reach her—made her stumble. The locket intended for Stewart skittered out of her grip.

The Dark Lord's gaze fixed upon it.

With a fleetness born of desperation, of screeching knowledge that her time was ticking away, heartbeat by heartbeat, Liz flung herself back into action, scrambling to her feet, snatching up the locket on the second try and scrambling to Stewart's side. Her bubble allowed Stewart inside with her. His broken wing shuddered with the effort of healing, and he watched the Dark Lord with the glowing eyes of a badger from hell. There was no quit in him.

He didn't see the locket in Liz's hand until she slipped the chain over his head. His powerful body stiffened as he realized what it was.

And then she opened it.

In a flash, Stewart was gone, and she was alone with the Lord of the Dark Realm, her back to the wall.

He walked slowly toward her, leaning against her bubble, and it gave way like pressing against a balloon, distorting it. In moments, the balloon would fail from the pressure. His grin spread impossibly wide, revealing hideously sharp teeth in a black maw hungry enough to eat the universe itself.

Her fingers fumbled with the locket at her throat, unable to find the clasp, and she dared not look way from the Dark Lord to find it. Her magic gushed away like liquid from a punctured bladder.

He began to chuckle, a dry, rasping sound. His eyes met hers.

Then she opened the locket.

In the split second before the splash of light took her away from there, she caught a smug grin on Baron Tyrus's face.

CHAPTER TWENTY-NINE

Liz experienced a timeless moment of pure vertigo, of floating un-moored by gravity. She was no longer moving forward through time, but experienced the past and future all at once, if only she could fathom it.

Then the grand hall of the Queen's mansion appeared in her vision as if through gauze, and she was standing in the center of the hall just a few feet from Stewart.

Stewart knelt doubled over on the polished wood floor like a man who'd just received a sledgehammer to the gut. His wings were gone. He looked *human* again.

Without a thought for her own safety or what she had seen him do only moments ago, Liz ran to him, only dimly aware she was far from alone. The kids stood about twenty feet away, staring at their father in hopeful confusion. The denizens of the Queen's mansion were emerging from back corridors and hurrying down the grand staircases. Among them, smiling, were Peaseblossom and Bob, who had also brought himself safely home.

The parquet wooden floor was vibrating like a gong, as if she had arrived amid the reverberating after-effects of a huge noise.

She knelt before him, lifting his face to look into it. "Stewart...?"

At the sight of her, pure joy filled Stewart's eyes, and he reached for her, tentatively, as if unsure they were both real. Her heart swelled until it was too big for her body, and she threw her arms around him and sobbed.

"You did it," he said, kissing her, "you brought me back."

"I can't believe it!" she repeated, over and over, as the throng in the hall grew. So many faces hurried into the hall. Too many?

She rained kisses on Stewart's face and lips, squeezing him against her. Hot tears poured down her cheeks. Too many emotions to think. Too much relief. Could it finally be over? Such words were probably bubbling from her mouth, but she wouldn't remember them.

Hunter came closer, and Stewart wrapped an arm around him and pulled him close, too. "It's good to see you, son."

But Cassie held back, frowning.

Liz held out her hand. "Cassie?"

Cassie shook her head and took a step back, her body stiff.

How long this joyful reunion lasted, Liz couldn't be sure, but when she could finally pay attention to her surroundings again, what she saw turned her body into wood.

Eyes glimmering with tension, fully armed and armored, the Queen's Royal Guard, scores of bright elves, surrounded them, and there was no friendliness in them. Lady Jocinda stood at a balustrade above, scanning the returned for signs of Jaclyn and Jazlyn, her expressionless doll-like face somehow expectant.

The dolls. Liz's heart cracked open at everything they had lost. Captain Ar-Chaheris. Claude.

The adult-sized automaton hurried down the stairs, looking for her daughters, increasing desperation apparent in her movements.

Cassie caught her at the foot of the stairs and threw her arms around Lady Jocinda's waist. Cassie only cried and squeezed. Through the tilt of Lady Jocinda's head, her movements, a cascade of emotions emerged. Sadness, grief, and then pride. Lady Jocinda laid a hand of metal and porcelain on Cassie's back, and the two of them grieved.

Then, in a flash of blinding cosmic light, the Queen and the Princess appeared at the edge of the encroaching throng. Their expressions were as blank as eggshells. They said nothing, only fixed Liz and Stewart with their implacable eyes. Even the Princess, usually so brimming with welcome and cheer, wore the face of someone steeling herself to do the worst.

Liz wiped her nose with her sleeve, her eyes with her palms, her joy receding like a tide revealing a shipwreck.

"Stewart?" she said. "Is it really you?" She hardly dared to hope.

"Yes, yes, it's me," he said. "I...can't feel the umbral anymore. Whoever made that locket, that was some incredible magic."

"I made the locket," the Princess said, "and I did not include the power to free you from the umbral."

"But I feel fine," Stewart said, confused. "I feel more like myself than...god, I don't even know how long." He stood, as if sensing danger. "It feels so good for that thing to be gone. Maybe it couldn't withstand being forced into the Light Realm. I—"

"No, Stewart Riley," the Queen said. "The umbral has the cunning and instincts of a beast. It knows when it is threatened. It has retreated, but you are not free of it."

"Trust me, if it was still here, I would know," Stewart said.

"Until it has been destroyed," the Queen said, "you will never be trustworthy again."

"But you can't destroy it," he said. "It's impossible. Nothing in the universe can be annihilated. Matter and energy can be rearranged, but it cannot cease to exist. It would break the laws of existence itself."

"Very astute, Stewart Riley," the Queen said. "You understand the cost of what we must do."

"You mean to annihilate it," Stewart said.

"Erase it as if it had never existed," the Queen said. "Otherwise, it will never fail to reconstitute itself, given enough time. It will hound you until the end of your days. And the Dark Lord has shown himself to be several steps ahead of us in his plan."

"I can show you how he does it," Stewart said, nervousness growing in his voice. "It's this Obsidian Tower, it's called, and it can—"

"I have extracted your experiences in the Dark Realm from all your memories," the Queen said.

Liz shuddered at the thought of the Queen being able to read her thoughts and memories like an open book, without Liz even noticing.

"I now understand the Dark Lord's advantage in raw power," the Queen went on. "He has been siphoning unused Source from both the past and future to feed his designs in the present. What he disregards is how his greed for power depletes the natural flow of Source in both realms and will eventually destroy us all. He must be stopped." She stepped closer, all nine feet of her, impossibly potent, impossibly wise, but her patience was running out. "Stewart can no longer exist in the Light Realm without the magic of that locket, and its power will soon be depleted, at which moment he will fall away from us forever and return to the Dark Realm. Stewart, you cannot exist in the Penumbra anymore, except for a short time, any more than a dark elf or a goblin."

Liz said, "He can't even go home anymore?"

The Queen shook her head. "Not until the umbral has been removed. And it is stronger now than before."

"I knew it!" Cassie said, her voice full of anger. "He's not Daddy anymore! He's a monster!"

Stewart stared at Cassie, heartbreak splashed across his face.

Cassie shrilled, "You let them kill Claude!"

It was Liz's turn for fresh heartbreak. Her ten-year-old daughter had just seen two former friends and playmates murder another friend in cold blood. What would that do to a child? What child deserved to carry such an awful burden?

Liz went to Cassie and hugged her, but it was like hugging a post.

"Get that thing out of him or send him away!" Cassie said.

"Oh, baby..." Stewart said, his voice cracking as he reached for her. Cassie slid behind Liz, never taking her eyes off him.

"So let's do it," Liz said. "We all want to go home."

"It is much more powerful now," the Princess chimed in. "We will require your aid."

"Now, hold on a minute!" Stewart said. "I keep telling you, I'm fine. If it was still inside me, I would know!"

"That is the voice of the umbral," the Princess said, "bargaining for its existence."

"No! I'm fine! Liz, you believe me, don't you?"

Liz looked deep into the eyes of the man she had missed so terribly, so badly it ached, and that's all she saw. She saw no hint of the creature that had just battled the Dark Lord hand-to-hand. "I want to..."

311

He turned to Hunter. "Son! You believe me, right? It's me! You recognize your old man, right?"

Hunter's eyes narrowed, scrutinizing, searching. "We're back, but I feel sick."

"Cassie?" Stewart said, reaching out to her.

She shook her head, frowning deeply, edging away. "You let Claude die."

Stewart sank to his knees again, tears glistening. "You're right. I did that. The umbral made that decision okay in my mind at the time, but now it's going to haunt me forever. I'm so sorry, sweetheart. I let you all down. Can you forgive me?"

Liz could see the yearning to do just that on their faces, but something held them back.

Then Liz noticed that the Princess's eyes had gone pure gold, shining like sunset on a breeze-rippled lake. Her voice reverberated from every direction at once. "The umbral has retreated. It senses its danger and goes into hiding."

"Retreated to where?" Stewart said. "I can't feel it anymore!" His voice sounded too strident.

"As it possesses no substance," the Queen said, "it can, when it chooses to, hide in the smallest of spaces, such as the nucleus of a cell, or even amid the bonds of a single molecule." Then she waved a hand as if stroking the air itself. A swirling mist like motes of diamond took form around Stewart and suddenly encased his body in a crystalline block, except for his head.

"Hey!" Stewart yelled, struggling in vain, but he was encased in a substance that resembled the urn in which the umbral had been imprisoned. "Am I a prisoner now?" His face reddened.

The Queen said, "This prison will hold you fast. You will not be able to flee to the Dark Realm until I will it."

A chill went down Liz's spine at the truth of what the Queen and the Princess were saying. She could still lose Stewart forever. The darkness within Stewart was simply hiding like a predator waiting to strike. The grand hall was not just filled with onlookers, but with the Royal Guard, scores of bright elf warriors, each of them a master of magic in his own right. They were not here to greet anyone. They were here to fight.

"Stewart," Liz said, "you know we're not going to hurt you. My Stewart would realize that."

"You're right, Liz, I'm sorry," he said, relaxing, as if the umbral were retreating deeper. "Do what you've gotta do."

The Queen said, "First, the umbral must be found and brought to the surface. Hunter, I believe you and Bob used a technique that would work here."

Hunter stiffened under her attention. "Uh, you mean like when we searched through the haunted house inside his mind?"

The Queen nodded. "All of you must go. You must search every cell, every atom, every synapse of memory until the creature is found, and coax it out of hiding."

"All right," Liz said, "let's go."

"I don't want to go in there," Cassie said, frowning. "It's an ugly place."

"It's the only way to bring Dad back," Hunter said.

"What if he'll never be Daddy again?" A tear glistened in one of Cassie's eyes.

Liz squeezed her hand. "We have to try, baby. Right?"

Cassie nodded reluctantly, sniffling.

Liz, the kids, and Bob sat in a half-circle around Stewart's imprisoned body and held hands.

Liz could still feel the magic reverberations through the living floor, like the waves of an asteroid dropped in the ocean. Then she turned to Cassie, "Cassie baby, I think you should sing us along."

Cassie blinked, as if she had forgotten her ability to do so.

Liz went on, "You saved me with your singing once. Now we all have to save Daddy. Can you do it?"

Cassie swallowed and composed herself, wiping fresh tears. "We have to try everything, right?"

Liz smiled. "Oh, *yes!*"

Cassie took a deep breath, closing her eyes. In the air around them grew the sound of music, the bright, hopeful melody of "Try Everything" from one of her favorite movies, *Zootopia*. Liz couldn't help grinning as she realized Cassie was creating a magical musical accompaniment for herself from her own memory of the song. Then she belted it out, a song about never giving up, never giving in, trying over and over again even though they could fail. Liz could almost hear Shakira's rich, angelic voice coming from her daughter.

Liz closed her eyes, took several deep breaths, and let her awareness sink into the ocean of Source swirling around them, feeling the nearby vastness of the Lake, a physical-seeming projection of the Light Realm's reservoir of Source. She breathed it in, let it fill her, let it renew her strength, her will. She breathed in the love in her daughter's song—because Cassie's anger had been born of deep, deep hurt, the kind of hurt only deep love makes possible. And she felt the courage of her son leading her toward a pulsating beacon of magical power.

Stewart.

But the beacon was not pure. Its light was tainted, sickly, greasy.

The three of them joined minds and plunged into the polluted brightness.

Stewart's voice echoed in their minds: *I'll try to help you find it...*

But they couldn't be sure the umbral wasn't trying to lead them astray, distract them until it could find a way to escape and Stewart returned forever to the Dark Realm.

With the exuberant melody driving them on like trumpets, they plunged into the heart of Stewart's body and mind and spirit.

Into the pulsating light they went, through vistas of cells and tissue and constellations of swirling Source. Through imaginary clouds they flew, until they found a dazzling mansion that, had it existed in the real world, would have covered several dozen acres, a structure of marble and jewels, balconies and gardens, gleaming windows and sweeping staircases.

But something about it felt wrong. This didn't feel like a place the real Stewart would care to inhabit.

Breathing deep of the Source billowing around her, Liz gathered it into a bubble of force that she blasted into the mansion. The mansion shattered into a billion shards, dissolving into nothingness. A facade.

Stewart would not make such a place his home.

Trying to contain his disappointment, Hunter said, "We should split up."

From somewhere outside them all, Bob chimed, "And if ye find the beastie, don't face it yerself. Call out to the rest of us. Who knows what such a thing could do to our minds?"

Somewhere in the distance, she felt the umbral's amusement at impending triumph, like a child about to win a game of hide and seek.

The deeper she went, the more she saw the inner workings of Stewart's body, great conduits of pulsing blood flow, bolts of bioelectricity crackling down the superhighways of nerves, firing the gigantic machinery of muscle fibers, the titanic framework of pale, living bones supporting it all. Through these endless pathways she searched, looking in vain for signs of Darkness.

Cassie's song rose and fell, rose and fell in the distance. She caught glimpses of Cassie zooming through hair follicles and skin cells. Hunter zoomed round and round through Stewart's consciousness.

Then from the mists of magic and thought emerged a small town Liz recognized—Mesa Roja.

Down through its empty streets she flew. No sign of cars or people, but she recognized every building. She checked the outskirts and found their home, their trailer, just where it should be, but it was empty. Flitting across town to the nicer side with the speed of thought, she found her parents' house, also empty. This was not her world, but Stewart's, and if the umbral had been formed from Stewart's darkest memories, if it operated on pure instinct, might it retreat into those memories when threatened?

Liz knew all the foster homes Stewart had grown up in, horrors most of them. One night, after they'd gotten engaged, Stewart had given her the tour of his childhood in Mesa Roja, and she'd been equally moved and amazed that he'd grown up to be as well-adjusted as he was. His steadfast belief in the reality of magic had been a big part of that. The other big part of that was the unshakable integrity born of his awful experiences.

But maybe his integrity was quite shakable after all.

Drifting through the streets of this illusory Mesa Roja, she wondered why this dream town existed. What secrets did it hold? Was it another distraction, or was this place the key to finding the umbral?

She found herself outside a ramshackle stucco house, little more than a shoebox, missing roof tiles, surrounded by a waist-high, rusted, chain-link fence. One of Stewart's foster homes. A *Beware of Dog* sign hung near the gate, and every square inch of earth inside the fence had been beaten bare by the endless pacing of an aggressive dog she remembered well from her junior-high years. A few savaged chew-toys and splintered ham bones scattered the hard-packed earth. The dog was a vicious conglomeration of Rottweiler, wolf, and pit bull, they said. She didn't remember the family's name, but she remembered that dog.

What had caught her attention and brought her here?

She opened the gate and stepped into the yard.

The front door crashed open, sending splinters and glass in every direction, and that dog flew toward her, a locomotive of bristling hair and fangs, eyes blazing with hatred, jaws trailing slaver.

A force bubble expanded around her with the speed of thought, caught the dog in midair, and sent it flying. It landed on the roof of the house, where it righted itself, then crouched to leap at her again, barking thunderously.

But she had all the Source she needed at her disposal. She seized the dog in an invisible fist and flung it away as hard as she could, so hard it disappeared into the sky. She would have felt terrible about doing that to a real dog, even one as vicious as this one, but whatever that thing was, it was *not* a dog. Maybe she was on the right track.

317

She walked into the dim interior of the house, which smelled like dog feces and cheap cigar smoke. A haze in the air suggested the smoker was nearby, but she heard nothing. The hideous sofa in the tiny living room sagged in the middle. A cigar-burned coffee table hosted a half-empty bottle of vodka, a full ashtray, and a layer of grime. A weird construction of aluminum foil wrapped the TV's rabbit ears.

Something was here. A presence inside the house.

She kept her protective bubble in place, letting it mold itself around the contours of walls and corners as she walked through the house.

In the bedroom off the dingy kitchen, a bedside clock-radio beside a rumpled, sagging bed played some best-forgotten hard rock song, Molly Hatchet or something.

A door to the basement stood ajar, and she thought she heard something down there, a surreptitious shift.

She opened the door and peered into the musty darkness. Shafts of light slanted through dust motes amid shelves of old tools, gas cans, and miscellaneous junk. One foot after another she descended the worn wooden steps, into smells of musty earth and cobwebs, into the leftover junk of a forgotten life.

The movement came again, clearer this time, from a tiny door to a crawlspace.

"Who's there?" she said, her voice sounding strange and hollow in this non-reality.

She approached a meaty-looking door. There was a bolt on the *outside*, as if it were intended to keep something in. The shiny, new lock slid easily aside, and Liz pulled open the door.

From the blackness, two eyes met hers with the intensity of coals from a blazing forge.

CHAPTER THIRTY

Liz's psychic yelp interrupted Cassie's song. Two distant cries of alarm instantly zoomed nearer.

A low growl, deeper than any living creature's, like a rumble from beneath the earth, emanated from the darkness of the dirt crawlspace and made her feel like a mouse facing a rattlesnake. Amid curtains of cobwebs, the vague, liquid outline of the thing swirled and seethed.

It lunged at her, boiling out of the shadows and enveloping her bubble like an octopus around its prey, its tendrils digging and clawing at her protection with profusions of hooked spines. If that thing got to her, it would tear her mind to pieces and leave her living body an empty husk.

Stewart's voice whispered to her, snippets of conversations, *...trust me...it'll be okay...just let me in...let's just go home...come with me...I love you...*

Fending off the viciousness of its attack expended a tremendous amount of her Source, shrinking her bubble. In her mind, she could feel the grating and gouging of its spines against the bubble, like the tines of a fork against a ceramic dish. Something got through and tore a slash across her upper arm. She gasped and redoubled her concentration.

"Cassie! Hunter! Stay back! It's here! It'll hurt you!" she shouted into the void, hoping the kids would hear before they got within the umbral's reach.

The umbral's attack ceased, and its attention turned outward.

The kids were unprotected, and this thing could rip their little psyches to shreds.

"No!" Liz shouted.

"We're coming, Mommy!" Cassie called, as if from just upstairs.

The umbral peeled itself away from Liz's bubble, and somewhere else, her heart almost leaped out of her body. "No!" she cried again.

Then, purely by instinct, she flipped her bubble into a net that enveloped the umbral. It surged with instant rage against the limits of its confinement. Pain shot like a railroad spike behind her eye, and she squeezed her eyes shut against a fountain of tears. She staggered and dropped to one knee, gasping at the effort of restraining such prodigious power. Her skin felt bathed in cool, comforting mist as Light Source flowed into her.

Then she felt Cassie's light touch on her "shoulder."

"Sing for me, honey!" Liz gasped.

Cassie launched into a fresh rendition of "Try Everything," and fresh Light Source gushed into Liz through the conduit of Cassie's touch, like a freshet of cool air in a hot, stuffy room, a drink to someone dying of thirst. Liz would *not* fail. She did not dare. If she did, she would lose not just Stewart, but her children, and probably herself as well.

Inside its prison bubble, the umbral boiled like black lava, seething with hate, distorting the bubble's shape with its convulsions. She concentrated on thickening the bubble, which increased the Source drain exponentially. She couldn't hold it for long.

Then Hunter was there, too, bolstering her courage with his, sending another gust of Light Source into her. The flow of it expanded her. She became larger than herself, as if her power had always been this big, as if the only thing holding her back all this time had been her own beliefs about how much space in the universe she should fill, how much strength and power she could muster.

Then, as if reading her mind, the umbral began to speak in her mother's voice. *You're useless...just a stupid cheerleader...never amount to anything...married to a loser...live in a trailer...could have amounted to something...*

"Shut up!" Liz snarled. And then she *squeezed.* The bubble shrank, compressing the umbral into a roiling black mass of burning eyes and rage the size of a basketball. "You will not beat me!" she shouted, punching the side of the prison.

"Come on, Mom," Hunter said from beside her. "Let's get out of here."

"Take my hands, kids," Liz said. They did, and she squeezed them tight. Help from their Source was the only way she would be able to control this beast long enough to extract it from its hiding place.

Hunter sent a blast of golden energy from his free hand upward, blowing the house above them into the metaphorical heavens. Liz leaped into the sky with her children, towing the imprisoned ball of evil with invisible magic tow cables.

Upward and outward through Stewart's psyche and tissues they flew, through networks of neurons and synapses, through mountains of bone, plains of skin, forests of hair, expanding, until they snapped their awareness back into their bodies.

The bubble containing the umbral hovered in the air in the Queen's grand hall above Stewart's imprisoned form.

Gasps of amazement and horror filled the chamber.

With mighty heaves the umbral threw itself against its confinement, distorting the shape of the bubble and sending another spike of pain through Liz's head. Her vision dimmed, shot through with sparks. She almost toppled until small hands propped her upright.

But the umbral was in full view of everyone now.

Liz felt another mind engulf her meager bubble, as vast and powerful as a thousand oceans, a thousand suns, a thousand galaxies. The Queen. The Princess. Two infinities working together.

Immense golden chains formed around Liz's bubble, bolstering its strength. The umbral struggled harder and harder.

Through tears of pain, Liz saw a look of surprise on the Queen's perfect face.

"It is more powerful than I imagined," the Queen said. Had Liz heard a moment of doubt in her voice?

Through the Source flowing into her, Liz's magical awareness sensed the Lake. Children of many colors and shapes played along its shore, swimming and splashing and laughing, oblivious to their jeopardy. But then chopping waves erupted across the Lake, whitecaps, whirlpools, waterspouts. Dark storm clouds coalesced above the expanse of "water," but the rain flowed *upward*.

Suddenly the waterline receded, leaving the children on soft, empty sand.

The umbral's bubble bulged and contracted with pseudopods of blackness as it fought in growing desperation.

322

Stewart looked to have fallen unconscious in his block of cosmic diamond. His eyes were closed, his head sagging to the side.

Light blazed through the grand hall as if coming from everywhere, from the air itself, forcing scores of Royal Guards and other denizens to shield their eyes. The rush of Source flowing around and through Liz brought a gasp, like stepping into a rush of monsoon flood down an arroyo.

The Queen blazed too brightly to look at, but Liz saw something emerging from her. The Queen's head was thrown back, hair standing on end, arms outstretched, as she floated three feet above the floor. Golden tendrils snaked from within her torso, coalescing into a throbbing mass in the air before her. The radiance grew and pulsated until it became a semi-solid entity. When two luminous eyes appeared in the thing, Liz realized what it was.

It was a negative of the Dark umbral. It was the essence of Light that resided within the Queen herself. A Light version of the umbral. As Liz realized this, she thought she saw emotions in its eyes—sadness, resignation, regret.

Then she understood. To annihilate the umbral, the Queen had to force the Light and Dark entities together, each into contact with its opposite, and then, like matter and antimatter, both would be annihilated.

But the Queen had created this anti-umbral from her own essence and drawn it out into the world. Was this the soul of the Light Realm itself? Liz's human mind boggled at the ramifications of what she was witnessing.

The anti-umbral enveloped the black ball of hate and began to squeeze.

The brightness in the hall flared, as bright as the sun but without a source, as if the air itself were aglow. Liz clapped her hands over her eyes. Through her clenched eyelids, she could see the shadows of her bones within her flesh.

All around her, the bright elves of the Royal Guard, so attuned to their Queen's wishes, lent their strength and will to the anti-umbral, forcing the two entities closer and closer. The umbral's psychic scream of rage tore through Liz's—

Silence.

As abrupt and total as if shut off by a switch.

Liz collapsed on the floor, opening her eyes into twilight.

Standing atop the Obsidian Tower, looking out over the beautiful, twilit desolation, Baron Tyrus, Lord of the Dark Realm, felt the universe fracture.

The pinhole he had sensed in the barrier between the Light and Dark Realms abruptly tore wide. From a tiny pinhole smaller than an atom to a tear the size of a mountain.

Through the rip, torrents of Light and Dark Source flowed in both directions, and the breach was spreading. On the scale of the universe, the breach was still infinitesimally small, but its size would increase, and as the Dark Lord's victories accumulated, it would accelerate.

His forces stood ready at the breach, unopposed by any sign of Light Realm defenders. Fools.

Somewhere, the bloodthirsty roars of the cyber-dragons, the war drums of his dark elves, the chittering of swarms of kniblings, the horns of goblin spider-riders, the rumble of war machines, the thunder of the El-Mithari Garkus Riders, all raised such a fanfare that it echoed across the breach into the Light Realm.

He raised a fresh goblet of blood and lifeforce in celebration. His endgame had begun.

The silence in the grand hall was deafening. Liz wobbled to her feet, hands on her knees. She stood amid a confused throng of stunned faces, all of them wearing thousand-yard stares that looked like she felt. A sense of terrible foreboding turned her heart cold.

As if something in the fabric of the universe itself had just...torn, and they'd all felt it, like an earthquake in the foundation of reality itself.

The umbral and its Light counterpart were gone.

The kids stood beside her, unsteady.

Liz looked around for the Queen. A knot of onlookers was gathering around the Princess, including Bob and Peaseblossom, both of whom looked beside themselves with shock and grief. The Princess's expression was one of sadness and resignation.

Pushing through the crowd, Liz came upon a white-haired crone lying on her back and staring at the ceiling.

She was normal human size, decrepit, but the Queen's features and costume were unmistakable.

Liz knelt beside her, and the Queen fixed her with a gaze so full of weariness Liz wanted to cry for her.

"It is done," the Queen said. "And I am...diminished." Her eyes closed as if going to sleep.

"What's wrong with her?" Liz yelled, taking up the Queen's cold, wrinkled hand and squeezing it.

Standing nearby, the Princess said, "We have done what we set out to do. The umbral is gone, utterly destroyed. But in so doing, we violated one of the laws of existence itself. The power required to do so—"

Just then Liz noticed a terrified hue and cry coming from outside and rippling through the throng inside. Hundreds of people, thousands, shouting in dismay. In the grand hall, several onlookers and Royal Guards ran for the windows.

The Princess went on, "The power required to do so has drained the Lake of Source."

"Forever?" Liz asked.

"Nothing is forever. The universe itself *is* change. Eventually it will replenish. That is the nature of things. But we used nearly all the Light Source in existence to manifest the umbral's counterpart."

"Will she...get better?" Liz asked, feeling a weight of guilt she had not known could exist. Had she just destroyed the universe to save Stewart? Such an act would be selfish beyond measure. Surely the Queen would not have allowed such a thing. But what might she have foreseen that motivated her to do it anyway?

The Princess shook her head. "It will soon become time for her to disperse and return her essence to the universe."

"What? No!" Liz said.

"This was her choice," the Princess said. "She knew the outcome. When she is gone, I will assume her role."

A new voice beside Liz, thick and trembling with emotion, turned her from her shock. "Thank you both for saving me." It was Stewart.

Liz jumped up and faced him, mouth agape.

A streak of white splashed one side of his hair as if he'd leaned against fresh paint, but there was no sign of raven-black wings or simmering Darkness in his gaze. He just looked indescribably tired.

She threw her arms around him again.

"I love you," he said into hair, kissing her temple, her ear, her neck. His embrace felt tremorous, overtaxed, but she could feel the true heart in it. She could count the times on two hands he'd said those words to her, and each one of those times meant the world.

They kissed tenderly, then looked into each other's eyes as if to make sure it was real. She gave a half-sob, half-laugh, and kissed him again.

"Dad!" came a cry as Hunter shoved through the crowd and flung his arms around them both.

Stewart squeezed his son close, then looked down incredulously. "Good grief, son, have you *grown?*"

"He's grown *up*, Stewart," Liz said.

"Have I been gone that long?"

"Growth spurts," Hunter said with a half-grin.

"I'm so proud of you!" Stewart said, hugging him again, kissing his head. "But we're missing one..."

He looked around.

The crowd parted for Lady Jocinda, who was leading Cassie with an arm around her shoulders. A frown creased Cassie's face and she faced them shyly.

"What's the matter, baby?" Stewart said, turning toward her.

She sniffed and wiped her nose.

Liz said, "Honey, come and hug your daddy."

"No, Liz," he said, "she's upset with me. And rightfully so." He knelt before her on one knee. "I'm so sorry, Cassie honey. You're right to be mad at me. I feel terrible about what happened to the dolls, and to Claude. I feel terrible about all the danger you went through to save me. I hope you can forgive me for all that and let me try to make it up to you."

Cassie wiped a tear. "I understand, Daddy. It wasn't you."

"Except that it *was* me, honey. That thing was as much a part of me as my fingers and toes, my heart, my lungs. But the Darkness brought out the worst things I'm capable of, made them easy. All it did was give me permission. I know this isn't what you want to hear, but here's what I want you to remember. *Everybody* has that Darkness, even the kindest people we know. But we have to choose not to listen to it. Some of us, our hearts are so big and bright, like yours, that the Darkness almost never has a chance to come out. But it's there. Never forget that."

Cassie said, "Like when I get so mad at Hunter I want to punch him in the face, but I don't? Or stop myself from squashing a bug that isn't hurting anything?"

"Exactly."

"Did you...you know, want to hurt us?"

"Oh, honey, no. I did everything in my power not to, and to stop the Dark Lord from hurting you. The Dark Lord wanted me to, but I could never hurt you, even if I was the most evil person in the universe." He turned back to Liz. "And now that that thing is gone, I'll never listen to that Darkness again. No matter what. It's finally over."

"It is not over at all," the Princess said.

Liz said, "What do you mean?"

But Stewart nodded in understanding, his face stricken.

"You felt it the moment the umbral was destroyed," the Princess said. "In so doing, we—"

"Tore the fabric of reality," Stewart said, rubbing his eyes and sighing deeply.

The Princess nodded. "There is now a rift in the barrier between the Light and Dark Realms. Such a thing has never happened before in this life of the universe. The Dark Lord means to come here and destroy us. His armies are already crossing through the breach, directly into the Light Realm."

"Then what are we standing around for?" Hunter said, alarm catching fire in his voice.

Many in the hall, especially the Royal Guard, seemed to share the same sentiment.

"We are taking a moment to mourn what has been lost," the Princess said, looking down at her mother's sleeping form. "And a moment to celebrate what has been gained." She looked gravely at Stewart.

"But isn't all the Light Source gone?" Hunter asked.

"It will replenish itself as Life in the universe goes on its way. It is the stuff of Life, after all," the Princess said.

"But will it be in time to save us?" Hunter asked.

The Queen's eyes opened—audibly somehow—and the circle around her drew back. She floated upright and rose from the floor, her white hair floating free as if she were underwater, her ancient face gray and indistinct, her formerly resplendent gown now dull and washed out.

"Prepare yourselves," the Queen said. "The Dark Lord is coming." A dimness surrounded her, like a candle starving of air, going out. Then she seemed to expand, pass out of focus, and disappear like white smoke.

Everyone stared, dumbstruck.

"What just happened?" Liz said in growing alarm.

"She's gone," Stewart said, voice cracking.

Cassie began to cry, and Liz hugged her close.

The Princess looked toward the ceiling, eyes closed, impossibly bright crystal tears flowing down her flawless cheeks.

Liz held Cassie close and let the sadness overtake her. They had just witnessed the passing of a being as vast and powerful as the universe itself. With the Queen gone, what hope did any of them have? The Queen's final words reverberated in Liz's memory. *Prepare yourselves. The Dark Lord is coming.*

For several minutes, only the sounds of weeping disturbed the silence, until...

"The Lake!" came a distant cry from outside.

A Royal Guard at one of the high windows called down to the throng inside, "The Lake is returning!"

Liz's magical awareness told her he was right. The Lake had partially refilled, but to nowhere near its original shores. It was a mere puddle compared to its former vastness. But it was something.

The Princess opened her eyes. "Mother has given the last of herself to give us a fighting chance. She has refilled the Lake as much as she was able before dispersing forever."

One of the Royal Guards stepped toward the Princess, his fine features stricken with tears and grief, and faced her. He raised his voice for all to hear. "The Queen is dead. Long live the Queen." Then he knelt before her.

Almost as one, everyone in the hall knelt to the new Queen. Unaccustomed to such etiquette, the Rileys were the last, but they knelt as well to the first-ever new sovereign of the Light Realm.

When Liz looked at the new Queen again, she had grown a foot taller, going from a little girl in appearance to that of a teenager, yet still somehow timeless, ageless.

"We must save our grief until such time as might honor it," the Queen said. "Come, everyone, let us to action."

The throng in the hall stood again and awaited her command.

She said, "The Dark Lord's forces are already moving. Captain Ar-Chaheris."

The new commander of the Royal Guard bowed before her. "Your mother's memory will become our battle songs, my Queen."

"Ready your lieutenants. We must prepare our defenses immediately," the Queen said.

Suddenly Bob appeared on Stewart's shoulder in the blink of an eye. "It's a great boon to me old heart to see ye yerself again, Stewart old boy. We've work to do, never fear, but the City has weapons deep in its vaults, and the Queen has given us an underdog's chance replenishing the Lake. This won't be our first pitched battle against the Dark Realm."

"But it will be the first on our own soil," said Peaseblossom.

The Queen said, "We must have faith in each other that we will prevail. The Dark Lord is coming, yes, but we have the most powerful human wizard in over a thousand years, one untainted by the Dark."

Liz squeezed her husband. "Is that going to be enough?" All she wanted was a little rest and relaxation time with Stewart, with the kids, but now she doubted she'd get the chance.

"It must be," the Queen said.

THE END

Billy Wright is a former professional boxer and author of the thrilling fantasy book series Earthly Worlds.

www.ingramcontent.com/pod-product-compliance
Lightning Source LLC
Chambersburg PA
CBHW020903200626
46814CB00001BA/150